# LAST SUMMER AT THE LAKE HOUSE

HEATHER DIXON

Storm
PUBLISHING

Ebook ISBN: 978-1-80508-282-8
Paperback ISBN: 978-1-80508-284-2

Cover design: Sarah Whittaker
Cover images: Getty Images

Published by Storm Publishing.
For further information, visit:
www.stormpublishing.co

ALSO BY HEATHER DIXON

**Summerville Series**

*Last Summer at the Lake House*

*Burlington*

*For Anna, Lauren and Paige—my most favorite set of sisters. You are, and always will be, the best thing that has ever happened to me.*

# ONE

## ALEX

After the phone call, Alex London sat as still as possible at the kitchen table. She needed a minute. Her eyes were closed, as if that would help her concentrate, while her youngest sister's words echoed in her head.

*Alex... it's Dad...*

A light tap, the gentle touch of a chubby, dimpled hand on her knee, told her that the minute was over. Alex opened her eyes and Molly was in front of her, asking something Alex couldn't hear. She looked down at her five-year-old daughter, into those beautiful green eyes that seemed too big for her small face. Molly was waiting. Alex crouched over in her seat to put her face directly in front of Molly's. When she was pregnant, she had read that you were supposed to get down to their level when you spoke to your kids so they could really hear you.

"Mommy? Not the purple bowl—the blue one."

Alex touched her bottom lip. "The purple one?"

"No, the *blue* one." Molly was getting impatient now. "Can you get me some strawberries cut up the way I like them, in the blue bowl?"

Alex straightened in her seat. She brushed her hand over

the top of Molly's silky hair and stood up, her knees cracking. Strawberries. She could do that.

"Sure, Mol. Strawberries, no green leaves on top, in the blue bowl."

Alex moved to one side of their bright, open-concept kitchen and rummaged through the drawer filled with hard plastic cups and bowls, water bottles and lunch containers. It was such a mess. Every time Alex saw it, she fought the urge to drop what she was doing so she could purge and reorganize.

"And cut up, okay, Mommy?"

"Mmm," Alex hummed.

"Mommy? Cut up? Okay?"

"Yes. Cut up. Blue bowl. Got it."

"Okay, I love you!" Molly turned and skipped out of the kitchen on her thin, delicate legs, a ribbon of light shining in a straight line across the back of her hair.

Alex opened the refrigerator and put her hand on the container of strawberries. She paused, head bowed, but only for a moment. Then her movements were swift and expert as she rinsed the berries under the tap, slicing them into quarters and sweeping them off the cutting board with the edge of the knife into the blue bowl.

The motions of motherhood were automatic for Alex by now, although it had surprised her at first that it didn't come naturally. It had taken her a while to settle into the role comfortably and to get to know her children. She assumed a gut, innate instinct would take over, the way her own mother always described it. When her mother had told her she would die for her and her sisters, Alex thought it was an overly dramatic statement. Now, with time, she understood. The mundane parts, like fetching snacks, arguing over bedtime, insisting they brush their teeth a thousand times before they would do it, even the hardest moments, could all be overshadowed by this odd sort of love. It was like a longing, this feeling she had for these two demanding little humans of hers.

And those little humans would need protecting now. She couldn't let them know yet what their Auntie Jess had said on the phone.

Ben walked into the kitchen, grabbing a mug from the cupboard and filling it to the brim with coffee. He blew a ripple into the top and then grinned at Alex as he nodded at the blue bowl. "Molly strikes again?" He found the girls funny when he wasn't the one on the receiving end of their demands.

"Ben..." Alex's voice sounded far away. Her arms fell to her sides, her shoulders slumping. Now that Ben was here, she could allow herself to come undone.

He put his mug down onto the counter and looked at her, alarm crossing his face. "What? Alex, what is it?"

"My dad..." she choked.

Ben's mouth hung open only for a beat and then he was next to her, his arms wrapped around her body. "What happened?"

Alex buried her face into Ben's wide, soft chest, running her forehead and eyebrows across the soft cotton of his shirt. He smelled familiar, clean and fresh, like soap. She pulled away and opened her mouth to speak but was interrupted by Lucy's voice coming down the hallway and into the kitchen with force for an eight-year-old.

"Mommy? It's Spirit Day, remember? I need a wild hairdo!"

Alex gave Ben a look. She couldn't pass this one off onto him, it wouldn't be fair to ask him to handle the task of wild hair. "Let's try to get the girls to school first," she said. "Then we can talk."

Ben held her gaze. "You sure?"

Alex nodded. She ran the back of her hand over her right eye, swiping at the tears, and handed him the blue bowl filled with strawberries delicately sliced just the way their youngest daughter liked them. "Can you bring these to Molly? I better go do Lucy's hair."

There were things to do, lunches to finish making, kids to help, work for Ben to eventually get to. She brushed her hands off on her hips and forced a smile.

"Who thought a Spirit Day during the last week of school was a good idea?"

Ben nodded, gave Alex a quick kiss on the cheek, and left the kitchen in search of Molly. She couldn't be far. Their home was relatively small, a raised bungalow with three bedrooms, the living room and kitchen all on the same floor. When Ben and Alex had first walked into it with their real estate agent for the showing, they knew immediately that it would be their forever home. Alex loved the warmth, the slick hardwood floors, the shiny kitchen and the carpeted, comfortable bedrooms. She especially loved how easy it was to keep tabs on the kids when they were little, with everything laid out neatly on one large floor.

They had chosen a home in the suburbs, knowing they wanted their kids to have the type of childhood they'd had. One where they could roam around a quiet neighborhood together, unsupervised, making snow forts in the winters and exploring creeks in the summer. Where they would come home only when the streetlights came on, their necks creased with dirt and their fingernails caked with mud. Ash Grove was like that. It was a sandwich town, situated between two larger suburbs, and relatively unknown and quiet. It was close enough to the city but secluded enough to give Alex the quiet she had grown up with.

Alex turned down the hallway and went into the main bathroom to find hair elastics. She scanned the countertop and found toothbrushes not put away in the cup, a book that belonged in Lucy's bedroom, lip balm. It was all a discarded mess that reminded her of her job as mom: to keep order. Alex touched a hand to her forehead. Her eyes were heavy, sore to the touch, and the skin underneath was puffy and darker than usual, almost purple now. It seemed that forty-one was the age when she started to show signs of youth slipping away. Although, this time, Alex thought the splotchy skin and deep creases around her mouth and eyes could be blamed on the phone call.

She'd known something was up when Jess had called instead of texting. A sharp stab of alarm went through her whenever she got a call from her little sister. Jess was the baby, and Alex and Sam had always worried about and fussed over her.

Alex could remember the day their mother had first brought Jess home from the hospital. Alex had been allowed to hold her. She had thought Jess looked like a baby pig—all pink and squishy, the fine white baby hairs on her head glowing in the daylight.

"This is Jessica," her mother had said, handing the baby to Alex who was propped up on pillows.

"I want a turn!" Sam had struggled to get in between Alex and their mother, sticking her face in front of baby Jess's.

"You'll get a chance, Samantha." Their mother was so patient. Three girls aged seven and under was no easy life to navigate, even with an involved father. And John London was hands-on.

As a kid, Alex had liked to follow her father around from room to room just to be with him. When he went to the kitchen to make Alex and Sam's breakfast for them, when he puttered around in the garage, when something needed fixing in the backyard, John would do it, and Alex would be there, too. The only thing she had never seen him do was laundry. That, for some reason, was solely up to her mother, but everything else was fair game, divided between the two of them. Sometimes, her father would take baby Jess into her room and set her down carefully on top of the changing table. Alex would stand at one end, watching him, grinning at the thought of Dad wiping a poopy bum, but it never seemed to faze him. He would delicately lift her feet, wiping at her soft skin and then placing the diaper under her tiny wrinkly newborn bum like an expert. Then he would dress her in her onesie again before lifting her gently, always holding onto the back of her neck, and settling her into the crook of his arm. He was a natural.

Alex pulled a hair elastic off the door handle in the bathroom and replayed the conversation with Jess over again in her head, as if she was still holding the phone to her ear.

"Where are you?" Alex had asked. "What's all that noise?"

"I'm at the airport, out on the tarmac right now. Sorry. It's loud here."

"What are you doing at the airport? I thought you weren't coming home for another few weeks. Are you okay?"

"No, not really." There had been a pause. An excruciating silence that felt like it lasted forever, until Alex could hear a crack in Jess's voice when she tried to speak again. It had wobbled and broken the way it always did when she was crying. A wave of cold had swept over Alex, her pulse beginning to thud.

"Jess?" Alex had said. "Jessica! What is it?"

"It's Dad. He had a massive heart attack. He's gone."

# TWO

## SAM

Sam woke to find the weight of an arm across her body.

She strained her neck to look to the side, thankful to find it belonged to her new boyfriend, Wes. They were in her bed, she was wearing her pajamas, he was in his boxers, but she had no recollection whatsoever of how they'd got there.

Sam lifted Wes's arm up and held it in the air, positioning it away from her chest before dropping it onto the mattress. He grumbled and snorted and then resumed snoring, a soft chortling sound coming from his parted lips.

When she moved, a thick wave of nausea rolled through Sam's stomach and up into her throat. Her head throbbed.

*Oh God. Thirty-nine is way too old for whatever we did last night.*

Sam gingerly sat up in bed, her head bowed so she could take a breath and collect herself before trying to move again. On her nightstand sat an empty wineglass, the dregs of last night's overindulgence staining the bottom red. The acrid smell of old wine flooded her nose.

*Gross,* Sam thought as she heaved herself up and out of bed.

She shuffled into the washroom to splash cold water on her

face, swiped at the black smudges under her eyes with some coconut oil and a tissue and looked in the mirror. Her curls were even bigger and wilder than usual, with a significant amount of frizz on top of her head sitting high, like a crown. The humidity in the summer air had that effect. Her hair would be frizzy now until the fall. She gathered it up into a high bun.

Bits of last night were coming back to her. The dress, the high heels, the restaurant with the great food. They had been celebrating—but what? Sam couldn't recall. At least she had today to recoup and recover. There were no sales calls scheduled until mid-afternoon, which meant the morning was hers.

Sam shook a couple of ibuprofen into the palm of her hand and gulped them down with water, throwing her head back and then regretting it when a spear of pain shot through her temples. She opened the bathroom door, wincing as it creaked loudly, and looked over at the bed. Wes hadn't moved.

They had only been together for just over a month; it was too new to know every little detail about how he slept, how he handled hangovers, if he even got them. She didn't want him to sleep this off at her apartment; they were also too new for that much togetherness. He would have to go home to shower and get clean clothes to pull himself together before work.

"Wes?"

He mumbled something.

"Wes. It's eight o'clock already."

Wes rolled over in bed and opened his eyes, blinking a few times and then smiling at her. "Good morning, beautiful."

"Ha. Good one. I look about as great as I feel." Sam stood at the end of the bed, looking down at the rumpled sheets, Wes's lean body tangled up in them. "What the heck were we thinking last night? People in their late thirties have no business going drinking on a Sunday night just for the hell of it."

"Speak for yourself. I'm four years younger than you, remember? I can handle this no problem." He smiled again and rolled onto his back, pulling the covers up to his shoulders and burying himself underneath. "Besides, it wasn't for nothing. You had a great week, it needed to be celebrated."

Sam sat down on the edge of the bed and smiled as it came back to her. The deal. Last week, she had made her first big sale in a while, and it came with a large commission. Media sales was an odd industry that was always changing. You had to adapt and get creative when you were selling space, and Sam had been finding it challenging lately. When she had called Wes after the deal had closed, she had been on a high. It was his idea to go out for a fancy dinner and order several bottles of wine to celebrate, but Sam didn't have to be asked twice. The beginnings of relationships were filled with snap decisions and spur-of-the-moment nights like this, and Sam loved the spontaneity. Until the next morning.

"You need to get moving, don't you? You'll be late for work." Sam twisted her body toward Wes. She wanted some time alone to nurse her hangover now. Her favorite way to start the morning was to sit on her couch in her pajamas, sip her coffee and browse through the news. Slow, quiet mornings were her luxury—one that she could afford because of where she was in life. No kids and the flexible work hours meant she could take her time each day, and she did.

"Yeah, I guess I should get going." Wes pulled at the covers and swung his legs over the edge of the bed.

Sam watched the lateral muscles in his back flex as he bent over and picked up his jeans and shirt. He was lanky and lean but had a muscular build and thick shoulders. His most attractive feature, though, had to be his messy hair, which was maybe a touch too long and always in need of a brush. It was a young look, but it worked on him.

"What are you doing later?" Wes moved to Sam's side, wrapping an arm around her waist. His lips brushed her neck, muffling his voice as he spoke.

"I don't know."

He stood, waiting for her to say more, but Sam hadn't made any plans yet. She didn't want to be pinned down by something that she would later feel like she didn't want to do. She half shrugged at him.

"Well, give me a call when you know what you're doing with your life," Wes joked.

Sam felt another wave of nausea sweep over her. "I will." She needed a glass of water. Maybe back to bed for a nap.

Wes pulled on his shirt and jeans and made his way to the door, pausing to kiss Sam again, then headed off, leaving the house quiet except for the soft whir of the overhead fan. As she listened to him go, her phone rang, the sound more startling than she expected. She looked at the screen: it was Alex.

"Oh good, I'm glad you answered." Alex's voice was thin and tight, an octave or so higher than she normally spoke.

"Hey. What's up? Are you okay?"

"Not really, no," Alex said.

The back of Sam's neck prickled. Alex was always okay. "What do you mean?"

"Jess called me."

"From Ireland?" Sam said. "Is she okay?" Now her stomach rolled. She paced towards the kitchen, the phone clutched to her ear. Something wasn't right. Jess was closest to Sam, so if something had happened, why had she called Alex first?

"She was at the airport—she's on her way home." Alex's voice went quiet. "Dad passed away."

The room seemed to move around her. Sam collapsed into a kitchen chair and tried to breathe, tried to make sense of the words that had come through the phone line. She must have misheard. Dad was a vibrant, healthy man. He wasn't sick.

"What?" Sam's voice was hoarse.

"He had a heart attack while he was at the cottage. Mom was with him. She called Jess and asked her to call us."

"Why didn't Mom call me?" It wasn't the right question to ask, but it came out before she could stop herself. This was how it had always been—Sam pretending it didn't bother her that she was overlooked in little ways, pushing down her disappointment when she discovered that she was last to know anything important going on in her family's lives, or that she wasn't included.

"We need to get there right away. Can you come pick me up?" Alex ignored the question the way big sisters do when they don't want to talk about something.

"Okay." Sam's ears felt clogged, her voice sounding strangely far away. "I'll be at your place in an hour."

After she hung up, Sam stared at the phone in her hands. When was the last time she spoke to her father? She couldn't remember. She couldn't recall what the last thing she said to him was. It couldn't have been anything of significance, they didn't often speak to one another in a deep and meaningful way because that wasn't the type of relationship they had. Her father liked to joke with her. The last time they saw one another, he probably teased her about something. She would have laughed, they would have had a glass of wine together, the way they often did, they would have said their goodbyes when the visit was done, and she would have left. Nothing very memorable.

She never could have known.

# THREE

## JESS

Jess sat in her car, stopped along the edge of the winding road that led to their family's cottage. She was only a few minutes from arriving, but she wasn't ready to make the last stretch of the drive yet. She tilted her head back.

The window was down, allowing the damp June air to blow its way into the car. It smelled like her childhood did: the woodiness of campfire smoke, earthy, fresh rain.

She would have to move eventually. She couldn't stay here much longer without Alex texting to see where she was.

Jess let out a slow sigh, raised her head until her eyes were firmly focused on the path ahead and put the car into drive. Then she made her way down the road that led back to her family.

Jess hadn't been back to the cottage in a while. Her mother would think it had been too long, though she would never say it out loud. Carol London was okay with her children growing up. She didn't push them or make demands on their time now that they were all adults, but Jess and her sisters knew she was thrilled when they all gathered there together.

When Jess did return, it always felt like coming home. The

quaint sand-colored cottage never felt too cramped or too small, no matter how many people were there. Jess thought of it as open and breezy, all warm and familiar. She loved every little part of it—the steps just to the right of the entranceway that led up to the open kitchen overlooking the modest eating area and living room, the scratchy plaid couch beside the giant windows that were always open, the creaky bunk bed in her and her sisters' room. When you walked around barefoot, grains of sand clung to the bottoms of your feet, and the floors groaned under your weight. Old games gathered in one of the corners of the living room, and tattered books—beach reads—could be found on the tall, floor-to-ceiling bookshelves lining one of the walls.

But Jess's favorite part was the beach. You only had to walk down a gentle slope of grassy land before you were at the sand and the water. Shadow Lake was one of the smaller lakes in the cottage town of Summerville, but it was still vast and gorgeous, and the beach—again, tiny in size—was their own private play area growing up. Jess and Alex and Sam used to spend hours in their bathing suits, discussing the logistics of sandcastle building and, when they got older, talking about school or their friends as they stretched out on towels, hoping the sun would turn their pale skin golden brown. Their shoulders and noses would freckle as their hair lightened, Mom and Dad reminding them to wear sunscreen as they sat reclined in their Adirondack chairs, resting plates of cheese and crackers on the armrests, sipping cold glasses of beer.

The lake had brought them together, but Jess wondered how it would feel now. When they sat by the water and Dad's chair was left empty, when they set the table for dinner, who would sit at the head of it? Or when they pulled out the board games at night and sat cross-legged on the floor, shouting at one another about how many times one of them had won, who would be the voice of reason? Life without him wasn't something Jess could comprehend, and yet, just like that, he was gone.

Maybe his death was some type of punishment. She shouldn't have left home for her retreat in Ireland. She shouldn't have been so focused on herself. Shame flickered inside her. She should have been there. At the end, she should have been with him. So many things had been left unsaid.

Jess pulled into the long gravel-filled driveway and got out of the car to stretch, tilting her face up to the sky. Soon, the work would begin. Funeral arrangements, banking details and tons of paperwork, Jess imagined. Alex would have to help with that; she was good with details. At least nobody would ask Jess to do it. She wouldn't know where to begin. She had been disorganized her entire life. Her mother told her she was the only kid in the history of their elementary school who lost a pair of jeans while at school. She had gotten better since then, but organization still wasn't her strong point. Anyway, Alex was good at compartmentalizing. She could set aside the grief while the work needed to get done. Jess couldn't.

Jess already understood that this type of grief was different for her. She hadn't cried much yet, and she worried about that. The deep, heaving sobs your body should be wracked with when a loved one dies, the kind Sam most certainly had already experienced, hadn't happened for her. What did that say about her?

She heard the familiar crack of the screened patio door slapping against the wooden doorframe and looked up in time to see Mom appear just outside the cottage doorway. She was thinner and looked frail, more so than the last time Jess saw her, like the wind might whip her away.

"Mom," Jess sighed. Her arms instinctively went up and out toward her mother. Mom's arms opened the way they always did when she greeted Jess and her sisters. Jess went to her, wrapping herself around her mother's petite frame, resting her chin on top of her shoulder, breathing in her light, floral scent.

"It's okay," Carol said eventually, her voice low and sad.

Jess pulled away so she could get a better look. Close up, the creases on her mother's face were more severe than she was used to, her smooth, buttery skin showing the signs of age and exhaustion. Her eyes flashed with a kind of uncertainty that made her look small. Jess's throat ached.

"You're just in time," Carol said, clearing her throat and then gripping Jess's forearms. "Alex and Sam have opened a bottle of wine." She tried to smile.

Jess put her keys into her purse and followed her mother through the front door.

Standing in the middle of the living room, a wine glass in one hand, was Alex. She had one arm crossed over her body and an impatient look on her face that softened when she saw Jess. "Hey, you." Alex put the glass down on the coffee table in front of her and moved toward Jess. Her dark hair was tied back at the nape of her neck and she had on almost no makeup. Even in times of distress, Alex managed to be beautiful and pulled together. "Did you just come from the airport?"

Jess nodded.

Alex came closer and wrapped one arm around Jess and then leaned back, calling over her shoulder. "Sam! She's here."

Sam came into the room, wiping her hands on the hips of her ripped jeans, a tea towel slung over her shoulder. She smiled at Jess for a brief moment and then pushed a strand of curly hair out of her face with the back of her wrist. It was only a second before Sam's face crumpled and, as if the act of crying in front of her family embarrassed her, held the same wrist up in front of her face to try to hide her pained expression.

When Jess was little, she could cry easily and often did, probably because she was the baby of the family. The more she cried, the more attention she had showered onto her. But, at some point, she stopped the crying—right around the same time she didn't want attention on her any longer. It suited her fine for most of her adult life. Until this moment. Now that she was here in the cottage, surrounded by her sisters, it was a good time to allow herself to finally cry for her father. Only, she couldn't. She pressed her lips together into a grimace and hoped her mother wouldn't notice her lack of tears.

Alex didn't seem to. She ran the palm of her hand over Jess's cheek and then touched the tiny mole Jess had just above her lip, the way she used to when they were kids. That was Alex's thing to try to make Jess laugh, their inside joke. Their mother used to tell them the story of how she had been in one of her early-motherhood sleep-deprived states when she was changing Jess's diaper and noticed it—a tiny brown mark above her baby's lip. She was certain it was dirt, maybe even a pinprick from a marker left behind by one of her sisters. Carol had wiped and wiped at Jess's lip, only to realize shortly after that her baby had a beauty mark. A sweet, little beauty mark that Carol had tried to get rid of with a damp cloth. When Carol told that story, she always laughed, and the girls did, too.

Alex gave Jess another squeeze, and then pulled away. "Okay, now that we're all here, would you like a glass of red or white?"

"White." Their summers at the cottage always involved lots of drinking and eating. Glasses of wine on the dock, tallboy cans of beer, bread and cheese, barbecued burgers, butter tarts and cookies from the bakery in town. It was one of Jess's favorite things about this place. "But I'm going to grab my things from the car first."

She kissed her mother's cheek again and paused, looking directly into her eyes. She held her gaze, wondering if her mother saw the *I'm sorry* she tried to silently communicate. There was so much to be sorry for.

"I'm good now," her mother said quietly, misunderstanding. "Anyway, how was Ireland? I want to hear about your trip."

"Oh yeah," Sam called over her shoulder as she walked toward the kitchen. "Doolin, was it? That's where you stayed?"

Ireland was so beautiful, Jess thought it was untouchable. She had thought that sadness couldn't find its way into the windswept ocean views and fresh salty air. She had no reason to think it would find her all the way in County Clare. When she had left Ash Grove and arrived in Ireland a week ago, she was filled with anticipation. She told herself she was there to write, to finally take her craft seriously, rather than just pounding out pithy little articles and blocks of copy that were dull but made her money. The truth was, she went to be alone. To write her novel, yes, but also to try to figure out who she was and what she was doing with her life now that she was in her mid-thirties. She didn't get a chance to discover much.

"It was beautiful," Jess said. It was easy to get swept up in County Clare. She hadn't thought of her family once while she was there and part of her had thought she might not come back. Her face flushed at the memory. Jess turned her back to the room so Sam wouldn't be able to see her.

The tiny home she had rented in Ireland had an other-worldly, magical quality. The living room had three massive floor-to-ceiling glass windows that overlooked the flat country-side outside. It was a farmer's home that had been restored with a quaint but simple design and aesthetic, and Jess had fallen in love with it the minute she had found the pictures online, especially the wood-burning stove and the cozy bedrooms. But it was the giant copper free-standing tub in front of more floor-to-ceiling windows in the master bathroom that had completely sold her. She would be isolated out there. No interruptions, no people walking by. Just flat, empty land to stare at and a secluded cottage in a tiny village in Ireland to escape to.

It had been as magical as she could have hoped for, but now

Jess couldn't shake the guilt of knowing that while she was there, her father was at home taking his last breath and her mother was alone while she tried to process it. Jess's bones felt like lead, weighed down by how much she had missed back home in one short week. Her father was gone before they could say anything to one another. They hadn't had a chance to talk, and the thought nearly undid her.

"Give me one second. I'll be right back," Jess said now.

The screen door creaked in its familiar way as Jess pushed it open. How many times had they run in and out of that doorway as kids, flinging it open with force, kicking their sandals off once they were inside? Everything here had a recognizable sound and feel. It was a small comfort for her at least.

At her car, Jess pulled open the door to the back seat. She bent over and stuck her head in to reach for her bags.

"Excuse me—" An unfamiliar voice came from behind her.

Jess's head instinctively snapped up and smacked the edge of the car opening.

"Ouch." She pulled herself out and held a hand to the back of her head.

A man she hadn't met before came towards her.

"Oh. Um. I'm sorry about that," he said. "Are you okay?"

"I'm fine." Jess felt her face warm. She lowered her hand and tried to play it off.

"Sorry," he said again. "I'm Hunter. From the cottage just down the road."

Jess looked to where he was motioning. "The Smiths' cottage?"

"Yeah. Well, formerly the Smiths' cottage. I bought it a few months ago."

"I had no idea they were selling," Jess said. Her mouth twisted into a frown. More change was unsettling.

"I got lucky." He smiled and extended his hand. He was directly in front of Jess now, and she was able to get a better look at him. He had tanned, toned forearms and broad shoulders that were emphasized by the tight T-shirt he wore. He must have been at least six foot tall. It felt like he towered over Jess when he moved closer to her. He was probably about Alex's age. Early forties, maybe. Definitely older than her thirty-four years.

"I'm Jess," she said, taking his hand.

"Good to meet you. So, this is your place?" He pointed behind her.

"Family cottage. My parents own it," she said and then frowned again. It wasn't natural yet for her to say "my mother" instead.

"Nice." He nodded and smiled.

Jess stood by her car, waiting for him to continue, wondering what he wanted, hoping she could somehow politely excuse herself before they got stuck making small talk for too long.

Hunter rubbed the back of his neck. "I was actually here because I was wondering if you might have a flashlight I could borrow? I'm working on some plumbing repairs in the kitchen and I somehow managed to leave every single flashlight I own at home. Rookie mistake."

"Oh. Uh, sure." Jess supposed she couldn't just leave him outside standing here. She grabbed her duffel bag from the car, slung it over her shoulder and started to make her way up to the cottage. "Come with me," she called behind her.

Inside, Sam's head popped around the doorway of the kitchen, her curls cascading around her face like a curtain. "Oh. Hello."

"This is Hunter. He bought the Smiths' place." Jess turned to Hunter and pointed at Sam. "This is my sister, Sam."

Sam held her hand up in a wave and smiled.

When Alex and Mom came into the room from the back

hallway, Alex's eyebrows furrowed. She shot Jess a quick look and then turned her attention back to Hunter.

"This is my other sister, Alex," Jess said. "And my mother, Carol."

"Hunter." He extended his hand and nodded at them both.

"Nice to meet you." Carol's voice was polite, but her words short. Jess could see exhaustion in her face. She had no energy for small talk right now.

"I'll grab you that flashlight." Jess went to the junk drawer and rummaged through it until she found one. "Will this do?"

"Perfect. Thanks. I'll have it back to you tomorrow if that's okay?" He stood close and looked down, his eyes focused squarely on her.

"No rush." Jess's face warmed again.

When he left, Jess stood in place and watched him go until she couldn't see him anymore. He was interesting. Not her type, but definitely handsome. Then she went to the living room to flop onto the couch next to her mother.

Sam sat cross-legged on the floor, picked up the bottle of wine and poured a generous glass for Alex.

"None for you?" Alex asked.

Sam shook her head. "I'm still queasy from my overindulgence." After she passed the glass to Alex, she grabbed their mother's phone and held it up to the room. "What should we do about all this?" The screen was lit up with missed calls and messages. A litany of condolences from well-intentioned people who wanted to see Mom, drop off food in foil packages, hug her and ask how they could help.

Mom shook her head. "I can't deal with it. Not yet."

"Here." Alex waved a hand at the phone, motioning for Sam to hand it over to her. "I'll answer them."

Carol put her feet up on the ottoman in front of her and held her head in one hand. The way she had slumped over, her shoulders rounding in on herself, made her look much older than she really was, as if a heaviness had settled on top of her and was pushing her down. Even as a grown-up, it was hard to see your parents weak. It caused a piece of Jess to break, like a little shard of glass cracking.

After a moment, Carol looked up at her daughters and spoke in a quiet voice. "I know you're worried, but I'll be okay. I've got you with me now. Dad would have loved this."

Dad probably wouldn't have come right out and said he loved it, but it would have been clear in the way he sat upright in his oversized comfy chair like he was holding court, his fingers pinched around the stem of a glass of wine, listening to soft music in the background and silently watching his daughters and wife. When all of them were together, he tended to shy away from taking control of the conversation. He'd once told Jess that he knew they needed time with Mom to chat, and he was happy to let them take over while he sat nearby listening. Even when he was silent in that way, Jess could feel his presence. Unlike now.

Jess looked over as Carol bowed her head. The clock on the wall ticked, filling the silence with a steady rhythm.

When Carol looked up again, she forced a small smile and took the glass of wine Sam handed her. She put her feet on the floor and sat up straighter. "For now, I only want to sit here and be with you."

"Okay." Jess reached over and placed a hand on her mom's leg, smiling up at her the way she had when she was little, masking the worry. They were all trying to make up for the vast emptiness they felt, but it wasn't working.

# FOUR

## ALEX

The sky was smudged with pinks and yellows the next morning. Alex watched it through the kitchen window while the coffeemaker's low hiss and crackle indicated it had started up. It was still early, and the cottage was quiet, so Alex moved as silently as possible across the floor to the fridge. Everyone would need a little extra sleep after the late night and the wine. Alex, however, was a creature of habit. She liked to be up early before everyone else to enjoy the stillness of the empty house.

"Oh good, coffee's on?" Sam yawned as she walked into the room a few moments later in a tank top and baggy pajama bottoms, her hair wild and tangled from last night's sleep. Even when messy, it was gorgeous, the way it framed her face. Sam was blessed with the perfect head of hair and, like most curly-headed girls, had absolutely hated it growing up. Alex, on the other hand, had inherited the kinky, frizzy hair gene from their mother and had to straighten it every day to get it to do what she wanted.

"Just got it on," Alex said. "You're up early." She took the milk from the fridge and poured it over her bowl of cereal. Alex ate the same breakfast every single day, and had done so for as long as she could remember—always a bowl of Shreddies and a cup of coffee. Mom made sure there was a box of it every time she came here. It struck Alex as such a Carol thing to do—taking care of your kids and making sure they had what they wanted, even when they were fully grown. Even when she was grieving.

Alex pulled two mugs down from the cupboard and filled them with coffee. She splashed milk into hers, watching the black liquid turn a caramel brown, and took it to the table, picking the seat facing the window. From this spot, Alex could watch the sun rise over the lake. It was flat and shining like a mirror, not yet disturbed by swimmers or boats.

"What's the plan for today?" Sam asked, her fingers wrapped around her cup of coffee. She pulled her legs up onto her chair.

"I guess we have to figure out what to do first." Alex dipped her spoon into the bowl, allowing it to fill with milk. "We'll have to decide what to do with—" She stopped. She couldn't bring herself to use the term "the body" to describe her father. "How to handle the details of cremation."

"Mom needs to go through the will and the banking, take his name off accounts. There's some other legal formalities, but she has the lawyer helping her with all that." Sam blew into her coffee before taking a sip. "Did she tell you she already wants to sell the house back home and move here?"

Alex sighed, leaning her spoon on the edge of her bowl. "It's too soon to make that kind of decision." Their mother lived not far from Ash Grove, where Alex lived. It was only a few hours away from Shadow Lake, but she seemed to spend less and less time at home and more up here at the cottage.

"Maybe." Sam shrugged.

Alex stretched her arms above her. Her shoulders cracked and her back was stiff from sleeping on a different bed last night. It bothered Alex how many things changed in her body as she got older. Her legs ached when she first got up in the morning, her ankles cracked often when she walked. She used to think her body was invincible.

When she turned around, she half expected to see Molly and Lucy stumbling into the kitchen to find her. Normally, this would be the part of the morning when they would appear in the kitchen, wiping sleep from their eyes, their bodies still warm from their beds. Her days always started the same way—coffee and cereal in silence, then the girls and Ben would get up soon after and the work would begin: rushing around to make them their breakfasts, pack their lunches and get their backpacks ready, help Molly get dressed and brush her teeth, while Lucy did most of it on her own. Always the same thing, day in and day out. After school, they would come home and Alex would unpack their bags, washing their lunch containers so they would dry in time to make lunch again that night. Get them snacks, take them to their activities, have dinner, showers when there was time, books and bed. And then all over again the next day. It was routine and comfortable, and Alex thrived on that.

Yesterday, Alex had tried to keep going with the morning routine, tried to focus on getting the girls to school before she let herself take the news in, but Ben and the girls had come to the bedroom and found her perched on the edge of her bed, her head in her hands and eyes wet. They'd enveloped her in a tangle of arms and then Lucy had pulled away first to study Alex with round, worried eyes. It alarmed both of her daughters whenever she cried.

"Come sit next to me." Alex had motioned to Lucy and Molly and then patted the bed on each side of her. Ben had run a hand over Alex's shoulder and then backed away to give the girls space, standing in the doorway. "You know how we talked about what happens sometimes when people get old or really sick?" Her throat was dry, and her voice had come out hoarse.

"They die," Lucy had said, matter-of-factly, the way kids do.

"That's right." Alex had nodded and then swallowed,

buying herself time to compose her voice. "Grandpa got sick and something sad happened. He died yesterday." She had reached both of her arms out and placed them on her daughters' legs. Something about their tiny bodies, their smooth skin, the way her hand rested on them like it fit, like it was meant to be there, gave Alex comfort. She had decided she would keep it to the plain and simple facts, that was all her daughters were ever looking for anyway. Little kids needed that basic knowledge so that they would be able to move on, and Alex knew, with time to process, they would be okay.

"That's really sad, Mommy." Molly's little voice had sounded far away.

Lucy had started to cry. She'd looked up at Alex, and Alex thought her chest might break open.

"It *is* sad. I'm very sad." Alex had pulled the girls close, her need to comfort them instinctual. After the learning curve when she'd first had Lucy, she had quickly discovered that when they were babies, or when they got a bit older and would hurt themselves, or when they would wake in the middle of the night after a bad dream, Alex reacted instantly to their cries, as if her body moved before her brain knew what she was doing. She had to wrap her arms around them, kiss their hair, run her hands gently over their faces. She had no choice.

They had sat and held one another until the cries eventually stopped.

Ben had moved closer to them and bent over to reach for Alex, pressing his lips to her temple, holding it that way. "I'm sorry," he'd whispered.

She had closed her eyes and leaned her head into his, then stood and folded herself into his body. He was stocky and muscular, but soft at the same time. He had been her safety and security for twenty years. She couldn't recall the last time she'd had to function in a crisis without him. But Lucy and Molly had a few more days of school to finish up, so they had eventually decided that Ben would stay at home with them, giving Alex time for the initial frenzy of arrangements and details to settle down at the cottage. After that, they would come and join Alex and the rest of the family, the way they usually did in the summers. They were lucky Ben was a teacher, which meant he had the same schedule as the girls, and Alex ran her own free-lance business so she could arrange her life in order to have summers free. They had so much to be grateful for, but in that moment, Alex had only felt a raw pain.

When Sam had showed up and they were ready to leave, Alex had hugged Lucy and Molly one more time. She'd stood close to Ben and kissed his lips, then closed her eyes as she ran her forehead along the side of his cheek. "Call me later."

Now, in the quiet of the cottage, Alex refilled her giant mug with coffee and added some more milk, feeling the absence of her family. She wanted to check in with Ben, wanted to know how the girls were, but it was still too early.

"I'm going to the dock," she said to Sam. "You want to come?"

Sam moved to the couch and stretched out, shaking her head. "Thanks, but I want to sit here and read my magazine."

Alex nodded and slipped into her flip-flops, pushing the screen door open, then closing it carefully so it wouldn't snap against the frame and wake her mother or Jess. She wandered down to the dock and took a seat in one of the Adirondack chairs, holding her coffee up close to her mouth with two hands, watching the lake.

It was still smooth, with only a few light ripples where a bird would land, or a small fish would jump. She could stare at the water for a long time and think. Quiet moments like these were rare—stolen snippets of time when nobody was asking her for something or crawling into her lap.

A kayak rounded the corner past the trees at the edge of the dock and floated in front of her. The guy from yesterday was inside it—the one who'd bought the Smiths' cottage. His head jerked when he saw Alex on the dock. He shifted in his seat and lifted a hand to wave.

"Hi," he said. "I didn't think anyone would be outside this early."

"I'm an early riser, against my own will. Two little kids means I can't sleep in anymore even when I want to." She forced a smile.

He put his paddle into the water, pulling against the shallow of the lake to stop his kayak near the dock. He smiled back. "That's nice. The kids, I mean. Not the forced early rising bit."

Alex laughed in spite of herself.

"How's the fishing out here?" he asked. He rested his paddle across his lap for a moment and looked around him, surveying the lake.

"Pretty good. You should probably ask my younger sister Jess about it, though. She's the fisherman in the family." Jess was the one who had no fear when it came to handling squishy worms and slimy fish. She was their father's right-hand man in the summers. Jess could often be found on the boat wearing a life jacket and an old ball cap, their father with his giant tilly hat, handling lures and worms, both of them enjoying the quiet of the still lake in the early morning or at dusk. They had been partners, until Jess had distanced herself, the way girls do with their fathers as they get older.

"I will," he said. He nodded at Alex, placing the paddle back into the water when the kayak started drifting. "It'll have to wait, though. I managed to forget all my fishing gear, too. I swear, I don't know what I did bring here."

"Are you staying for a while?" Alex asked.

"The rest of the week. Then I'm heading back home to grab a few things before I come back for the rest of the summer. The perks of being self-employed. You?"

"Also self-employed." She raised her hand up the way she used to in elementary school. The freedom that came with running her own business was a gift, especially now. She managed her own website full of healthy eating tips and recipes for parents with little kids. She had enough experience in the area with Lucy and Molly and she had always loved making them healthy lunches or snacks for after school. Eventually, she had figured out how to make a decent income from her passion. She sold ads and subscriptions to her newsletter, and it afforded her a life she had always wanted, a regular income and all the time she needed for her family. "My husband and daughters usually come up here for most of the summer, too—as long as my mother doesn't mind having four extra mouths to feed, anyway."

"I didn't think I heard any kids?" He looked past Alex and back up at the cottage.

"No, not yet." Alex's shoulders tightened up around her ears. "My sisters and I came up to help my mom go through my dad's estate and will. He just passed away."

"Oh. I'm so sorry," he fumbled. "I shouldn't be asking so many questions. Feel free to tell me to get lost."

"No, you're good." She forced a smile again and then changed the subject. "Anyway, we have loads of fishing gear here somewhere in the shed if you want to borrow a rod and some lures?"

"That would be great. Thanks, Alex."

Her eyebrows shot up. "Good memory. You met four of us all at once; that's a lot to keep track of."

"A family full of women willing to help out a neighbor," he said. "That makes you memorable."

His words surprisingly warmed Alex. What a nice thing to say. Alex knew she wasn't the memorable type. She was somewhat plain: dark hair, dark eyes, average build, average height. She didn't have wild curls or a big personality. She wasn't petite and sweet, like Jess, something that people seemed to like in a grown woman. She fiddled with the edge of her shirt and hoped he couldn't tell she had completely forgotten his name already, but she was terrible with names.

He nodded. "Anyway, I should keep going. I planned on kayaking across most of the lake this morning. It's my thinking time."

"The lake is a great place to think." Alex stood up. Her mug was almost empty, and she could use another refill. "I'll grab one of our spare fishing rods for you. Drop by whenever you want."

"Thanks," he called over his shoulder as he lifted one arm to wave. "It's Hunter, by the way."


Alex made her way down to the shed to fetch the fishing gear. She might as well get it now and have it ready in case Hunter came back later. She smiled to herself at his sense of humor. He must have realized she didn't remember his name. For an attractive guy, he had a touch of self-deprecation to him. She liked that.

Inside, the shed was dank and cool, with only a dim light coming through the window on the far wall. When was the last time she had come in here? It was a storage area, holding boxes of Christmas decorations, old pool noodles, dirty garbage bins, rows of tools; another thing they would eventually have to go through with Mom. When they were growing up, the shed had been their father's escape. He would come out here to fiddle with his fishing rod, or to work on some project he had going on. There was always something to do: a chair needed a fresh coat of paint, or a few small tables had to be built to rest food and drinks and bottles of sunscreen on by the edge of the lake. Dad was a worker. He had to be busy, and sometimes he liked to escape the chaos of three loud little kids.

Alex's eyes scanned the room, searching for fishing gear. She wouldn't give Hunter Dad's fishing rod—he could borrow hers, or Sam's. Neither one of them had touched them in years.

Along one side of the shed, buried under a shelf, was a tackle box she didn't recognize. There was bound to be something in there that Hunter could use. She crouched down and pulled it out with both hands, setting it on top of the wooden bench Dad had built.

After opening it up, Alex surveyed the lures. There were wormy, wiggly pieces, shiny silvery ones, something that looked like a spoon on a hook and another large, aggressive-looking lure that looked like a fish with a knife sticking out of its mouth. Alex shook her head. What kind of fish would ever fall for that? Anyway, this would do.

She went to put a lure back, but her finger caught on an edge along the side of the box. There was an extra layer to the tackle box—a tray that came out of the bottom. Alex lifted it up, curious as to what else she would find.

Underneath the top layer lay a fat stack of folded pieces of paper, held together by a rubber band. More paperwork to go through, Alex thought. She picked it up and flipped it over, looking for a letterhead or something that would indicate what it was. There was neat handwriting across the back of one of the pages. Her eye caught sight of a phrase and stopped.

*I love you.*

It stood out among a sea of scrawled words.

Alex's cheeks warmed with embarrassment. Love notes? Dear God, had she found a stack of love letters between her mother and father? How cute, but also grotesque, in the way it was to think of your parents having sex. Then again, the handwriting wasn't familiar to her. Maybe her father had held onto some letters from an old girlfriend before he had met Mom.

She put the papers back in their place. Mom knew about the couple of girls he'd been out with before they'd met, and would probably think it charming he'd held onto these mementoes. Alex would come and get them later and put them with the rest of her father's paperwork for sorting.

She was about to close up the tackle box when her eye caught something else on the back of one of the pieces of paper. A sentence that confused her.

*I'm sorry for showing up at your home, but you weren't returning my calls.*

# FIVE

## ALEX

Alex whipped the elastic band off and peeled one of the pieces of paper away. A sour taste formed in her mouth and the back of her throat ached. She put the paper down on the bench and smoothed it out in front of her with shaky hands. It was yellowed around the edges and worn soft from time.

*John—*

*I know you're busy, but I miss you. When do you think we'll see each other again? What about our weekend away?? You said you were going to tell her you had a business trip, and we were going to be together. I haven't forgotten. I hope you haven't forgotten me.*
*I keep thinking about that new restaurant we went to the other week, and the steak and aged wine. Just you and me and good food, and then after...*
*Hope we can do that again.*
*Talk soon. Call me as soon as you're alone. I know that's hard with your little ones around, but try. Please.*

*xoxo*

*P.S. I'm sorry for showing up at your home, but you weren't
returning my calls. I love you. I won't do it again.*

Alex took a step backwards, and almost fell over a stack of
old flattened cardboard boxes. It was suddenly hot and suffo-
cating inside the shed. She looked around, her eyes searching
for something, and then back down at the note. Her stomach
lurched when she saw the words again. It wasn't what she
thought it was. It couldn't be. This note was to her father from
another woman.

She shook her head. John London was not this man.

Shoving the letter into her pocket, Alex picked up the rest
of the notes and pushed them down into the other pocket of her
sweater. She couldn't look at them now, she had to get out of
there. She had to go tell Sam and Jess so they could try to make
sense of this together without letting their mother know. Alex
couldn't understand at all. If anyone had told her that her father
was the type of man who would receive love notes from a
woman who wasn't their mother, Alex would never have
believed it. Not a single word. But the evidence was in her
hand.

Inside the house, Sam was still on the couch with a mug of
coffee and a magazine perched on her lap, her bare feet resting
on the coffee table. The rest of the cottage was quiet, except for
the hum of the refrigerator and the call of mourning doves
coming in through the open window. Jess and Mom were the
late risers of the family. They must still be sleeping. Alex was
thankful for that fact in the moment.

"Sam. *Sam*," Alex hissed, urgent and insistent. Her movements felt awkward as she made her way to Sam's side, her
limbs wobbly and light as air, the way they always were when
she was nervous or scared.

"What?" Sam looked up.

"I found something weird." Alex spoke quietly as she sat on the edge of the couch and pulled her sweater around her torso. Her forehead was tight and throbbing.

Sam sat up straighter in her seat. "What is it?"

Alex pulled the piece of paper from her pocket and handed it to Sam. "Read this."

Sam's forehead wrinkled, but she took the paper from Alex, opening it up to reveal the curvy, loopy handwriting scrawled across it. Her eyes scanned the words and Alex watched as her face went pale and ashen, as it always did when she was uncomfortable. It was just like the time when they were finally old enough to get their ears pierced. Alex was older, so she got to go first, and Sam had stood in front of the chair at the store in the mall, waiting her turn, watching the woman place the plastic ear-piercing gun on Alex's lobes. When Sam had heard the crack of the gun and saw Alex flinch, she'd sat down in the middle of the store and told their mother that her stomach didn't feel so good. Sam's small face was waxen—almost gray-green in color, and it took hours for her to recover. Ever since then, Sam couldn't hide when anything unsettled her. It was written all over her face.

A chill ran down the back of Alex's neck, causing goosebumps to spring up along her arms. "Who the hell do you think this is from?" she demanded.

Sam looked up from the note. "I don't know." Her mouth hung partially open.

"What does it mean?" Alex asked, pointing down at it. "I mean, I know what it means, but—" Her voice wobbled. "This can't be true. How old do you think this is?"

They both looked down at the soft, yellowed paper. Sam ran her pointer finger over it. "It feels pretty old. Where did you get it?"

"I was looking for something in the shed and found it buried in an old tackle box underneath a bunch of lures, along with these." She took out the rest of the notes and held them up.

Sam's eyes flicked over Alex's shoulder and then back to the stack of notes. "Have you read them?"

"No. I only just found them. I looked at that one and then came to find you."

Alex could say with confidence that this scenario would have never, ever crossed her mind in a million years. John London was a good man, a devoted father and attentive husband. Alex knew how lucky she had been. She grew up with the image of a perfect family around her: a mother who was patient and loving, three healthy, relatively happy girls, and an involved father. John changed diapers and did hair, he made the girls their breakfast, took them out on the boat, brought them with him on his errands. People always asked him if he wanted a boy, or assumed they would have another child so he could try for a son, but John always shrugged those kinds of comments off. In fact, Alex had once overheard him telling their mother that there was nothing you could do with a son that you couldn't do with a daughter. The fishing and camping and digging around in dirt and wrestling, those were some of Alex's most vivid memories. They were always together. When would there even have been time for him to cheat? Her stomach dropped at the thought of it.

"How old do you think we would have been?" Alex needed to know. She liked all the facts laid out in front of her when it came to any question or problem. "How long do you think he was cheating on Mom for?"

Sam only shook her head in response, her mess of curls shaking around her face. She folded up the paper and handed it back to Alex. "We don't know the full story yet. We've only read one note. I think you're jumping to conclusions here," Sam said.

Alex flinched slightly. "You don't think this is pretty clear?"

"We have no idea who this person is, or how involved Dad was. I'm only saying let's not completely freak out," Sam reasoned.

Alex was convinced she was right about this. She rubbed at her forehead. A dull ache was forming at her temples. They sat in silence for a moment until Alex spoke again. "How could this have happened without us knowing? I never noticed any signs at all."

Sam ran a hand through her hair. She frowned. "I guess there was a time when... I remember thinking that something wasn't right."

"*You what?*" Alex stiffened. "What do you mean? Did you tell Mom?"

"Of course not. I was too little. I had no clue what was going on." Sam looked at her lap and examined her cuticles.

"When?" Alex wondered why Sam hadn't said anything at the time. "How old were you?"

"I don't know. Maybe ten. I remember Dad being different, and I wasn't sure why, but I thought it had something to do with him and Mom." Sam's voice shook a little when she spoke.

"But you never talked to me about it. Did you talk to Jess?" It bothered Alex to think of Sam, so little, not fully under-standing and carrying this worry around on her shoulders. She reached out for Sam's hand and squeezed it, although she wasn't sure who she was trying to reassure.

"I vaguely remember mentioning it to Jess once," Sam said. "She sort of brushed it off, like she didn't want to hear it. You know how she gets with anything confrontational. Besides, I did talk to you—don't you remember?"

Alex's back straightened upright in surprise. "You did?"

"I was lying in your bed one night when I couldn't sleep, back when you used to let me." She smiled a little sadly when she said it. "I told you I thought something was wrong with Dad and that I was worried about him. I said that I used to hear

Mom and Dad arguing a lot. The only reason I remember all of this so clearly is because you laughed at me."

"I laughed at you." It was more of a statement than a question. It sounded like something Alex could very well have done back then. The things they had said and done as kids, before they realized how their words and actions could sting, it made her cringe as an adult.

"Yeah." Sam raised her chin into the air. "It upset me. Actually, it embarrassed me. That's why I remember."

"I had no idea. I didn't mean to," Alex said.

"You probably thought I was overreacting. Mom and Dad used to argue a lot, remember? You used to think I was being paranoid."

"I guess you weren't." Alex flopped back onto the cushions of the couch, crossing her arms over her body. She wished she hadn't reacted that way to her sister. She could only imagine what might have been different if she had taken Sam seriously. "He couldn't really have been having an affair, could he? He wouldn't do that to Mom." Her eyes darted to the piece of paper on the couch between them. "Or to us."

If these letters turned out to be what Alex thought they were, their father had betrayed not only their mother, but all of them. He had put their entire childhood in jeopardy. It didn't make sense. Was it just about sex? If it wasn't, Alex didn't want to even begin to think about what it could mean. He couldn't possibly love someone else the way he had loved them.

"What are you going to do with them? Are you going to put them back?" Sam asked.

Alex sat upright with a new resolve. "I'm going to read them all and find out what was really going on." She picked up the papers and shoved them into her pocket again.

"You're not going to tell Mom, are you?" Sam asked, her eyes wide.

Alex's underarms were getting damp. It was humid, and the

air inside was sticky, like it was going to rain. She gave her head a small shake.

"Don't bring this up to her, whatever you do, okay? She doesn't need this now," Sam said.

"I know. But we have to tell Jess." Alex motioned for Sam to follow her as she got up to leave the room.

"Now?"

"Yes, of course. We can't pretend things are normal now that we know about this."

Alex stood in the middle of the cottage, waiting for Sam to get up from the couch. Her entire body tensed. She rolled her shoulders and tried to ignore the tingling in her limbs.

Who knew what else they would find out?

# SIX

## JESS

When they were little, the three of them used to share two beds between them at the cottage. Every summer after school let out, they would arrive in Summerville, the small community situated across three islands. The girls would be in the back seat of the car, pressing their fingers up against the inside of the window as they approached the town, watching familiar scenes whip by.

There was the little pie and coffee shop on the corner of one of the main intersections, next to an independent grocery store that was surrounded by pots of flowers in brilliant colors. Just ahead of it was the abandoned steepled church nestled into a bend in the road. Another tree-lined street was always filled with locals and vacationers milling about, strolling in and out of shops, eating ice cream. There was a giant shoe store on the main street that seemed out of place in the quiet town, where Mom would take them at the end of every summer to get new shoes for school. Restaurants with floor-to-ceiling windows lined the street, with people spilling out onto the patios.

If you went down a side street, you would find the town bakery, the fish and chip shop where they got takeaway on

Friday nights. Hidden along another side street was the dairy, where they served scoops of ice cream through the front of the building, out a narrow window. If you ordered three scoops on your cone, the story was that the servers had to come out a side door to hand it to you because it was too tall to be handed out the window. John and Carol didn't allow the girls to order three scoops; it would make their stomachs hurt or cause them to bounce off the walls. Sam protested the most, even though she was the one who had the weakest stomach. It was known in the London house that if Sam had too much junk, she would throw up. Yet, she was the one with the sweetest tooth and often had two scoops instead of one.

Separating the main street in town from the area with all the cottages was a swing bridge over a set of locks. Jess used to love getting stuck at the red light by the swing bridge so she could watch the long wooden arm come down, lights flashing and a bell clanging out as the locks opened up to make room for the boats slowly chugging through, moving from one lake to the other. Kids would stand on the bridge, waving madly at the boats, delighted whenever anyone waved back at them.

Once they arrived at the cottage, Jess would go straight for the bedroom the three girls shared. Mom usually followed behind to push the two twin beds tightly together and cover them with fresh sheets. For as long as they were little and could fit, they slept side by side, three in a row in those twin beds, where they would whisper and giggle long after they had been told to close their eyes and go to sleep.

Eventually, the bunk beds came in, along with renovations for more space. Mom and Dad had known the girls would outgrow the twin beds—they were only a short-term solution anyway—but Jess wished they hadn't gotten rid of them. She loved being in between her sisters where she was huddled close and safe. Alex and Sam used to argue over who had to sleep in the crack where the two beds came together until Jess gladly took that spot.

As the baby, Jess was used to feeling protected and doted on, especially by Sam, and being in that bed was no different. At the end of each day, they would collapse on top of the covers, usually with dirty feet and tangled hair but wearing a fresh nightgown, exhausted after a day of sunshine and fresh air and lake swimming. The girls shared that space, shoulder to shoulder, their heads pressed so close to one another that Jess never had to worry or struggle to be heard.

The bunk beds were still there now, mostly for when Lucy and Molly came to stay, but when Alex, Sam and Jess were here together, it didn't take much convincing on Jess's part to get them all to share the bedroom again.

That morning, Jess was lying on her side on the bottom bunk, awake, but with her eyes closed, dozing in and out of morning sleep when Alex whisked into the room first, followed by Sam.

"Jess, are you awake? We need to talk to you." Alex's voice was urgent.

Jess's eyes popped open. "I'm awake. Where's Mom? Is she okay?" Mom was the first thing that came to Jess's mind when she woke up these past couple of days, and the last thing she thought of before falling asleep.

"She's still in bed. She's fine," Alex said. "Listen to this."

Alex and Sam filled her in on the note, the woman with the big loopy handwriting, the details they never wanted to know about their father. Sam mentioned the fighting, and how she suspected something hadn't been right for a while when they were little.

Jess stayed silent, but her bones were buzzing with unease. This wasn't happening. She felt dizzy when she hauled herself up in bed and sat cross-legged, like the world was tilting from side to side. For this to come out now, after he was gone. There was nothing they could do. Her gut reaction was to hide, to crawl back under the blanket and think, but Alex's voice was already so angry, so insistent. It was too early for this.

Jess thought she had done a good job of ignoring her memories, but now they started to swell beneath the surface. The anxiety was coming back, too. After all those years of therapy she hadn't told anyone about, she felt good. She thought she was at peace with herself and her family. In truth, ever since she got the phone call from Mom about her father's death, something was bubbling up that made her weary and anxious at the same time.

"What are you going to do?" Jess asked.

"I don't know." Alex sat next to Jess on the edge of the bed and bent over, her head in her hands.

"We can't tell Mom. She's dealing with Dad's death, and she's already making snap decisions." Sam stood over them with a hand on her hip. "She mentioned she wants to sell the house and move here, but first she wants us to get rid of all his things. Already." She squeezed the bridge of her nose.

"It's too early." Alex sighed.

"There's no timeline for this. Everyone grieves in their own way." Jess wanted them to leave Mom alone. She wanted them to leave all of this alone.

Alex shot her a look. Her face was pinched. "There are more notes," Alex said. "A whole stack of them. I took them from the tackle box in the shed." She held up a pile of papers bound together by an elastic band.

Jess froze, a heavy feeling settling into the base of her stomach. *Don't go there, Alex.* "Did you read them?"

Alex shook her head. "Not yet, but I'm going to. I'm going to get to the bottom of this."

"Why?" Jess couldn't understand her sister. What was the point? Dad was gone, Mom was grieving. The truth was, opening that box was a very slippery slope, and how much did they really want to know?

"What do you mean, *why*? I want to know if our entire childhood was a lie. We thought we had a great family life with parents who loved each other, but it turns out Dad was lying to us." Her voice rose an octave and sped up, the way it always did when she was angry or upset.

"Alex, this could have been a one-off thing. Maybe he had a short fling with this woman and was done." Sam rested the edge of her hip on the wall, crossing her arms over her chest.

"Or maybe there are more secrets." Alex frowned. "I want to know."

Jess rubbed her eyes and stood up to grab a pair of shorts from the floor. She took off her pajama pants and stepped into the clean shorts, then picked a tank top out of her duffel bag and pulled it on over her sports bra. There was a tension in her shoulders, a feeling of dread. This would likely play out the same way as things had played out when they were kids. Alex would decide how it was going to go, she would make all the rules until Sam grew tired of it and refused to go along. Then Alex would be mad, Sam would be mad, and nobody would notice that Jess hadn't said much at all. She wanted to be left alone for the most part, and right now, she didn't want to stick around to hear what else Alex had to say on the subject.

"I'm going for a walk."

"I'll let you know what else I find out," Alex called after her.

# SEVEN

## SAM

Sam and Alex stood in the kitchen, hovering over plates of food and tinfoil packages that well-meaning people had dropped off. Sam picked at a piece of ham before placing it back onto the plate and thought about how excruciatingly long the last twenty-four hours had felt. Everyone was exhausted, but they had barely even gotten started. The funeral was planned for Saturday, here in Summerville rather than back at home. Mom and Dad had spent more and more time in Summerville as they'd got older and less back in the city, which meant it made sense for her mother to hold a small funeral here. It also made sense for her to sell the house and stay here permanently, but Sam didn't like the thought of her mother being alone. Especially during the long winters.

Sam knew her father would ideally have liked no funeral at all. He hated the idea of all that attention on him. He despised any kind of fuss like that. When he had turned fifty, and then again at sixty, he had flat out insisted that Carol not hold a big birthday party. He wanted a cake and a quiet night with the five of them. It was all he needed. Sam remembered how hard that had been for her mother. She had wanted to decorate their home with balloons and streamers, invite their friends, play music and pass around drinks.

But the fact was, a wake and a funeral weren't for the deceased. They were for the family to grieve, and her mother wanted to hold one, so Sam would push down these newly conflicted feelings she had about her father and the notes and would help her mother.

When Carol came into the room, Sam reached out her hand and touched the edge of her mother's arm, hoping that she was okay.

Carol turned to Sam. Her eyes looked tired. "I can't bring myself to do his laundry," she said.

Sam's chest tightened at the weight in her mother's tone. "What do you mean?"

"There's a big pile of his clothes... Your father's dirty clothes are still sitting in the laundry basket, and I can't bring myself to look at them, let alone do them." Her eyes had a glazed look. "But that's not realistic. I can't leave there forever. When do you think I'll be able to do simple things like look at his dirty clothes without crying?"

It was the way her mother's voice cracked at the end that crushed Sam. Sam wished she were more like Alex. The last thing her mother needed was the extra work of comforting her daughter on top of all her grief.

Sam did her best to compose her voice. "This just happened, Mom. You've got to give yourself time."

"You don't have to do anything until you're ready," Alex added. "And we can help."

"I want to clear everything out, but I can't seem to," her mother said. "It's too hard seeing reminders of him all around me."

Sam glanced around her. Dad's things were everywhere— his glasses perched on top of a book on one of the end tables, his coat hanging by the door, a pair of slippers at the edge of the room. Her mother hadn't moved a thing, so the girls hadn't either. It stood out, like a mistake. They were signs that he was alive and well, that he would return soon to find his wife and daughters happy to see him. But he wouldn't, and they all knew that. Sam shivered.

"How about one step at a time?" Alex went to Carol's side and wrapped an arm around her frail shoulder.

Carol's voice was small and far away when she spoke. "I don't know how else to handle this."

Sam didn't know either.


Outside the cottage's front door, Sam almost walked into somebody. It was the neighbor. The tall one Jess had introduced them to yesterday. Hunter? Was that it? He was standing on the porch, like he was about to knock. Was he going to be the type of neighbor that dropped by all the time? Sam wasn't sure how she felt about that. The Smiths had owned that cottage forever and barely ever said more than hello to Sam's family. She was used to it.

"Sorry, I didn't expect you," he said. His voice was deep. Actually, Sam could see he was quite good-looking now that she was close up.

"That's okay," she replied.

"You wouldn't happen to have a flat-head screwdriver, would you?"

"The number of times I'm asked that in a day," Sam quipped.

He laughed, low and throaty. "That's funny."

"What can I say?" She smiled at him. What was she doing? It sounded like she was flirting, but that couldn't be right. It was the most inappropriate time to be acting flippant. Her world was crumbling, and her family was in crisis, but she liked the way he stood in front of her, his arms crossed over his muscled chest, smiling wide. His expression was full of light, like a million suns. It was a distraction from the sadness, and Sam welcomed it. "Weren't you here borrowing a flashlight yesterday?" she asked.

"That was me."

She raised an eyebrow at him. She was definitely flirting.

Nothing wrong with some meaningless fun, she thought.

"I'm still moving in, and I forgot a lot of things at home," he said.

"It happens." She shrugged. "I can look for a screwdriver for you. A flat-head?"

"Yeah, do you think you might have one?" Hunter asked.

She moved past him, off the porch and towards the shed where her father kept the tools, when she stopped abruptly. She didn't want to go in there. Not after what Alex had found.

"I'm sure we do somewhere, but I was just about to run an errand. Could I look a little later?" That was partially true. She planned on going into town to get ice cream. She bolted from the house at the first opportunity because anywhere but within the cottage would be better. She needed to be doing something right now.

"Of course. I'm sorry to keep pestering all of you."

"It's no problem. I've always said that to have good neighbors you also have to be one."

Hunter tilted his head an inch to one side. "I like that." The edge of his mouth turned up into a half smile.

Sam liked the way her limbs tingled when he smiled. She wouldn't admit it if asked, though.

# EIGHT

## JESS

Jess had seen the first clear sign that something wasn't quite right with her father when she was seven years old. She had been playing outside and the streetlights had come on—her usual sign to head home. Alex and Sam were somewhere else, with friends maybe, so Jess was by herself when she took a shortcut through the catwalk close to the creek and down the path behind the row of houses on her street.

After slamming through the front door and kicking off her shoes, she had turned and saw him. Her father was sitting on the stairs that led to the upper level, perched on the third step from the bottom. His elbow was leaning on the stair behind him, and he was reclined, with one leg resting on a step and the other stretched out. His eyes were red and far away.

"Dad?" Jess had stopped in her tracks and stared at him, her head tilted to one side. He didn't move for a long time, but when he finally looked up and met her gaze, his expression was distant.

"It's you." He had clasped his hands together.

It was an odd thing to say, especially directed at her. Jess and her father were the most alike, so she always thought he knew her the best.

Of course it was her. Jess had frowned. "What are you doing?"

Dad had looked away and out the window, saying nothing else.

Jess had tentatively taken a step forward, toward him. The look in his eyes bothered her, the way it made him seem so weak. She wasn't used to the fragility he was radiating. Her father had thick hands and broad shoulders that carried her around. That was the man she was used to, strong and reliable. He used to like to take hold of her hand and intertwine his fingers in hers, pretending to squeeze them. "Let me crush those cute little fingers," he would joke. "They're so skinny and squeezable." He always laughed when he said it, and Jess would laugh, too, liking the feel of his warm, sturdy hand on hers.

Dad had looked at Jess with a hint of surprise in his expression, as if her movement snapped him out of his trance. He had stood up before she could get too close, turned around and walked up the stairs in silence.

Jess had waited for him to pull himself back together, to come down the stairs and ask to crush her fingers with a laugh, but it didn't happen. When her mother had found her sitting on the stairs, her head bowed and her shoulders slumped, she'd gathered Jess up into a hug and asked her what was wrong. Jess didn't know how to answer, so Mom had brought her to her room to get ready for bed, holding her both softly and firmly, but Jess had been shaken after finding her father like that, in a way that her mother couldn't fix.

That moment had been the beginning, as far as Jess could remember. Later, she had overheard bits and pieces of one of her father's phone conversations. They were different, Jess could tell because his voice wavered between soft murmurs and the angry hiss of a whisper threatening to get out of control. Jess had pressed her ear up against the cold wall in the hallway outside the room her father was in to try to hear through it, but she couldn't get a grasp on what was happening. Not until she heard him say it.

"Yes, I love you. But I have a family. Give me time."

She was a little older than seven when she'd overheard those words, maybe eight or nine, but she would have known they were wrong at any age. She had stood frozen, unable to move, wondering why those words weren't directed at her mother, the only person he should love that way.

Maybe that was why she had followed him into town one afternoon that summer. He had said he was going to run some errands and Jess knew a shortcut into town. By this point, the girls were allowed to wander around unsupervised. She'd hopped on her bike and pedaled to Main Street, just in time to see him standing out front of the bakery. He had looked over his shoulder once, scanning the area, but he didn't see her. Then he'd leaned in toward a woman Jess had never seen before and kissed her.

The pressure in her chest had been debilitating. Jess had fought for air because it felt like she couldn't breathe. After that, she was numb. So numb, she kept silent. She was torn between loyalty to her mother and her father. She wanted her mother to know, but she couldn't betray her father. It wasn't fair that she was in this position. None of it was fair.

Because she didn't know what else to do, Jess had let the secret fester inside her. Throughout the rest of her childhood, as a teenager in high school, even as she went off to university, Jess was forever pushing it down, trying to forget. She had tried to push it down so far that it didn't hurt anymore, hoping it wouldn't affect her relationship with her father, but it did. Of course it did. She was wary of him after that, especially when he showed his affection to Mom. She would still go fishing with him, still enjoy her summers on the lake, talk to him about her homework over the dinner table, but she kept him at arm's length. She never let him pretend to crush her little fingers again. It hurt her more that he didn't seem to notice anything was wrong.

Jess's fingers tingled as she walked. She knew that if her mother had ever found out back then, there was a very good chance their father wouldn't have been involved in their lives. He would have missed out on soccer games and dance recitals and first days of school and graduations and friends and jobs. Everything.

The memories of her father's betrayal made her sick to her stomach, but they weren't enough for her to say anything to her sisters. Not yet. She didn't want to add to what they already had to carry around. If she was being completely honest with herself, she didn't want to add to her own shame either. They would be mad at her for keeping this from them and she would feel worse. She didn't know if she was strong enough for that.

Jess made her way down the road, swatting away bugs, the heat of the late-morning sun on her shoulders. She turned automatically to the right, the way she always did. Jess liked going this way, past the Smiths' cottage, because they were hardly ever out front. That meant she didn't have to stop and make stilted conversation with people she didn't really know, even though they had owned that place for almost as long as her family had owned theirs. It slipped her mind that it wasn't the Smiths' place anymore just as a voice called out.

"Hey there." Hunter stood on the front porch, fiddling with a set of tools. He stopped what he was doing and waved.

"Hi," Jess called back. For a split second, she thought about continuing to walk by with only a polite wave, but instead, she stopped and stood in place.

"How are you?" he asked, waving her over to him.

Jess hesitated and then went to the edge of his porch. "Fine, thanks." She studied his eyes now that she was closer. She couldn't pin down what color they were. They looked brown, with bits of hazel and even a little spot of blue all mixed in. He looked directly at her when he spoke, and something about the way he did it caused her chest to flutter when she took a breath in.

"Can I make you a coffee, or are you on your way somewhere?"

Jess's plan was to go for a walk to clear her head, but Hunter stood looking down at her, and she found herself saying yes. "I'm not going anywhere. That would be nice."

She followed him inside to the open living room. In all the years they had been coming to Summerville, Jess had never been inside the Smiths' cottage. It was surprisingly homey and neat for someone who had recently moved in. There was a soft, plush-looking loveseat to one side of her, a matching recliner on the other side and a small wooden coffee table in the middle of the room with a few books scattered on top of it. Everything faced the big sliding glass door that led out to the dock. The view of Shadow Lake was perfect from here.

"Incredible, isn't it? Though I'm sure you're used to this view," Hunter called from the kitchen over the clatter of mugs and utensils.

Jess was overcome with a sweeping wave of sadness as she looked out at the lake. Dad had brought Jess and her sisters up on this lake. He'd taught them how to fish and had let them drive the little tin boat when they were much too young. He swam with them for hours with fins and snorkel masks, searching for fish and discarded lures and other treasures. He had jumped with them from the middle of the floating dock, listened to them shout and scream with delight and excitement, and cuddled them on his lap in front of campfires at night. That was what she wanted to remember, but it was so long ago.

"You never get used to it," Jess said to the open window. Her voice sounded weird.

"Hey—are you okay?" Hunter stood beside her now. His shoulder was almost touching hers. She glanced up at him and he smiled.

Damn it, she was in trouble with him. She could tell by the warmth flooding her insides.

"Do you need a moment?" he asked. "I know things are hard right now, with your father. I could leave—or we could go sit on the dock." He was fumbling over his words, and Jess was struck by the softness of his voice, his eagerness to help find a solution.

She turned to him and tried to smile. And then she found herself reaching for him, clasping her hand onto his forearm like she knew him, like he was familiar, stretching her body until it came close to his, her face right in front of his, her lips searching. She kissed him, a soft kiss, and felt his body stiffen at the shock and surprise of it. He pulled away first.

"I'm not sure why I did that." Jess's face went hot. She looked down at her feet and wiped at her mouth. What had come over her? Maybe it was because she wanted to feel something in the moment. It was a desperate kind of reaction, one she regretted instantly.

"It's okay." Hunter's voice was quiet, a little hoarse.

Jess almost laughed at herself then, a crazed laugh, but she managed to hold it in. It was so bizarre. Here she was, standing in the middle of a man's living room, a man she'd just met, and she was trying to kiss him. Instead of being with her sisters, or helping her mother, Jess had run away and directly into an uncomfortable situation. It was typical of her. She was unable to face things head on, unable to tell it like it was, the way Alex could. "I'll leave," she said, looking down to avoid his gaze.

"You don't have to."

Jess was too embarrassed to look at him, but she couldn't

ignore the stiffness in Hunter's body. She had been stupid; she knew better. The only thing she could do was get out of there. "I'm actually not feeling all that well. I really better go."

"You don't have to leave," Hunter said again. He put the mugs down on the coffee table in front of him and moved a step closer to her. "I'm sorry if I made things awkward."

Jess wanted the earth to open up and swallow her. Now he was apologizing—but for what? For not wanting her the way she wanted him in that moment. This was awful.

"It wasn't you. It was me," she said. "I shouldn't have—I'm sorry." She turned to leave, and Hunter was standing behind her now. She could sense his body close to her, although he wasn't moving. He didn't reach out for her. "Thanks for listening to me."

She went for the door in a hurry.

Outside, it was a relief to feel the air again. She moved quickly over the driveway, the dusty gravel crunching under her sandals. What had she been thinking? When was the last time she had acted on impulse like that? She was an expert at pushing down her feelings, not letting them take over. She had to get a hold of herself.

She moved quicker, a light jog now, until she got back out to the road and close to the edge of her driveway. She bent over and put her hands on her knees and then jumped in alarm when a squirrel ran across her path.

Jess breathed out and shook her head.

Seriously, what the hell had she been thinking?

# NINE

## SAM

The timing was bad, but Sam had invited Wes to come visit. He'd caught her off guard in a moment of sadness when he'd called. All she knew was that she wanted comfort, and Wes was the closest thing she had to comfort outside of her family. The ice cream wasn't cutting it.

"Wes is on his way. He'll only stay for a night," Sam said to Alex. They were back in the kitchen, where everyone seemed to gather if they weren't outside by the water.

"We just got here yesterday. You think that's a good idea?" Alex closed the refrigerator and turned to Sam. Her voice had a tone to it. It was laced with judgment, the kind that she'd used with Sam and Jess most of her life.

Sam took in a calming breath. Alex had an innate ability to raise her blood pressure without even trying.

"It'll be fine. You'll barely notice he's here."

"But we're trying to help Mom settle things," Alex said. "And now this." She touched the side of her pocket where the notes were still sitting.

"You should get rid of those instead of carrying them

around," Sam said. Alex was being careless; she should know better.

Alex gave her a look, but refrained from saying anything and then left the room. A tiny victory over Alex was still a victory.

When Wes appeared in the doorway of the cottage late that afternoon, he stood slumped over, as if standing were too much effort. He grinned a lazy, lopsided grin at Sam.

"Hi." She leaned into his body and let him hug her.

"How are you?" he asked.

"Been better." She let go of the hug and looked up at him. What did she think of him? The newness of their relationship still made her question her feelings. It was hard to tell if she was infatuated by his looks, his body, or if she truly felt a connection. She had called him and asked him to come see her in her time of need, and he had come. That was something. Sam put her hands over his wrist and pulled lightly as she turned to walk away. "Come meet my family."

Inside, Wes tossed his bag down at the edge of the room and stood stiff and rigid as Sam introduced him to Alex and then her mother.

"This is Wes," Sam said.

She wondered why his back was so straight, his smile forced. Maybe it was her family, they were a lot all at once. It could have been too soon for him, Sam wasn't sure, but she hoped he wasn't going to be like this all night. She realized that she didn't know much about him at all.

Last night, when Mom had wanted to know more about Wes, Sam didn't have much to say. She had eventually come up with a shrug and said he was fun. She had tried, but she wasn't sure she'd hidden the defensive edge in her voice very well.

Alex had looked at Sam, as if she was waiting for more.

Sam had shifted her seat on the floor, lifting one edge of her thigh and then the other. "There's not much else to say."

"Okay," Alex had said, a slight uptick at the end of the word, like it was a question. Like she didn't believe Sam. It had set off a stab of irritation in Sam, the way Alex spoke—not the actual words, but the tone of her voice.

This was Alex's thing, to judge the way Sam did things, though she didn't even know she was doing it. When they were kids, Alex had once crushed Sam with only a few words. It was a brief, fleeting moment that had meant nothing to Alex, but had wounded Sam for days. The kind of thing that she remembered vividly even though she was an adult. It still stung a little, if she was honest with herself. There was a school project in the third grade and Sam had chosen to study Paris. Already at eight years old, Sam knew she desperately wanted to go there. Audrey, Sam's best friend at the time, had planned to travel with Sam as soon as they were old enough, agreeing that they should first go eat chocolate croissants and see the Eiffel Tower. Sam had spent hours working on Bristol board, cutting out block letters, writing neatly printed sentences about the population, tourist attractions, foods like baguette and crêpes and macarons. After she had finished, Sam carefully picked up her project with marker-smudged hands and brought it to the kitchen to show everyone. Mom and Dad had been delighted, showering her with compliments on how hard she had worked. It was only Alex who had remained quiet, her face revealing nothing but a mild interest. When Mom had nudged Alex's arm, asking her what she thought, Alex had looked from Mom to the project and then directly at Sam.

"It's kind of messy," she'd said flatly. "And you're not supposed to use that size of Bristol board."

Sam's stomach had dropped. She had worked so hard on it, was so proud of her drawings and the little touches she had put into it. When she had looked at it again, she only saw the places where her markers had colored out of the lines, where she had accidentally spelled a word wrong. Alex had been scolded by their mother and father, but she had also been right.

Now, Sam was hoping Wes would show them how comforting and adoring he could be when he was with her. Then Sam would be the one who was right.

"Nice to meet you." Mom held out her hand and smiled.

"I'm sorry for your loss," Wes said back.

Alex, thankfully, did her best to keep the conversation moving. "How was your drive?"

"Oh, you know," Wes said. "Not bad."

Sam picked up his bag and slung it over her shoulder, tugging on his wrist again. "Let's go out to the dock." She could see he needed saving from small talk, and she wanted to escape, too. Especially from Alex, who was watching Wes with an eyebrow raised.

Wes followed her to the guest room, where she placed the bag on the bed. He glanced down at her now, putting his palms on her bare arms, rubbing slowly.

"Thanks for being here." She leaned into him and he kissed her forehead. Then she pulled away. "You have to come see the lake. Let's go sit. Do you want something to drink? I can make you a coffee."

"Do you have any wine open?"

Sam thought it was a bit early for wine, but then again, Wes had made the long drive, and all bets were usually off when it came to food and drink at the cottage. They had convinced themselves that the calories somehow didn't count. Sam had once eaten three butter tarts in a single day and felt no shame whatsoever about it.

"Sure."

Sam went to the kitchen, leaving Wes behind to wait in the living room with her mother and Alex. She quickly grabbed a bottle of wine and two glasses and motioned for him to follow her to the lake.

Out on the dock, Sam sat as close to the water as she could get without actually being in it. "It's beautiful here, isn't it?" She squinted her eyes into the sun and waved her hand in the air.

Wes hummed in agreement and took a long sip of wine. After, he reached for the bottle and filled his glass again, pouring until it almost reached the brim.

"We won't run out." She tried to sound gentle, but she didn't want him getting sloppy, not here in front of her family.

Wes glanced in her direction. "So, how are you? Like—really? Are you okay?"

Sam softened. "I will be."

They were silent for a while.

Wes tilted his head back and closed his eyes, pointing his face up to the sun. "Is there a funeral planned yet?"

"It's on Saturday."

He raised his head again and opened his eyes. Maybe it was the sadness she couldn't hide in her voice that caused him to look over at her. The kindness in his expression suddenly made Sam want to talk.

"I just learned my dad had an affair. When we were kids." She regretted it almost as soon as the words were out of her mouth. It was too personal to share. They weren't there yet in the relationship.

"Really? How did you find out?" Wes asked.

Sam supposed she had already opened Pandora's box and couldn't exactly end the conversation without questions, so she continued. "My sister found some old notes."

Wes shook his head. "Who keeps written proof of their affair in the same place they spend summers with their family?"

"I don't know." Sam turned to face the lake. It was a good question. She hadn't had a chance to dissect it all with Alex and Jess. Maybe the affair had happened here, in their oasis. That made it even worse. Summerville was filled with nostalgia and good memories, but now it would be tainted.

"What are you going to do?" Wes asked.

Sam thought about it. Alex planned to read the other notes and see what she could discover. Jess, on the other hand, hadn't said much. She would probably avoid all confrontation, the way she usually did, and wait for someone to solve her problems for her. It was funny to Sam that her two sisters could be such polar opposites, and yet she was so different from them, too. They knew how they were going to handle this, but Sam didn't know what she wanted.

Sam shook her head. "Not sure." She needed to change the subject now. "Anyway, what do you think of the lake?"

Wes looked out at the water and then down at his wine, swirling the glass in one hand. "Nice." He tilted his head back and closed his eyes.

It struck her that she didn't feel close to Wes, then. She had opened up to her boyfriend and then regretted it. She didn't have the energy to try to analyze why she couldn't feel close to Wes in that moment. Instead, she turned her head back to the lake and watched the water ripple in front of her, billowing out into perfect circles and then disappearing.

# TEN

## ALEX

The house was quiet. Jess was out for a walk, Sam was with Wes, and their mother had gone for a nap. For the first time, Alex had a moment to herself alone, so she went directly to the bedroom and pulled her suitcase from under the bed. When she flipped open the case, they were there, in front of her.

She didn't want to read the letters again; Alex knew it was a bad idea to put herself through this, but it was like being unable to turn away from a car crash, and it was the only way she knew how to handle the situation. Examine every fact, think about it exhaustively, discuss it within an inch of her life. That was how Alex made sense of things. Somewhere in those notes she might find a hint or an answer about why her father had done this, or who this woman was.

Alex only wished Ben were here. When she had called him earlier, after she had spoken to Sam and Jess, she wanted to go over it with him—he was the one she always turned to in tense situations.

"Wow," he'd said at first. "Are you sure?"

"Sure of what?"

"Are you sure they're notes for your dad?"

"Ben. What kind of a question is that? His name is at the top."

"I don't know—I'm grasping here. I'm trying to think. I can't believe your dad would do that."

"I know. Me neither. I wish you and the girls were here."

"I wish we were there with you, too," he'd said. "I really don't know what to think or say. This one totally came out of nowhere."

"Can you imagine playing around with Lucy and Molly's lives like that? Threatening everything safe in their worlds so you could have sex with someone else?"

"I'm guessing it's a bit more complicated than that," Ben had replied.

Alex had stiffened. It wasn't more complicated than that to her. She'd crossed an arm over her chest. "When you get down to it, he cheated on my mother and could have ruined everything we had as a family. He's an asshole. Not that complicated."

"Alex." Ben's voice was quiet.

"What?"

"I know you're angry, but—" His voice had trailed off. He was only silent for a minute before he'd continued, "What are you going to do now?"

"I want to find out more, like who this woman is, how long they were together, if he was leading a double life or if it was nothing more than a fling."

"But why? Why do you need to know all of this? He's gone. It's not going to change the past."

*Has my husband just met me?* Ben knew Alex needed the facts laid out in front of her.

"I need to try and understand." This wasn't what families did. It wasn't love. So, what was it? "We must have been young when it started, I could tell by how old the notes are—what if he had other kids?" she'd continued. The idea of another family was so odd to her, but there was a chance it was possible.

Now, Alex crouched down on the floor in front of the suitcase and picked up the thick pile of folded notes held together by a rubber band. They didn't look like much, but she knew they had the power to potentially change her world, and her history.

Alex removed the rubber band and glanced over her shoulder again to be safe. She opened a note and scanned the words.

*John,*

*I miss you. I know the girls are young and it's hard to get away, but could you please try a little harder? I'm lonely. I want you. Call me when you get this.*

*Xoxo*

The back of her neck prickled. This was going to be worse than she thought, if that was possible. She hated how this woman referred to her and Sam and Jess as *the girls.* Alex and Ben called Lucy and Molly the girls all the time to one another. It was too casual and familiar for someone who didn't know them, and too violating seeing it written in someone else's handwriting.

Alex scanned a few more notes, finding much of the same— the woman wanted to know when they were going to meet up again, she was lonely, she missed him. She talked about the things they did together, the places they went and the getaways they took. She referenced little inside jokes between them. That might have been the hardest to read.

Folding up the notes again, Alex touched her forehead. She was too lightheaded to get up, but she couldn't keep reading.

She closed the suitcase and pushed it under the bed. A heavy feeling weighed her down, pushing her into the floor. She couldn't pinpoint it. Sadness? Yes. But she was also angry. Her grief was confusing to her. How could she properly mourn her father when he wasn't who she thought he was?

Alex never doubted that her father had the kind of life he wanted. A simple life, but a fulfilling one. He went to work, he paid his bills and raised a family. They spent summers here, they went on day trips to museums and hiking through parks, they made dinner and sat down to eat together every Sunday night. He read bedtime stories to the girls and went to bed early and got up and did everything all over again the next day. He seemed to like it, but now Alex couldn't help but wonder if sometimes it all got too boring for him, if he felt overcome by the monotony of it. What was his breaking point?

A shred of terror rippled through her. If her father wasn't immune to the pull of something, anything, that would take him away from the dreariness of adult life, would the same thing happen to her? There was no denying that family life could be very dull sometimes. When you were an adult, you had bills to pay and people to take care of, and at times, it could be boring and predictable. Then again, Alex knew the difference was in how they looked at life. Alex was carefully in control. She hadn't realized her father wasn't until now.

Her phone rang, surprising her, the way it always did when she got a call. She looked at the screen and saw Ben's name and face. She picked up. "Ben?"

"Hey."

"What's up?" Alex asked. "Is everything okay?"

"I wanted to check in on you again. I'm worried about you. This is a lot."

Alex's shoulders softened. Her body had been so tense without her realizing it. Sometimes during tense moments in her life, when she was in bed at night and right before she fell asleep, she caught herself grinding her molars. Ben would lean over in bed, usually around the same time as she realized she was doing it, and tap her arm lightly. "You're doing it again," he would murmur. "It's okay. I'm here." The sound of Ben's voice always calmed her.

"I know." She breathed out, long and heavy, and stood. She placed a hand on the wall next to her.

"Do you want me to bring up the girls earlier than we planned? I could be there tomorrow if you need us."

Alex would love to see Lucy and Molly. Watching them run in and out of the lake, whipping their heads around to make sure she and Ben were looking, sitting together at the table to eat dinner, listening to their high voices tell silly stories and then erupt into laughter would be wonderful. But she wasn't ready to be distracted yet. She hadn't figured out how to handle the news about her father. The thought of juggling her two kids and her sisters and mother, all while trying to keep the notes hidden and work through her own thoughts, it was overwhelming.

"I would love that, but we haven't done any of the things we're here to do yet. Mom hasn't even had any visitors." People had called, dropped off platters of food, had asked to come visit, but her mother had told them she wasn't ready. Everyone would love to see Ben and the girls, but they had details to go over and things to accomplish that needed all her attention. In the past, Alex had tried working when the girls were with her; it wasn't possible to do it well. Once the work was done, Ben and the girls could come to the cottage and Alex could give them all her attention. "Come up on Saturday for the funeral. After it's over, I'll be able to focus on you and the girls."

"If you're sure."

"I am. Thank you, though. I love you."

"I love you, too, and I'm worried about you," Ben said.

"I know. I'm okay, I promise."

"Listen," he said. "Until we get there, what do you think about looking into grief counseling?"

Alex shook her head, the phone still up to one ear. She was about to cut him off and end that kind of talk when he interrupted.

"And before you say no, think about it, please." He knew her too well. "You're going through a lot. It could really help to talk about it. Especially when I can't be there."

It was only a few more days until he would be here, but Alex knew where this suggestion was coming from. It wasn't the first time she had taken on the weight of the world and tried to survive it all on her own.

Motherhood was harder than Alex had expected at first, and when you had high expectations for yourself, failure wasn't an option. Back when the girls were little and Alex didn't feel like she had a handle on anything, when the clothes would sit wet in the washing machine for several days and she couldn't remember the last time she washed her face, she almost fell apart.

Ben had called her one afternoon when she was home with Lucy, just a toddler then, and Molly, a baby. Alex wouldn't answer the phone. She couldn't talk because of the lump in the back of her throat. The worst part was that Alex didn't know why she was about to cry. The girls were okay for the moment, but Alex felt like she was slipping, like she didn't know who she was now that she was a mother. She was grieving who she used to be, a woman in control and on top of her life. She had felt like a disorganized mess, and she couldn't see a way out. That afternoon, Ben had called six times and then come home early from work, he was so worried about her. He had found her sitting on the floor in the basement alone. It had scared her how unlike herself she had become, and so quickly.

She supposed she could admit that he was right about this being a lot to handle, too. It was easy to understand why he was concerned. She wanted to carry on and be organized like everyone expected her to be, but she couldn't risk losing herself again.

"I'll think about it," she said eventually.

"Alex."

"I will. I promise."

They said goodbye and she ended the call. Thank goodness for Ben. When anything got to her, he pulled her back. Ben and Lucy and Molly were living, breathing reminders of how much she had, how wonderful life could be, how lucky she was.

Why hadn't she and Sam and Jess been the same for their father?

# ELEVEN

## JESS

The next day, in the early evening when the sky was starting to dim, Jess walked into the kitchen and found her mother moving around in a swift manner, chopping vegetables for a salad, then stopping to whip up her homemade dressing. "Can you grab an extra plate for the table?" she asked.

"For who?" Jess reached into the cupboard and grabbed the plates.

"I ran into the man who bought the Smiths' cottage when I was coming back from town. He's all by himself over there, and we've got room and tons of food. I don't want many visitors right now, but it seemed only right to invite him."

Jess stiffened. "Hunter? Do you think hosting a dinner is a good idea? Don't you think we should be focusing on some of the things we need to do and tying up loose ends?" She placed the plates on the counter.

"Your father wasn't a loose end, Jess." Her voice was thin.

"I didn't mean that. I meant you need time to grieve. How can you do that if you're hosting dinners?"

Mom stopped what she was doing, her shoulders slumped. "I know. But I also need to keep busy. It's been really hard."

Of course it had. This was very hard, and it was hard on Jess, too. Having Hunter here for dinner though, after she had stopped into his place for coffee yesterday and... The thought made Jess cringe. Maybe he didn't want to see her either. Maybe Jess was better off somewhere else, back in Ireland, where she could be away from everyone and write her novel, where she could be her own person. Not the baby sister in the London family who made embarrassing mistakes.

Her mind went to her father, and she couldn't help but think about what life would be like now if he had been a different man. Jess would be more certain of everything, that was for sure. She wouldn't constantly study her mother's face, looking for signs that she knew, signs of depression, wondering how she was going to be after all of this had settled down, or how she would be if she found out.

"I promise I'll finish up the paperwork and all the other legal stuff tomorrow, with a clear head. Tonight, I want to have a nice dinner with my girls." Mom put a hand out to touch Jess's arm. "Well, my girls and two men I don't really know at all." She laughed. It was encouraging to see Mom laugh. Enough so that Jess realized she could get through the evening, no matter how awkward, for her mother's sake.

A few minutes later, Jess wandered down the hallway and stood by the edge of the doorway to the bedroom, arms crossed over her chest, watching Sam looking for something. "Hey."

"Oh." Sam jumped. "Hey. Where did you come from?"

"I was out for a bit." She walked into the room and sat on the bed across from Sam. "Did I see you and Wes out having a drink on the dock?" She thought he was leaving today, and assumed it would be before dinner, but she didn't want to sound rude and ask why he was still here. They hadn't had much of a chance to get to know Wes yesterday. Sam and Wes had gone into town to grab a bite to eat at dinner, which meant they hadn't sat down with everyone yet and had a decent chat. Jess wasn't sure what she thought of him.

"You did. I thought he was going back home earlier," Sam said, as if she could read Jess's mind. Her voice was low, the way it always was when they spoke about things they didn't want everyone to hear. The cottage was too small for secrets, especially in their tiny bedroom, but they had always tried anyway. "I guess he's staying for dinner. Anyway, I came in here to find my sunglasses." She motioned to the duffel bag she had been rooting through.

"I kissed Hunter," Jess said suddenly, without any explanation.

"What?" Sam's eyes widened. She stopped what she was doing and turned to face Jess. "The guy next door?"

Jess nodded, her face grim.

"Why?" Sam asked.

"I don't know. I was walking by, he invited me in for coffee and I was so sad all of a sudden, I wanted comfort. The kind of comfort you can get from Wes, and Alex gets from Ben." Humiliation cascaded over her like a wave. "I'm so embarrassed."

Sam stopped moving around the room and came over to Jess to place her hands onto her shoulders. Her eyebrows drew together and her features softened. Jess almost couldn't bear the look of compassion on her sister's face.

"Things are messed up right now and we're all trying to figure out how to deal with it," Sam said. "Dad died, we found out he was a cheater, and we're hiding everything from Mom. No wonder we all need a little release." She studied Jess's face, likely trying to read it, but Jess did her best to avoid her sister's stare. She pushed a piece of hair away from her forehead and covered her eyes with one hand.

"Now he's coming to dinner," Jess said.

"What? Why?" Sam's mouth fell partially open.

"Mom invited him."

Sam's hand shot up to cover her mouth, but she couldn't stop the laugh from erupting.

"Sam! This is serious," Jess said. "I'm really embarrassed." It was absurd, the way she acted, and the situation she was in. She had kissed their neighbor and now he was coming for dinner. Maybe it *was* kind of funny. "We're such a messed-up family."

"Maybe." Sam shrugged. "But, more importantly, was it a good kiss?"

Jess grinned. "It was nice. But it was clear to both of us it was a mistake. It's not happening again."

Sam touched Jess's shoulder again and smiled before leaving the room. "Never say never."



Later, when she walked into the living room, Jess found Sam and Wes sitting together on the couch, and Hunter in one of the recliner chairs. His hands were clasped in his lap and his body was rigid. Maybe he was as uncomfortable with this as Jess was.

"Hey," Jess said.

"Hi," Hunter said, shifting in his chair. He smiled at her and sat upright.

"Come sit," Sam encouraged. She patted the couch seat next to her, the one that was closest to where Hunter was sitting.

Jess avoided making eye contact with everyone.

"Is dinner almost ready?" she asked.

"I'm not sure. We're trying to get Mom and Alex to join us for a drink, but they're too busy up there." Sam nodded in the direction of the kitchen.

"I'll go help," Jess said.

"No need! We've got it—and we're almost done." Alex's voice called down to the living room from the open kitchen.

Wes took a sip of his wine. "Smells great in here." His lips were tinged with red and his cheeks colored pink.

"My mom is a great cook," Sam said, turning to Hunter. "I hope you're hungry?"

"I am. Thanks for having me. It's nice to sit down with a group to eat. I haven't done that in a while." Hunter placed his hands in his lap again, his broad shoulders squared.

"It's all part of being a good neighbor." Sam smiled at Hunter, and he returned it in a way that was almost intimate, like they were sharing a private moment, an inside joke. A twinge poked at Jess's stomach. This was going to be awful, wasn't it?

"It's ready," Alex announced. She came into the room and motioned to the table.

Sam and Jess went to their regular seats. Jess saw Carol freeze when Wes went directly to the head of the table. He couldn't have known it was their father's seat.

Hunter eyed Carol and then glanced at Sam. "Here," he said as he stood. "Take this spot, I'll grab another chair." He offered his seat to Wes, who seemed oblivious to it all.

Jess's shoulders softened.

"Thank you," Carol said. "I guess I'm not quite sure how to do all of this. I never know what's going to get me."

Hunter nodded. He was so understated and calm, like nothing ruffled his feathers. It was an admirable quality.

"Is there more wine?" Wes asked.

As Jess reached for the bottle and handed it to him, Sam bowed her head and tried to speak quietly. "How about some water?" she asked.

Wes shook his head in response. "I'm good with this."

Sam looked around the table at everyone, like she was checking to ensure they didn't notice anything amiss. Only Jess seemed to pick up on the look Hunter gave Sam. It was a kind one, like he didn't want Sam to feel bad. Only it lingered. After

Sam looked away, Hunter kept his gaze on her, and Jess noticed. Her stomach dropped.

"Sam, how's work going?" Carol asked. "We didn't get a chance to talk about it much yet." She piled roasted potatoes onto her plate, sprinkling them with salt.

"It's good," Sam said.

Mom stopped dishing food onto her plate and shot Sam a look. *It's good* wasn't an acceptable answer, they all knew that by now. As kids, they had tried to get away with *fine* or *good, it was okay,* or sometimes even *I don't know,* as their answers to everything. How was school? Good. Who did you play with? I don't know. After a while, Carol and John had made it clear that those types of one-word answers weren't allowed—and they still weren't.

Sam rolled her eyes, but laughed lightly. Then, as they ate, she told them about the targets she was meeting and the customers she had. She sounded impressive when she talked about the things she was good at.

"I'm hogging the entire conversation, aren't I?" Sam said. "Nobody can get a word in and I'm sure you don't want all the details. You don't want to listen to me."

"I do," Hunter said. He watched her when he spoke. "I like the sound of your voice." His hands were still, clutching his fork and knife. "I like listening to you."

Jess's neck went warm with secondary embarrassment. For an excruciating moment, nobody spoke.

Alex raised both eyebrows and Carol took a sip of water. Jess looked down at her plate, and then snuck a glance at Sam. Her face didn't show any signs of embarrassment, although Jess could tell Sam was trying to hide the start of a tiny smile. Hunter's face had reddened by then.

After taking a long sip of wine, Wes finally seemed to take notice. "Wait, what? What did you say? That's a bit off, don't you think? I'm sitting right here."

"It's nothing." Sam put one hand on Wes's lap.

"It's not nothing." He stabbed a finger in Hunter's direction. "Some guy I just met told you he likes your voice." Wes's words weren't coming out crisp, a hint of a slur at the end of each sentence. How much wine had he had? "Who is this guy? How well does he even know you?" Wes asked, his voice full of accusation. He was speaking like nobody else was gathered around the table, like he wasn't a guest in someone else's house, or he'd forgotten why they were all here.

"What are you talking about?" Sam asked. "We just met." She poured him a glass of water and pushed it in front of him, trying to play this all off as nothing.

Jess grew increasingly unsettled. She glanced at Alex and her mother in an attempt to read their expressions, but she couldn't tell what they were thinking.

Wes turned to Hunter and spoke angrily. "You don't know her."

"You're right," Hunter said, one of his hands up in the air like a stop sign.

"She and I are together," Wes slurred.

"We all know that, it's okay," Carol said. She spoke in a calm voice, as if she could defuse the situation with her tone. It was clear to Jess that it wouldn't work. Wes was beyond messy.

"I wasn't talking to you," Wes snapped.

Jess dropped her fork and it clattered and clanged louder than she expected. Her breath hitched. Who the hell was Wes to talk to their mother that way?

Carol must have thought the same thing because she flinched.

Alex's mouth fell open.

"That's enough," Sam hissed. Her neck was splotchy.

"I'm sorry," Hunter said. "I should go."

Sam stood up, her chair scraping on the floor behind her. "No, we're going. Please stay."

Wes was piling more potatoes on his plate, oblivious. "Why? I'm eating. He should be the one to leave."

Hunter put his napkin down and stood now. "He's right. I'm so sorry. Thank you for everything, Carol." He glanced at Jess and held her gaze. "I would offer to help clean up, but I think I should probably leave."

Jess's shoulders tightened. As awful and embarrassing as all of this was, she didn't want him to go.

"No, please—" Sam said.

But Hunter had already noticed Carol nod, a silent acknowledgment that maybe it was for the best. He left the room as quickly as it seemed he could manage.

Sam snapped her head around to face Wes. "You're drunk. Let's go," she seethed.

His eyes narrowed, but he stood and followed her into the bedroom, stumbling a few steps behind her as he went.

Nobody else moved until after the bedroom door slammed.

Alex was the one who finally picked up her plate and spoke. "I guess we should clear up."

They tidied up in an uncomfortable silence for a while, talking about little things, like the weather, their plans for the next day, but Jess's mind wouldn't stop racing. What had happened in front of her? What did Hunter mean by what he'd said? He'd only met Sam the other day, he barely knew her. He barely knew any of them. It was just like Sam to get the attention. She always did because of her big personality. She was the fun one, and, undeniably beautiful, she stood out in a room, while Jess blended into the background. It had happened again, right in front of everyone.

Annoyance pierced at Jess, like a bee sting. It was a sharp, painful stab of jealousy that she wished wasn't there.

# TWELVE

## ALEX

After dinner, Alex went to the bedroom to be alone. She sat on the bottom bunk and pulled out the notes again, placing them flat in front of her. Something compelled her to keep looking at them, even though it hurt. At the very least, it was a distraction from the disaster of an evening they had just had.

Hunter was a surprise. She couldn't think of the last time she had heard a man say something so honest. It was touching, even if it was ill-timed. Then again, it wasn't a surprise that someone was interested in Sam. It was like an energy she had, exciting and captivating to both men and women. Alex would feel bad for Wes being right in the middle of it all if he didn't seem like such a mess. She wanted to talk to Sam, but the spare room had gone silent. Hopefully, Wes would sleep it off and all of this could be chalked up to too much alcohol and nothing more.

Still, she worried about her sister. She didn't need a bad partner weighing her down. Alex didn't want Sam to waste another minute of time on someone who wasn't good enough for her. Sam deserved much better than what they had just witnessed.

Now, Alex bent forward and pored over the notes in front of her, searching for something—anything. She was looking for a random detail that would give her a lead as to who this other woman was. Once she had a thread of information, Alex wanted to pull it. She wanted it to unravel until she had a solid answer in front of her. There had to be a reason why her father would cheat on his entire family, something that caused him to act in a way that was so unlike him. It couldn't be that he was simply a bad person.

She scanned the notes over and over, but found nothing she could use. Reading them gave her such a sweeping, overwhelming sense of pain and embarrassment, so she gathered them back up, folding them and securing them with the rubber band again. Then she hid them in the bottom of her suitcase.

When her phone buzzed, Alex picked it up and saw a text from Ben.

*Hey. Miss you. Love you. Have you checked out grief support yet?*

She typed a message back. *Love you, too. Will check soon.*

He wasn't going to let that go. Alex sighed.

She clenched and then unclenched her jaw. He meant well, even if it was annoying how persistent he could be.

Pulling her legs underneath her in her spot on the bottom bunk, Alex clicked open her phone to search for local counselors or meetings. She thought she was fine right now, but she should be careful. It was easy to slip up when you were in pain. This would be the sensible thing to do, and Alex was nothing if not sensible.

The local listings didn't turn up much. In a town as small as Summerville, that wasn't surprising.

Alex clicked on a listing for a place called Calm Waters in town and read the first page that came up.

*At Calm Waters, we understand that everyone grieves differently, and in their own time. That's why our groups are ongoing, meeting every week in an open and safe environment, giving you the opportunity to come and go as you please. You may choose to stay with the Calm Waters community for as long as you need to actively explore your grief, with no time limits.*

Alex tilted her head to one side. That seemed fairly flexible and low commitment. She could go and check it out and easily leave again if it didn't suit her, and she would still be able to tell Ben she'd given it a shot.

She clicked around the website, trying to determine if this place would work for her. Calm Waters seemed as good as you could expect. At the same time, Alex had trouble imagining herself telling a room of strangers about her father's infidelity and all the questions he had left unanswered. It felt too private and personal. Still, in the end, she clicked on the email address and sent a message asking when the next meeting would be. Several minutes later, she got a response. It looked like she was going to do this.

The next morning, Alex used the quiet as her excuse to leave. "I think I'm going to go for a drive. Can I take your car for a couple of hours?"

"Where to?" Carol didn't look up from her book. She was in the living room, in the middle of the couch, with the book flat on her lap, one hand pressed down on top of it to hold the pages in place, the other grasping a mug of coffee. Sam and Wes were still in bed and Jess was at the dock, sipping a cup of coffee with hunched shoulders.

"Just around. I might explore a few towns nearby. Do a little shopping for the girls. Unless you need me?" Alex wanted to keep this close to her chest. She wasn't ready to admit to everyone she might need help.

Carol looked tired, but she tried to smile. "No, no. You go and enjoy yourself. I'm fine." Her robe was draped around her body, her hair a kinky mess from sleep. In spite of last night's drama, her mother appeared relaxed. It was a good sign.

"Anything you need from town?" Alex leaned in to kiss her on the cheek.

"Nope. I want to start getting rid of things, not adding to this pile of stuff." She glanced around at the little reminders everywhere—Dad's stack of books on the bookshelves, his spring coat hanging on the rack by the door, a set of tools on the floor, tucked away in a corner of the room. It surprised Alex that her mother wanted to clear it all away so soon, erasing any evidence of Dad right after he'd passed away. Grief did strange things to everyone.

"Okay, see you in a few hours." She grabbed her purse and her mother's keys from the table by the door, slipped into her flip-flops and went out to the driveway.

"Alex." It was Jess's voice.

"Oh. Hey." Alex turned and saw Jess approaching from the dock.

"Where are you going?" Jess nodded at the purse slung over Alex's shoulder.

"To check out a few towns nearby."

Jess gave her a puzzled look. "We've been coming here our entire lives. What haven't you seen yet?"

"I need to get some new clothes for the girls, and you know the options aren't great in town. I thought I'd go further out." Alex moved the strap of her purse off one shoulder and slung it over the other, hoping Jess wouldn't notice how she avoided her eyes. Why was it so hard to lie to her sisters? This was only a little white lie.

"So you're going to leave me here with Sam and Wes? What did I ever do to you?" Jess raised an eyebrow while taking a sip of her coffee.

"I'm sure he'll leave as soon as they get up. If he has any sense, anyway," Alex said.

Jess shot her a look. "You think after last night that he has sense? What the hell was all that anyway?"

"I have no clue. We need to discuss this later." Maybe they could sit Sam down together and tell her that Wes was clearly not good for her, that he might have a drinking problem. Sam honestly couldn't think there was any future for them, could she?

Jess hummed her agreement.

"I'd invite you to come with me," Alex started. *But I don't want you to come. I need to be alone for this.* "But I'm going to be doing boring motherly type stuff. You know how exciting my life is." Alex tried to appear casual and relaxed when she laughed.

"It's fine. I've got some writing to do, so I actually thought I would try to sneak away for a while today, too."

"Nice." Alex nodded at Jess, eager to get going. "I'll be back soonish."

When she arrived at Calm Waters, Alex was struck by how regular it looked. It was a small white house with a long walkway leading up to the doorway, nestled back, away from the edge of the road, which gave it privacy from outside eyes. Alex appreciated that.

She pulled on the door handle and went into the front room where she looked around her, taking in the surroundings. It was all very warm and homey; soft chairs lined the wall in the waiting area, big windows allowed in sheaths of sunny light. There was a desk in one corner, where a woman with bouncy blonde hair and a giant pair of glasses sat. Her smile was wide and genuine.

"Hi there. Can I help you?"

"I've never been here before. I emailed yesterday."

The woman stood up and came around her desk. She went

to a door to the left of Alex and held it open for her. "The first meeting is usually the toughest, but everyone here is very kind and welcoming." She touched Alex's arm lightly. "When you're ready, head down the hall. First door on the left. It's our weekly adult grief meeting. Just started about five minutes ago."

Before having kids, being late made Alex twitch with stress. She had to arrive ten minutes early to everything or she was late, in her opinion. She couldn't recall when she had relaxed on this, but now she didn't care as long as she wasn't holding anyone up. Maybe she could sneak in quietly without anyone noticing and sit in the back.

Inside the room, a small group of people were sitting in a circle on hard metal chairs. A few of them turned their heads when the door shut behind Alex. She smiled apologetically and made her way over to the circle. No sneaking in, she supposed.

"Hi there. Welcome." A woman with a loose white top and jeans stood up. She had long sandy brown hair tied back in a braid. "I'm Laurelle. Please, come and have a seat." She held out a hand, gesturing to the circle. "You don't have to speak unless you're comfortable with it. Many of us find comfort in listening and learning we're not alone."

Alex took a seat next to a woman with a pink floral dress. The woman turned to her and flashed a smile, though there was a hint of annoyance behind her eyes. Alex understood, she would have felt the same way several years ago when someone showed up late to something.

"Do you want to continue what you were saying, Joan?" Laurelle asked another woman. This one was an older woman with the most beautiful shock of white hair Alex had ever seen.

She nodded and spoke. "I find the whole thought of getting rid of my partner's things incredibly depressing. I don't know. How did you all handle it, if you've had to?" She looked out around the circle.

Alex sensed the person on the other side of her move. She

turned her head and saw a woman with short ashy hair frowning deeply and then glancing down at her hands before she spoke. "I've kept everything."

"Don't you find it to be too much? So many memories. So much pain," Joan said.

The woman shrugged. "He was my husband." She looked like she wanted to say more. "I can't even bring myself to throw out a box of crackers." She ran her hands over the tops of her thighs. "They were his favorite kind and I bought them right before he died. I don't like the damn things, but I can't throw the box out because they were his."

Alex felt her own eyes dampen. She pointed her face down so nobody could see. If she was going to cry every time someone shared something sad, this wasn't going to work.

A few more people spoke and Alex listened to each of them, silent, until the meeting ended. Some of the men and women went to refresh their coffee, others folded up the chairs and stacked them on one side of the room.

As Alex stood, the woman with the ash-blonde hair looked over. "First meeting?"

"Am I that easy to read?" Alex asked.

The woman laughed. "Nobody ever speaks at their first one." She stuck out her hand. "I'm Michelle."

"Alex."

"I'm sorry you're here, but it's nice to meet you."

Alex nodded. "Thank you."

Laurelle came over and stood in front of Alex. "If you'd like to stick around and chat with me about anything, I'm available."

Her voice was so soothing, Alex found herself warming to the idea. It wasn't what Alex wanted, though. She tucked a thick piece of hair behind her ear. "I've got to get back—"

Laurelle smiled. "Absolutely. Just know that we're here. No one should have to grieve a death without support."

Being here felt a little like lying. She hadn't lost a

husband, she didn't live in the community. Was she allowed to be here? Then again, her father had messed up her grieving process and left behind a whole bunch of issues. She could admit to herself at least that she needed some help.

Laurelle walked away, stopping to touch the small of another person's back, looking directly into their eyes when she spoke.

"The next meeting is in a week. Same day and time," Michelle said.

Alex could see the fine lines around Michelle's mouth, in between her eyes. She was older, maybe in her sixties, but dressed young—in a gray T-shirt and a pair of denim shorts, thick chunky sandals. She looked a bit like a hippie. She slung a colorful woven bag over her shoulder.

"Thanks. Although, I'm not sure if I'll make it." Alex put a hand in her pocket and looked over Michelle's shoulder as she spoke to hide her discomfort.

Michelle grabbed hold of her chair and folded it up, then rested it against her hip. "Up to you, definitely. But it's been really helpful with my grief. It's a great place."

"I think my grief is different than yours," Alex said. She couldn't shake the imposter feeling. She had lost her father, not a partner, not a child.

Michelle shrugged. "It might be. Or maybe sadness is just sadness for everyone."

Alex looked down at the floor, thinking about it.

"Loss is awful. It feels like it's impossible to see the good around you again, right?" She didn't wait for Alex to acknowledge before she continued speaking. "But despite the tragedy, I'm consciously choosing to remain open and optimistic. I want to believe the best in the world, and in everybody I meet. I hope the same for you."

Alex looked up and met Michelle's eyes. Could she do that?

It seemed an impossibility now that she had so much knowledge. If only she had remained in the dark.

"Anyway, I have to run." The tone of Michelle's voice changed, like she had a sudden burst of energy. Her eyes were round and bright. She reached out and put a hand on Alex's elbow. Everyone touched here, Alex noted. "Listen, if you don't make it back—" Michelle took her hand back and smoothed the hem of her shirt. Then she looked into Alex's eyes. "I hope you're able to find peace in your grief."

Outside, Alex pulled her keys from her purse and squinted into the sunshine. She glanced around her, making sure there was no chance one of her sisters or her mother had come into town, and then made her way to her car. She waited until she slipped into the front seat before she allowed herself to break down.

# THIRTEEN

## SAM

Sam left Wes behind that morning, still curled up in bed, blankets wrapped around him like a cocoon. After getting dressed silently in the dark, she slipped out of the doorway and ducked into the bathroom before seeing her mother or sisters.

Wes had crossed some lines last night, and this was going to be hard to bounce back from. Of course, her mother would be great about it. Actually, Jess and Alex would likely be fine, too. Still, she was embarrassed.

The scene with Hunter made her lightheaded whenever she thought about it.

*I like the sound of your voice.*

It was undeniable that it was nice to hear those words, anyone would like to have someone say that about them, but it was complicated, so Sam pushed it to the back of her mind. She placed her hands on the sink in front of her, holding herself up for a moment as a wave of nausea rolled through her stomach. She didn't think she'd had too much to drink last night. It was Wes who wouldn't stop knocking back the wine before dinner, long after everyone could see he had had enough.

She splashed some cold water on her face and then slurped

some of it up from her cupped hand, staring at her eyes in the mirror, rimmed with red. Another surge of nausea went through her and Sam waited for it to go before she moved.

This was kind of sad, being hungover this frequently when you were approaching forty. What if she had a drinking problem? The truth was, Sam knew it was Wes's influence. She wouldn't drink wine as regularly, nor as much of it, if he didn't seem to enjoy it so thoroughly. She would have to get a handle on it. Then she would think about how to bring it up with Wes. If this was going to work between them, they had to get a few things sorted out. First, Sam wanted Wes to apologize. If he did, she was fairly certain she could forgive his behavior from last night. Alcohol made you act in awful and embarrassing ways, so they would just have to cut out the drinking. Although, she could tell she would have to be delicate about it when she brought it up. He clearly had issues and maybe he didn't realize it.

After the nausea had subsided, she went down the hall and into the living room, where she found her mother and Jess on the couch, sitting side by side, surrounded by papers.

"What's going on?"

Carol looked up. Her eyes were soft even though they were sad. She had her laptop perched on her knees in front of her. "Morning. I'm going through some things. You know—figuring out what to do about Dad's pension and survivor benefits, canceling his passport and license, settling taxes," she said. "It's time to get on top of all of this."

"Why isn't Alex helping?" This was Alex's thing, not Jess's.

"She went out for a while. Shopping for the girls." Carol slid her glasses down from the top of her head onto her nose and glanced down at the papers in her hand.

"Can I help?" Sam asked. She wanted to be useful.

"I think I've got it," Carol replied. "Where's Wes?"

"Still sleeping. He'll probably head off when he gets up."

Sam hoped he would, anyway. She had thought it would be nice to have him here, that he would comfort her and help take the sting away, but she could see now it had been a mistake to invite him. He wasn't family; he didn't fit in yet. They all needed more time. If her father had been here, it would have been easier. Another male in the house to balance it out. Dad had joked about that; how they were never allowed to get a female dog or cat as a pet. "I'm outnumbered enough as it is," he would say, but Sam knew he loved it. She thought he had, anyway.

"I can help you," Sam offered again.

"Why don't you make some coffee?" Carol said. "You look tired. Maybe you could use a cup?"

Sam bristled. "I'm fine." She watched them for a minute longer and then, when she could see they were wrapped up in what they were doing, she went for the door, calling behind her, "I'm going to apologize to Hunter. Be back soon."

She didn't wait to hear their reaction. It was something she had known she needed to do since Wes had behaved so rudely. Might as well face the embarrassment head on and get it over with.


The Smiths' cottage—Hunter's cottage—was a little shack of a building on the outside. This side of the lake wasn't the fancy side. The fancy side was the one they could see down the shore and across the water, lined with enormous homes that were oddly still referred to as cottages. According to Sam, cottages weren't supposed to be massive in size, decorated with nicer furnishings than most people had at home. Where was the roughing it in that? Sam always thought cottages should be more rustic and casual, filled with old, outdated furniture and mismatched dishes. You weren't supposed to care if the floors were sandy and the décor was old.

Sam liked the way the Smiths' cottage looked on the

outside: warm, reddish-brown wood with big windows and a wide porch out front. She pictured it looking similar inside: simple, but quaint and comfortable. She stood on the porch now, in front of the door, and knocked, her chin jutting straight out in front of her, almost defiant. She was sorry, and she would admit it, but she wasn't about to look sheepish. That wasn't something Sam did.

"Hi." Hunter opened the front door all the way, leaning up against the edge of it. There wasn't a hint of awkwardness in the way he stood, arms at his sides, hands in his pockets, one leg crossed behind the other. His loose T-shirt draped over his torso but was tight at the shoulders.

"Hey," Sam said. "I came here to apologize for Wes. I'm really sorry about the way dinner went."

Hunter waved her off with one hand, shaking his head. "Don't be sorry. I was out of line." An uncomfortable expression flashed across his face for the first time.

"I don't know—" Sam shifted position. What he'd said was sweet. Had anyone ever said something like that to her before? She couldn't deny how much she liked it.

A truck rumbled from behind her, and Sam turned to see two men in city uniforms hopping out of it, a big plastic bag in their gloved hands. The truck sat at the edge of the long drive-way, along the dusty dirt road their cottages resided on. The men were shouting to one another over the booming sound, words Sam couldn't quite make out, as they bent over to look at something.

"What's going on?" she asked.

"There's a partially eaten baby deer on the edge of the forest." Hunter ran his hand over his jaw, sweeping it down his neck and putting it back into his pocket.

"Oh, how gross."

There was a pause, silence for a moment as they both

turned to watch the men arranging the bag, pulling and tugging at it to cover something—the dead animal—on the ground.

When Hunter spoke again, his voice was quiet. "It's one of the saddest things I think I've ever seen."

Sam looked back at him. His mouth was turned down at the edges, his eyes far away. There was a tugging inside her—not desire, but something softer and warmer. An affection for the type of man who could feel things for a baby deer and say them out loud to a woman he barely knew.

He gave his head a small shake, then his eyes went to hers. He was focused on her intently. "Want to come in? I've got coffee brewing."

It was a bad idea. Wes would be furious, and Jess—maybe she liked Hunter? Enough to kiss him, anyway. There was an unwritten rule among sisters about this kind of thing.

Everything rational inside Sam made her want to say no, but the lightness in her stomach, the tingling in her limbs made her want to say yes. She wanted to spend more time with him.

Sam pulled at the end of one of her curls and then gathered her hair in her hands, securing an elastic band around it that had been on her wrist.

Later, long after Wes had left, she would think back to this moment and wonder if somewhere inside her she'd known what was coming. If, somehow, she had a sign that her world, her purpose, and everything she knew to be true about life, was about to change. Intuition.

Sam opened her mouth to answer Hunter, and then swiftly turned to the right, ran over to the edge of his front porch and bent over, examining the cracks in the old wood for a second before she threw up what was left of last night's dinner.

# FOURTEEN

## JESS

Early one morning, when she was a kid, a sound coming from the kitchen had woken Jess from her sleep. She'd crawled out of bed, careful not to jostle Alex or Sam, and wandered out in search of the source of the noise. Her father was sitting at the table, head bent and resting in his hand.

"Daddy?"

How old had she been? Young enough that she only remembered snippets up until now, like how cool the August air was that morning, the old jeans her father was wearing, the coffee cup in front of him.

"Hey, Jess. What are you doing up so early?" He had lifted his head and turned his body to her. His eyes were sad, his face grayish.

She'd scrunched her brows and narrowed her eyes, studying him. "I couldn't sleep," she had said finally.

"Come here." He had motioned her over, holding one of his arms out to her. She wanted to fold into his body, she had always loved the way he felt—big and solid and warm. He was a good hugger.

Jess had gone to him and buried her face into the crook of

his arm, while he wrapped it around her. He had kissed the top of her head and then asked her to join him out on the boat.

"For what?"

"For some early-morning fishing. You and me." He'd smiled down at her.

Jess had rushed off to get a sweater and then raced back into the kitchen, a thrill shooting through her at the thought of getting to go out on the boat this early in the morning, just the two of them.

They had spent that morning on the lake, an easy silence surrounding them, enjoying the slow catch and release of fish, talking about the ins and outs of casting and reeling in their line. There was a simplicity about fishing that Jess loved.

At one point, Jess had sat with her legs straddling one of the bench seats in their tin boat and asked her father what she thought was a relatively simple question.

"Daddy, are you sad?"

His eyes had flashed with a certain type of gloom, Jess thought. She could sense it even as a kid.

"Sometimes, I guess." He had busied himself with a worm and fishing line.

Jess had accepted the answer and decided not to push. Instead, she had asked him about lures and types of fish, and yelped with delight whenever she got one on the line.

Now, back in Summerville in the same quiet kitchen where she had been with her father, Jess stood alone and wondered what had compelled her to ask the question, and what those words had meant. Was he sad because he was sorry? Or was he sad because he was unhappy with his life? She wished she knew.

It was early on Friday morning, which meant everyone was sound asleep. Jess filled a glass with water and then stepped outside in her flannel pajamas and bare feet, careful not to let the screen door bang. She went over the damp grass, the sharpness of the cold dew shocking to the skin on the bottom of her feet. Even with the chill in the air, she was comforted by the familiarity here. She loved it despite the harder memories.

It was the right decision to stay in Summerville a while, and Jess was glad she'd made it. Alex would be here with Ben and the girls, and Sam had flexibility with work and had mentioned staying for most of the summer, too. There had been no talk of Wes after he left. Jess didn't ask about what that meant. She would leave it alone for now. Anyway, with her sisters here, Jess couldn't be the only one to leave. Besides, she could work from anywhere. Getting back to writing and submitting her articles to her usual publications would be a good distraction. She still held onto the hope that she might be able to work on her novel, too. Since she had arrived, she had barely written a word. That would have to change.

Jess stretched her arms high above her head and then lowered them behind her as she bent over at the waist. She stood tall again and breathed the air in deeply. Her eyes were heavy with exhaustion this morning. After Alex had found the notes, Jess had worried the pain and anxiety that came with knowing too much would come back as quickly as she had forgotten it. She was right. But she also knew she wasn't ready to leave. Her mother needed her.

The cottages next to theirs and across the lake were all still and silent. Jess walked down to the dock to take a closer look at the water. The docks that surrounded the lake were empty. It was too early in the morning for vacationers to be out yet. Jess was glad. She had always liked the quiet of the lake in the still moments.

Instead of taking a seat on the Adirondack chair, Jess sat cross-legged in the middle of the dock and stared out at the glassy surface in front of her. It was so smooth, with barely any movement, except for tiny little bugs creating ripples on the surface of the water as they hopped across. This view would never get old to her. It was stunning.

Jess tilted her head back, looking up at the sky above her. It was morphing into a beautiful blend of light that seemed to span the width of the earth, above the trees, and as far as Jess could see.

She stood up and glanced around her, double-checking to be certain there were no early-morning fishermen out on boats. Satisfied that nobody was near, Jess took off her pajamas and abandoned them on the dock. She stepped off the wooden platform and walked back onto the tiny sandy beach right beside the little stretch of water, feeling vulnerable and exposed, but willing herself to go with it. She put her hands on her hips and eyed the lake in front of her, then she dropped her arms to her sides, gave them a quick shake and ran straight ahead into the shallows. She didn't stop when the sharpness of the cold lake gripped her legs. She kept running until it got deeper and deeper. As soon as she was covered up to mid-thigh level, Jess flung her body forward and raised her arms, tucking her chin down and diving. She closed her eyes as she went underwater and felt the lake surround her, swishing through her hair and across her body.

She ignored the iciness as it weaved through her legs and twisted around her waist. It glided over the front of her face, cooling her eyelids and sliding over her warm cheeks as she pushed and pulled herself under the surface of the water, swimming hard for as long as she could.

When her chest tightened and teetered on the edge of burning, Jess broke the surface of the lake and came up with a loud gasp. She let her lungs fill again as she opened her eyes and saw she had startled a nearby bird. Jess turned her body around to examine the edge of the shoreline, wanting to see how far she had made it in one go. It was much further than she had ever gone before in one stretch.

Flipping onto her back, Jess swam across the surface toward the shore. It felt good to be naked underwater. To run in, plunging her body headfirst without knowing what to expect. It felt good to feel anything. When she was alone in Ireland, this was what Jess was searching for. Something to remind her that she was more than the little girl who'd held onto a devastating secret her whole life.

Jess's ears dipped below the surface as she swam. She liked listening to the water. It didn't stay silent. She could hear every odd squeak and hissing sound that came from underneath, wondering where they were coming from, what they were trying to say.

Once she got back to shore, she walked onto the beach, over to her abandoned pajamas. She looked down at them, lying on the dock like snakeskin that had been shed. If only it was as easy to rid yourself of pain.

Jess picked them up and struggled into them, then went back to the cottage to help her mother and sisters get ready for the funeral.

# FIFTEEN

## ALEX

"Mommy!" Molly flung her body into Alex's arms as soon as she was free from the car.

Alex bent over and wrapped her arms around her daughter, burying her head into Molly's neck and nuzzling her nose into that sheen of perfect, little-kid hair. It was so silky, it almost felt impossible. Molly wriggled in Alex's arms, but didn't try to get loose.

When Alex looked up, she saw Lucy slam her door shut and walk around the front of the car quickly, a wide grin on her face. She nestled herself into Alex's outstretched arm.

"Hi, Luce."

Lucy let Alex cover her face with kisses for a moment before pulling away and wiping it with the back of her hand. "Ew, Mommy!" Lucy admonished. Her eyes were narrowed, but she had a large smile, revealing adult teeth that her small face hadn't grown into yet.

"I missed you both so much," Alex said. It was Saturday morning now, and almost a week apart had been more than enough for Alex. Anything longer and it would have become physical; a dull, aching need deep in her gut. Getting a break from the day-to-day of raising little kids was great, but Alex could only handle a short stint until she wanted them near again.

Ben stood next to the car, his arms stretched above him and head tilted back, his T-shirt raised to reveal a line of bare skin at his waist. He lowered his arms and looked at Alex. "Hey, you. We missed you, too." He walked toward her, his eyes creasing when he smiled, and wrapped an arm around her waist. "How are you?"

Alex nodded. "I'm okay."

He leaned in to kiss her and his mouth smelled sweet like oranges. The cheek wasn't where Ben focused when he first went in for a kiss. He always wanted the lips. Alex had never given it a second thought, the way he always needed to touch her, running his hands down her back whenever they were in the same room, wiggling his eyebrows at her after a long kiss, always hopeful for a little more, like they were teenagers. That was Ben. She would sometimes roll her eyes in mock exasperation at him, but she knew that if he stopped wanting her, needing her body, she would notice. She would miss his touch.

"We're together now. That's what matters," Lucy said, using her big-girl voice.

Ben looked at Alex and tried not to smile. Amusement flickered in his eyes.

"You're right. Let's go see Grandma." Alex ran a hand over the top of Lucy's head and let it glide down the side of her daughter's face. It felt almost like ice, her skin was so smooth and cool.

Inside, Lucy and Molly ran for Carol, turning their heads and resting their cheeks on her stomach when they reached her.

Carol bent over halfway and wrapped her arms around them, kissing the tops of their heads. "Hello, my favorite granddaughters. How are you? How was the drive?"

"Good," Lucy said. "But, Grandma, we're your *only* grand-daughters." She giggled when she said it.

"You're still my favorites. Now, come to the kitchen and I'll make you a snack. You can tell me about your last few weeks of school."

The girls dutifully followed Carol into the other room like a pair of baby ducklings. Alex reached for Ben's hand. Thank goodness she had them all here now.


Later that afternoon, Alex helped Lucy and Molly get into the black and navy dresses Ben had brought up for the funeral. She brushed their hair and wiped their faces clean before getting herself ready. She hadn't worn anything formal in ages, and only had one dress that would suit for today. It was going to be a small funeral, a quiet affair. They didn't announce it in the paper and had asked the funeral home to keep it private, out of respect for their father. Mom had said he would have wanted that at the very least, so she had only invited immediate family and a handful of close friends. You would never know he was a well-loved man.

Alex stepped out of the car at the funeral home into the mid-afternoon sun. It was only the first of July, but already an oppressive heat surrounded her. The kind that made a trickle of sweat roll down the middle of your back, between your shoulder blades and all the way to the top of your underwear line. She hoped her face wasn't as red as it felt.

Sam looked particularly miserable. Her hair didn't hold up well in the humidity and her face was pale and sunken. She had been more subdued than usual since Wes had left. With Alex's mind bouncing between the letters and her own grief, she had lost track of how her sisters were doing. She made a note to talk to Sam when this was done and they were back at the cottage.

Alex smoothed the front of her dress and watched as Jess

went to one side of her mother and Sam the other. They linked arms with her, as if she would need help walking, and a quick stab of pain in Alex's stomach made her stop in place. Her mother looked so weak and frail, like she had lost everything. She *had* lost so much. A lifetime with her partner was gone like a puff of smoke. Only her mother didn't know what he had done to her and how much of their life was a lie. Alex wasn't sure she could ever forgive him for that.

The funeral went by in a blur. Lucy and Molly were well behaved, Ben held tight onto Alex's hand. There was quiet sobbing and hunched shoulders, soft voices up at the front, and then the next thing Alex knew, it was over. She was glad it hadn't been a big thing. She wouldn't have known how to act.

# SIXTEEN

## SAM

The morning after the funeral, Sam had a sinking feeling she knew exactly what was happening. It was intuition. Or maybe it was the vomiting. Either way, when she ended up in the bathroom on her knees over the toilet trying to silently expel the contents of her stomach, she knew she was pregnant.

"Sam? Are you okay?" Jess's voice came through the closed door. You couldn't do anything alone here.

Once the vomiting stopped, she could speak. "I think so, yeah. Must be a stomach bug."

Silence. Jess must have gone down the hallway and into another room in the cottage. Thank goodness. Sam didn't want to face Jess in that moment.

She stood, rinsed her mouth out and washed her hands. She dabbed her damp, cool hands on her closed eyelids, over her cheeks and then opened her eyes back up and looked at herself in the mirror. She was pale, but, otherwise, she didn't look as bad as she felt. She smoothed her hair before opening the door.

Jess stared back at her from the other side, worry settled into her face. "A stomach bug?" Her hair was wet, dangling in stringy vines, and she was dabbing at it with a towel. She had on her bathing suit, even though it was first thing in the morning. She was swimming again, the way she used to when she was a kid; always alone. Sam had asked Jess once when they were kids why she liked to go by herself. Sam always thought half the fun of swimming was having someone there to do it with. "I like to think," Jess had said back then. She didn't offer up much more. Sam had thought it was weird, but didn't push. Eventually, with time, Sam noticed a pattern. Jess would swim alone and often when something was wrong. It was how she processed things. She never would tell Sam what was wrong, though, and that always bothered Sam. She thought they were closer than that.

Now, Sam tried to avoid Jess's stare. "I don't know. I guess it's a stomach bug." She brushed past her sister and went down the hallway toward their bedroom, rubbing her stomach as if to calm it, to tell it to relax.

Jess followed behind. "I feel like you've been avoiding me," she said.

Sam could tell her sister was trying to come off as light-hearted, like she was teasing, but there was a hint of worry in her voice.

Sam was silent for a beat. "No, not avoiding. I'm over-whelmed."

"What's going on?" Jess asked.

Sam put one hand on her hip and lifted the other to her face, pressing her fingers to her closed eyelids. She let out a deep breath of air, steeling herself. She would have to be honest. It was the only way to handle this.

Sam swiveled around to face her sister now, standing in their shared bedroom. "I think I might be pregnant."

Jess stumbled back a step. Her eyes bulged. "*What*? Pregnant? Who—Wes?"

"Shh!" Sam said. She wasn't ready for Mom to hear yet. "Of course Wes, but I don't know for sure. All I know is I've been sick to my stomach off and on. And I think I'm late."

Jess's mouth hung open. "That sounds like pregnant to me."

Sam lowered herself to the edge of the bottom bunk, resting her elbows on her knees and placing her head in her hands. What now? There was enough on her mind with Dad's death and her grief. Now this. And Wes. She didn't even know how she felt about it. When she was sick to her stomach, and when it had finally dawned on her that she was late, Sam hadn't once thought about whether or not this was a good or bad thing.

"Aren't you guys careful?" Jess asked.

"Of course we are," Sam snapped. "Most of the time. I mean, I guess we got really drunk once and I thought it was an okay time of the month to get away with it." She knew how dumb it sounded as the words came out of her mouth. Sam looked down at the floor, examining the scratched-up hardwood underneath her feet.

When she had daydreams about her future as a kid, she had a hazy picture of life as an adult, and it usually included children. Oddly enough, she could never picture a partner in the scenario. Sam didn't know what she wanted in a spouse. Children weren't something she thought much about. She assumed that one day she would be a mother, but not this way. Not with her new boyfriend, who clearly had some issues. Now they would be tied together forever, and the thought of it depressed her.

"But what's going on with you and Wes? Are you two okay?"

Sam knew Jess was sidestepping the other night. She wouldn't come right out and say what a disaster dinner had been, but nobody had questioned Sam either when Wes didn't come to the funeral. She hadn't spoken to Wes much at all since he left—they hadn't had a chance to talk it out. Maybe they wouldn't. It was telling that she didn't care enough to rehash it all yet.

Sam flopped backwards, flat on her back, and rested her

palms on top of her stomach. She used to lie there on the bottom bunk as a kid and wonder what would happen if the top bunk collapsed on her. It was morbid, the way kids thought sometimes.

"I thought we were having fun, but it was so weird when he was here." She spoke without moving, directing her words up into the air, at the underside of the top bunk. She didn't want to admit out loud that she didn't really know him. He could have been anyone, but he had turned out to be complicated, and not in the good way. Now she was stuck with him. "I don't want his baby," she said, surprising herself as she heard the words.

From the corner of her eye, Sam could see Jess stiffen. "Well, I guess you don't have to have it," Jess said.

Sam sat up again. For whatever reason, that thought hadn't crossed her mind. She wasn't a teenager; she had her own home and a good job. It hadn't occurred to her to not have the baby, even if it was Wes's child. The words hung in the air uncomfortably between them.

"No, if I'm pregnant, I'm going to have it," Sam replied. "But I'm not happy about it happening with Wes, I guess."

Jess shrugged. "When are you going to tell Mom and Alex?"

"Soon." She needed to figure out how to approach it with them first. "Why?"

Jess stood and picked up the towel she had been drying her hair with. She draped it over one arm and rested her other hand on her hip. She looked down at her hand when she spoke. "I don't like secrets." She paused. Her voice was a little strained. "What's Alex doing with the notes, by the way? Has she found anything else out?"

"I know she's read them, but she hasn't said much," Sam replied. She shook her head. "You were right when you said we're all a mess. When did this happen?"

"I don't know. Always?" Jess shrugged. "I'm going to go make breakfast. Want anything?"

"No, thanks." Food was not something she could stomach right now.

Sam closed her eyes and thought about how she would tell her mother. Years ago, Mom had made Sam promise she wouldn't drift too far away. It was a typical Carol thing to say— she was only concerned and wanted Sam to stay close, literally and figuratively.

"You're the middle child," her mother had said, standing in her kitchen at home. "You have a free spirit, and you aren't tied to us in the way your sisters are."

"What does that mean?" Sam had been immediately defensive.

"I mean you don't feel the responsibility Alex feels as the oldest child, which she puts on herself by the way, and you aren't the baby. Everyone gives in to the baby. I tried to always be fair, but it's hard."

"You were great," Sam had said.

Mom had looked at Sam and reached out with one hand to brush the curls away from her face. "I used to worry about you the most, but now I think Alex and Jess are going to need you. You're much stronger than you know, and you've always been that way." She'd sighed. "We should all be like you."

What would Mom think when she heard that Sam was pregnant with Wes's baby? She couldn't be a calming presence for her sisters, she could barely take care of herself. On top of it all, to have to worry about actually raising a baby. A living, breathing thing that she had to take care of for the rest of her life.

Sam knew she was going to keep it, but she had no idea how to be strong enough for herself or her sisters, let alone a baby. Motherhood appeared exhausting; Alex was constantly on the go with Lucy and Molly, getting them what they needed, helping them do things, taking them places, playing together, putting them to bed and then doing it all over again the next day.

Sam gazed at her flat stomach and pressed one hand on top of it. Now there was one more thing to worry about.

Jess came back through the open door and grabbed her brush off the dresser. "I forgot this," she said. She noticed Sam and stopped. She rested one hand on the side of her cheek. "You're having a baby, Sam. A baby." Her eyes went wide and a smile crept across her face.

A baby. Sam looked down at her stomach again and frowned.

# SEVENTEEN

## ALEX

In the early days of motherhood, when everything was startling and new to Alex, she used to stare at Lucy's tiny face and wonder how she could ever get it right. This perfect blank slate of a person she cradled in her arms when she was nursing in the dim quiet of the baby's room. This gorgeous human made Alex feel so many deep, guttural things. Alex instantly began to worry, and she even worried she might never stop worrying. At first, it was worry over how she was going to raise Lucy and not completely ruin her. Then it was the immediate things. Was she nursing enough? Would she ever sleep long stretches at night? When would she learn to turn over and crawl and walk?

One night, after a particularly long stretch awake, Alex had found herself on the floor of Lucy's bedroom, laid out like a starfish next to the crib, staring into the darkness and shushing in a rhythmic pattern because she had heard if the baby could hear you but not see you, they would go to sleep without needing to be rocked.

That was only the beginning. Soon, those worries were replaced by concern over what she was eating, how much sleep she was getting at what times. Then it became social things:

why wasn't she saying as many words as the kids in the play group? Did she have friends? Did she like school?

After eight years of motherhood, Alex had finally come more into her own, but she still found herself riddled with anxiety every now and again. The difference was, she had learned how to manage it. The place all the worry and fear came from was still there; it was ingrained in her as a parent. To raise a kid meant to get knee-deep into the hard stuff. You had to, no matter how much it sucked. And it sucked. Parenting was hard as hell. Which was why part of Alex understood her father's choices. She would never admit that out loud to anyone, though.

The truth was, it took a strong person to not let the tough times you faced day in and day out cause you to break. Having an escape would be so easy. Yet, there was a larger part of Alex that would never be selfish because she knew now it wasn't only her who would eventually have to suffer the consequences. It was also her children.

Her muscles tensed and her body went stiff whenever she thought about how little she and Sam and Jess must have mattered to their father when he was with the other woman. He was thinking only of himself. Plain and simple.

That day, Alex was on the couch, alone in the living room, her feet resting on the coffee table in front of her and her phone in one hand. She still hadn't found out anything from the letters about the other woman. She didn't sign off with her name, and there were no clues as to her identity, but Alex needed to know.

She clicked through buttons on her phone until she got to one of her father's rarely used social media pages. There were news articles posted, a random photo. Nothing much she could use. Her fingers froze, however, when she saw a comment from a woman she had never heard of. It wasn't completely uncommon, Dad had parts of his life she didn't know much about, but something made her pause. Maybe it was the excessive exclamation marks being used. Alex's heart stopped for a split second when she saw the way the woman had ended her comment. *xo*.

She sat up and narrowed her eyes, moving her face closer to her phone screen. Alex could see the woman was smiling in her profile photo, standing next to an older-looking man, her arm slung over his shoulder. *Maria Fraser*. It didn't ring any bells for Alex, but she zoomed in on the photo, as if that was going to unlock something in her brain.

Ben came into the room and Alex jolted in her seat. He looked at her and asked, "What's going on?"

"Nothing," Alex said.

"So why do you look like you were caught doing something you're not supposed to be doing?"

Alex held her phone up and waved it around. "I'm trying to see if I can find out anything more about her."

"Who?" Ben sat next to Alex on the couch and put his feet up, too.

Alex said, "*Her*. The other woman." She widened her eyes and jutted her head forward for emphasis.

Ben's jaw clenched. "What do you mean?"

"I've been searching through the notes and now I'm looking online for some hint or clue. I'm hoping I might find her."

"Alex, are you sure that's a good idea?" Ben's eyes widened.

Alex knew him well enough to know that he thought this was a very bad idea.

She looked over her shoulder to make sure they were alone. "You know I want to figure out what other secrets my father had. Finding her is probably the best way to do it."

Ben let out a long exhale. "This is a lot to handle."

Alex nodded. She crossed her arms over her chest. Ben's forehead creased when he looked at her. He was processing it, she could tell. It didn't make rational sense to him. Everything had to be logical for Ben.

"Have you looked into any grief support yet?"

"Yes. I went to a group session the other day." That would appease him at least.

"How was it?"

"It was okay." Alex shrugged. She didn't have the energy to expand.

"So, now what?" Ben asked. "What do you want from the searching? What if you find her?"

"I'm not sure." There was a tug inside of her, something telling Alex to try to make sense of what her father had done, so she could feel safe. If she could rationalize it and understand it, then she could also compartmentalize what had happened and put it away. She could tell herself that she was loved by her father, that her life wasn't a lie, and then she could close that book and put it on a shelf, never needing to look at it again. If she could do all that, it would be easier to believe that this wouldn't happen to her. She wouldn't risk losing everything—Ben, the girls, the life they had. Her father had done that, but she wouldn't have to fear her own weakness.

The one thing Alex knew for certain was that if she ignored the whole thing and discarded the notes and tried to forget the fact that this woman was out in the world somewhere without ever knowing more, it would all build up. It would slowly but surely gnaw away at Alex for the rest of her life. She had never been able to let things go. The anger always subsided, and she often wanted to forgive and forget the fights she had with her sisters or with Ben, but they had to talk about it first. There had to be some kind of resolution.

Ben let out another long breath. "Alex, this seems like it'll turn out bad."

"I understand why you think that, but you know me. I need closure."

He reached for her hand and held it gently. "I don't think you ever get closure when your father dies. Especially when you find out something he can't explain. You might have to let this one go before someone ends up hurt."

For the first time in a long time, Ben's words stung more than they comforted her. He was typically a kind and careful husband. His considerate and easygoing nature meant he didn't tend to say things that hurt. Even this wasn't harsh, he was being as gentle as ever, but Alex wanted support. She didn't want to be talked out of it.

"I'm not going to hurt anyone," Alex said. "I'm trying to help us. If I can make some sense of all of this, then I can let it go. I can't pretend I don't know, Ben." It amazed her how he could not know how she operated after all these years.

Ben shifted. He squeezed her hand again and then heaved his body forward to stand up. "Okay. But please be careful. Your family has gone through enough already."

Alex felt a pang of defensiveness at those words, but she didn't respond. Instead, she tucked her legs underneath her and looked out the window, listening to the sound of the breeze in the treetops. Ben was right that they had all gone through a lot, but it wasn't her fault. Finding out what else her father might have been hiding wasn't going to make it worse for anyone. Nobody needed to know details unless they wanted to. Alex wanted to know.

Later, when the girls were on the dock fishing with Ben, Alex sat in her chair by the beach alone. She pulled out her phone and looked through the non-private part of Maria Fraser's profile, the woman who had commented on one of Dad's photos. There wasn't much to learn about her. She was an older woman standing next to an older man; in the next picture, she was sitting in front of a lake.

Alex needed something to go on, but she wasn't sure what. She went to Dad's profile again and clicked through his photos.

He was standing outside somewhere holding an ice cream cone up to the camera, then he was leaning on his car during one of his and Mom's vacations. In another, he was holding Lucy when she was a baby. He looked so vibrant and alive.

Alex slumped into her seat. Her throat thickened. He was gone. One moment he was here, and the next it was all over. It saddened her even more that behind that smile, those familiar eyes, he could have been thinking about someone other than her mother. He could have been thinking about anything, really. It struck her that you never really know someone, no matter how close you thought you were.

# EIGHTEEN

## SAM

Now that it was confirmed by two little blue lines, Sam had to call Wes. She had only been at the cottage for just over a week and had only suspected she was pregnant for a few days, but it felt like much longer.

At first, Sam had hoped she was wrong about the pregnancy. For a day or so, she'd thought it was all a coincidence. The nausea seemed to be over as quickly as it had started. It was bizarre the way her body was acting, but she wasn't convinced it meant anything yet. It could have been the grief; it worked in weird ways, didn't it? There was a part of her—a part deep down that she would never, ever confess to—that hoped something would happen. Something to take care of the pregnancy for her, so she wouldn't have to worry about the way her life was going to end up. But the thought was always fleeting and replaced with a hot shame.

When Sam had gone into the kitchen that morning with the plan to make a cup of coffee, the smell of rich beans and the thought of drinking it had disgusted her. That was how she was certain there would be no denying this. She had headed to a pharmacy in town shortly after and hurried back home to take the test. Now she knew for certain.

As much as her stomach dropped when she thought about a baby and Wes, and despite the shameful wish she had allowed herself to think, there was no doubt in her mind that an abortion was out of the question. It didn't have to do with anything particularly moral, she simply couldn't do it. On the one hand, she didn't feel like mother material, but on the other, there was a shred of protectiveness blooming inside her, growing alongside this tiny little cluster of cells. No matter how complicated it made her life, she wouldn't get rid of it.

Sam rinsed and wiped the test off with some toilet paper and slipped it into the pocket of her cardigan before washing her hands and leaving the bathroom to find her phone. It sat on the kitchen counter, amongst the food Mom had set out for lunch. A platter of meats—prosciutto, salami, shaved turkey, and slices of cheese. There was a small container of olives next to a bowl full of fresh baguette and another large platter of fresh vegetables and fruit. Her mother was getting a little more like her old self, always feeding everyone she could when they were around.

Sam grabbed a piece of cantaloupe and bit into it. Fresh fruit was all that appealed to her. The thought of meat was as gross to her right now as coffee.

"Ready to eat? We're going to take this and sit in the living room." Mom entered the kitchen and grabbed three plates from the cupboard. "Here." She handed one to Sam.

Sam set it down on the counter in front of her.

"I'll join you in a minute. I've got to call Wes first."

"Sure. Whenever you're done."

"Done what?" Alex came into the kitchen, eyes widening at the sight of lunch laid out for her. Sam thought it must be nice for Alex not to have to think about taking care of someone else. It was something Sam would have to get used to.

"I have to call Wes." There was no point in keeping this from them. Yet another secret. "Because I'm pregnant."

Alex's eyes widened.

Carol stopped moving mid-step, put her plate down and looked at Sam. Her face was unreadable. Was this a good thing?

"You're... pregnant? When? How?" Mom fumbled over her words.

"I'll spare you the details of how, but I just found out."

Alex remained uncharacteristically silent. She stood still, in shock, Sam supposed.

Sam didn't know how she felt either. It was like asking the universe for something good to happen to you and it turned out to be a big mix-up. A mistake.

Mom took hold of Sam's arms. "Oh, Sam. This is fantastic news! A baby!" She folded Sam into a tight hug.

Sam's back straightened. "You're happy about this?"

Carol pulled back and held onto Sam's forearms. She looked Sam squarely in the eyes. "Of course I am! Why wouldn't I be? It's wonderful being a grandmother."

Relief flooded Sam's body. "I thought you might be under-impressed with my situation," Sam said. The memory of their last encounter with Wes at the dinner table hung in the air.

"I want you to be happy. That's all that matters to me. Are you happy about this?" Carol asked.

Sam didn't have to think about it before answering, but she made it look like she was. "I don't think so," she mumbled eventually. And then she started to cry.

Alex slid next to Sam at the same time as Carol and slipped her hand over Sam's shoulders. They held onto her, a bundle of arms tangled together.

"You can do this," Alex said. "And we have each other."

"Exactly. Family is all anyone needs in the end." Carol's voice had a hint of sadness to it when she spoke.

"You'll be an excellent mother," Alex said.

Doubt nudged at Sam. She brushed a tear from her cheek and tried to smile at them. It wasn't true, she didn't think she could be an excellent mother. Good mothers were like Alex, with adorable, well-behaved kids like her nieces. Alex had probably never wished she hadn't conceived them.

Sam unraveled herself from the hug and squeezed Mom and Alex's forearms lightly before she turned to leave the room.

"I better call Wes."

She picked up her phone and went down the hallway to the bedroom. She flopped onto the bottom bunk and stretched out flat on her back. She could do this. She could make this one, simple phone call to tell Wes the news. The next day, she could make a doctor's appointment and then start taking vitamins. It was a series of small steps that she could handle, one at a time.

Sam waited for Wes to pick up. His voice was gruff when he answered, like he had just woken up. "Hello?"

"Hey, Wes. It's me."

"Hey. How's it going?" Wes was casual. He wasn't one to hold a grudge or stay annoyed for longer than a day. That was a positive when you were a parent, Sam thought.

"Not too bad. I have some news."

"About what?" Wes asked. "Is it your dad?"

Sam frowned. She had almost forgotten about her father and the other woman. How was that possible? It seemed sad to her, that she could have forgotten him so easily.

"No, this is about me and you," Sam said.

"Listen, Sam. I don't think we need a long, drawn-out conversation to rehash what happened. I drank too much. It was a mistake. Did you apologize to your mother for me?"

"I'm pregnant. We're having a baby."

There was a silence on the other end, for what felt like forever. Finally, Wes managed to speak, his voice hoarse. "Are you sure?"

"Yes, I'm sure. I took a pregnancy test today."

"When could this have happened? We're careful, aren't we?"

"Not careful enough, I guess," Sam said.

"Are you sure it's mine?"

Sam flinched and then sat up. *He can't be asking me that. He doesn't actually mean it.*

"Yes, it's yours, Wes. I wasn't seeing anyone else." Her stomach flipped. "Were you?"

"No. No, of course not."

She waited for him to say something else. She wanted him to be happy about it, even though she knew it was irrational. Why should he be happy when she wasn't? Still, she wanted Wes to take control, to comfort her, to tell her this would all be okay, that they would figure this out together.

Wes cleared his throat. "I'm not really sure what to think. I didn't plan on having kids. I don't think I ever thought I would be a dad."

Sam's head dropped. Her limbs went heavy. She realized she had been hoping so much for a different answer. "I know this isn't ideal, and I didn't think I would ever want a baby in this way either, but it turns out I do. I want this baby." Sam cleared her throat. This was the only thing she knew for certain. If Wes wasn't going to jump in and be the steady, strong presence she needed, she would have to do it herself. There were things to think of. She lifted her chin. "I'm going to raise it." She would have to find out if she was having a boy or a girl so she could stop calling them it.

Wes's voice was dull when he spoke. "I need some time to think about it."

"Think about what?"

"I mean, I guess I could be involved in raising it."

Sam shuffled her body to the edge of the bunk bed. What did she want from him? It was hard to know because of how little time she had spent with Wes.

She did her best to keep her tone light. "Sure. It would be nice for the baby to know you." Her father was so involved, so much a part of parenting with her mother that, for most of her life, Sam thought that was what all men were like. It wasn't until her Intro to Women's Studies class in university, when the professor had left a comment laced with annoyance on one of her papers, that Sam knew this wasn't the case. Sam had written a simple sentence—one that indicated that men did their fair share in this day and age, citing her father as an example. It was embarrassing now to think back on how juvenile that must have seemed. Her professor had circled it with a red pen and scratched a note into the margin: *You think because your father was a good man that all men are??* Still, even now, Sam had to be reminded that some men didn't act the way she thought they should—perhaps even her father.

"I think I better go. I need to process this." Wes's voice was tight. "Can we talk more about this later?"

Sam's breath was unsteady. "Yeah. Sure."

The phone went dead on the other end. Sam watched the screen flip to black and shut off, just as the hope she had been holding onto disappeared, too.

# NINETEEN

## JESS

"I'm going for a swim." Jess had a towel slung over her shoulder and her bathing suit on this time. "Who's coming with me?"

She swished past Lucy and Molly, grinning, knowing full well they wouldn't be able to resist the invitation. Having them here lightened Jess's mood. Their presence radiated through the cottage.

"Me!" shouted Molly.

Lucy had already left the kitchen, thundering down the hallway and yelling that she was going to get her swimsuit.

Jess noticed how Alex's face was serious most of the time these days, but now it softened. "I'll come, too. It's so hot out today."

Ben laughed at the way Jess walked through the kitchen, flicking her towel around. She was uncharacteristically silly, but Molly and Lucy did that to her.

Sam entered the kitchen and stopped at the entranceway. Her eyebrows shot up. "What's with you, Jess?"

"We're going swimming," Jess said. "Want to come?"

"That sounds perfect. I couldn't be hotter right now."

"Now we just need you," Alex said to their mother.

"You go." Carol sat at the table, finishing up her lunch of a toasted tomato sandwich, flipping through a newspaper. "It'll be nice for the three of you girls to spend time with Molly and Lucy."

Down in the water, Jess dove under, did somersaults when Lucy asked her to, swam with Molly on her back. They laughed at the way Alex refused to take her sunglasses off or get her hair wet, only swimming up to her neck, doing the breaststroke forward in one direction and then turning to come back again.

"Watch this," Sam shouted. She did a handstand and came back up again, sputtering.

Molly's eyes went wide. "How did you do that?" she asked, her voice filled with awe.

Sam winked at Jess and Jess laughed. This was nice. The time Jess had been spending here, hanging around the cottage with her family, was meant to be a time to grieve, but it had got to be too heavy. She didn't know how much she needed moments like this with her sisters until she was here, in the water. It helped her forget that most of the time her body was constantly humming with anxiety.

Keeping the truth about her father from everyone had taken a toll on Jess. It was only a small relief that her sisters finally knew and she could somewhat share the burden, even though they still weren't talking about it. Having to focus on not letting it slip in front of their mother brought it all back to the surface, however. When nobody knew, it was as if Jess could bury it down deep and not think about it. Now, she had to be careful about what she said and when, which meant she was always thinking about her father, what he had done, and how much she had kept hidden. That was why Ireland had felt like such a release. It was an escape, where she could live outside of the lie that had defined her childhood.

The truth was, even though Jess had been to therapy and worked through her feelings, she couldn't remember a time before her father was cheating. She didn't know who she was without his secret, and that frightened her.

Long after swimming was over, after the girls were inside the cottage with pink cheeks and dry, sandy skin, after Alex had gone to shower them off and Sam went to change into clean clothes, Jess stayed out on the dock. She eased back into one of the Adirondack chairs and smoothed her hair out of her eyes as the wind pushed it around, tickling her cheek. It was dusk, the best time of the day to be by the lake.

A gentle lapping sound, a paddle gliding through the water, came from the right. She would know the sound of a paddle and a canoe anywhere.

Jess sat up straighter. Hunter was coming around the bend, wearing a big hat and life jacket, upright in his seat, with his arms extended as he pushed the paddle through the water. He spotted Jess and raised an arm to wave. Jess waved back. She watched the canoe carve its way through the water as he came closer to her. A wisp of something exciting fluttered in her chest, but she didn't want it to.

"Hey." Hunter smiled easily, stopping the canoe in front of the dock.

"Hi." Their last exchange had been a week ago at dinner. It was a cringeworthy night, but at least it had overshadowed when Jess had kissed him at his cottage. Still, Jess was careful around him. She didn't want to say too much.

"How are things?" Hunter asked. He eyed the cottage behind her.

"Not bad," Jess said. She looked down at her bare feet; her heels were smoothing over from walking around in the sand so much. When she looked back up, Hunter was studying her from his place in the canoe. Jess pushed her hair out of her face again.

"Are we going to talk about that day at my cottage?" he asked.

The kiss. A flush crept across her face.

"I hoped we wouldn't," Jess answered. She looked away.

"I know it was a week ago now, but I've been thinking about you. We're not starting off on the wrong foot, are we? We're neighbors," Hunter said. There was a lilt to his voice, like he was slightly distressed.

"It's already forgotten," Jess replied. She waved a hand, hoping she looked casual and it would be enough of an explanation for him.

The truth was, Jess thought about it more than she would like to. She wasn't sure why she'd acted on that impulse, but when it had happened, she'd liked it. His mouth was full, and his arms and shoulders were broad. When she had looked at him in the cottage that day, there had been a longing within her. It had made no sense for her to react so quickly to a feeling, especially when she didn't know him at all, but maybe that was the reason she did it. She had wanted to act. To do something to make her feel, to forget what was happening in her life. Maybe it was her way of trying to be assertive, to get what she wanted. Then again, maybe she only needed comfort, like she had told Sam.

Whatever the reason, it was hard to forget the moment after it had happened. Sometimes at night, right before she fell asleep, he would pop into her mind, and she would imagine what might have happened if he hadn't pulled away. Then she would give her head a shake, because that wasn't reality. It was a silly, made-up moment.

A silence fell between them. Hunter moved his paddle to avoid drifting away on the current.

"I'd like to be friends with you," he said. "If you think that would be okay."

Did she want that? Hunter seemed like he would be a nice person to be friends with, but the attraction might get in the way for her. When she was younger, Jess had been on the receiving end of attention from guys—you were bound to be when you had two older sisters who went to the same school— but she tended to be wary of boys in general after what she learned about her father. She didn't trust that they would be good. She was certain they would eventually show their true colors, and Jess didn't want to bother with the heartache. She saw Alex and Sam often enough, crying over someone who had broken up with them, or treated them unkindly. Who needed that? Instead, Jess had put her energy into her schoolwork and her writing and kept boys at arm's length. Eventually, they grew tired of being friends with her. They almost always wanted more, and it ruined what they had. Maybe Hunter thought Jess might want more with him. Her face warmed again. All of this was complicated and awkward.

When Hunter eyed the cottage behind her again, Jess had a feeling he was looking for Sam. Sam and her gorgeous face and easygoing personality would solve this for Jess, simply by being Sam, the one all the boys liked. She thought about letting it slip to Hunter that Sam was pregnant, but that was a momentary, fleeting thought. She would never do that. She wasn't the type to betray her sister for a man.

"Sure. I'd like to be friends," she said instead. Then she stood up. "Do you want me to see if she's around?"

Hunter did a double take when he looked at her. "Who?"

"Sam."

"No. That's okay." He put his paddle back into the water and moved the canoe around in a circle, like he was ready to leave.

"It's okay," Jess said quietly. "Wes hasn't been around all week."

Hunter's face went red. He looked down at the water.

The longer Jess stood there, the more awkward it got. She would have to get over it, she supposed.

"No, really. It's okay. I better go. I want to get a little fishing in." Hunter lifted his paddle and slid it back into the water. "You wouldn't want to come with me sometime, would you? Your sister said you were quite the fisherman."

Jess avoided the question. She loved to fish with her father, and she might have enjoyed fishing with Hunter, but it would have been confusing. Instead, she smiled and said, "I used to be good at it. I've never caught Big Mama though."

"Big Mama?" One of Hunter's eyebrows arched.

"She's been seen around this lake since I was a kid. Giant bass. Nobody has ever caught her."

Hunter smiled. He was floating away now, so he put his paddle into the water on the other side of him and moved slowly in the other direction. He turned and looked over his shoulder as he left. "I'm off to find Big Mama, then. See you later, Jess."

"See you," Jess called.

She stood on the dock and watched him glide away and around the corner. Then she looked out at the beach. By the edge of the water, their canoe had been pulled up onto the sand and now lay on one side, abandoned.

Jess walked toward it and turned the canoe over, maneuvering it back into the water. She waded into the cool lake. When she got it far enough, Jess got inside and carefully positioned herself in the middle. One of the life jackets had been stuck into the narrow end of the boat and she placed it underneath her. She reached for the paddle and pushed and pulled along the edge of the lake, in the opposite direction to Hunter. After a while, she changed course and made her way further out, closer to the middle. It was there that she stopped.

Jess knew she should move over to one side, closer to the shore, to make way for boats going from Shadow Lake to the next body of water, but it was quiet today, so instead, she sat there, slightly hunched over, and closed her eyes.

She listened to the water. It sounded like it always had. The soft whoosh of the breeze pushed small waves towards the shore. The splash of a bird as it landed on the surface. It calmed her. When she didn't know who she was or what she should do next, the water helped center her.

# TWENTY

## ALEX

"Can you make me some cereal please?"

Alex didn't have to open her eyes to see her. Molly would be standing by the edge of the bed in her nightgown, her hair wild with bedhead, ready to get up and start the day. This was the way they always woke up on vacations and weekends back home. Molly first, ready for breakfast immediately, followed by Lucy sometime after. Lucy took her time in the morning. She usually wasn't ready to eat until she had been up for at least an hour. Alex was the one who would get up with the girls; Ben always needed more sleep.

Alex had been dreaming about the letters. They seemed to be in her thoughts, awake or asleep, as if her brain was trying to solve the mystery of who the woman was even when Alex herself thought she was distracted or escaping into sleep.

She opened her eyes and pulled her hand out from under the covers to reach for Molly. "Good morning, Moll. Come here, I need a hug."

Molly grinned and bent her body forward, resting her head on Alex's face and wrapping one small, soft arm around Alex's body.

Alex closed her eyes again. There was nothing like the feel of your child's warm arm wrapped around you.

"Good morning, Mommy. Now can you get up?"

Patience wasn't Molly's strong suit. Then again, not many five-year-old kids could count patience as one of their best attributes.

"I'm up, I'm up." Alex rolled herself out of bed and followed Molly into the kitchen.

"Auntie Sam!" Molly squealed like she hadn't seen Sam all week already.

Sam had her head inside the fridge. She stood upright and pulled out jars of cream cheese and jam. "Hey, Moll!" She set her things down on the counter and hugged Molly's head to her.

"You're up early," Alex said. Sam had already toasted a bagel, poured herself juice and cut up berries.

"I'm starving. My appetite is back."

"Where did it go?" Molly asked.

Sam looked down at her and laughed. "Hey, want to share some berries with me? They're so good."

"Sure!" Molly's head peered up over the edge of the counter. "Can I share your bagel, too?"

"I'll make you something," Alex said. "Let Auntie Sam eat her breakfast."

"It's okay. I don't mind."

Pregnancy agreed with Sam, Alex noticed. Her skin was clear, her hair so thick and shiny. Alex thought Sam was doing quite well, considering. How awful to find out you were pregnant and then not be thrilled about it because your boyfriend was an ass. Wes wasn't good enough for Sam, though she wouldn't say that out loud, no matter how much she wanted to.

Molly grinned up at them before she skipped over to the table and sat down, waiting for Sam to join her.

"What are you up to today?" Sam asked over her shoulder. She spread a thick layer of cream cheese on her bagel and then picked up her plate, grabbed as many things as she could and went to the table to join Molly.

It was Thursday already, wasn't it? Days often jumbled into one in the summer, especially at the cottage where nobody wore a watch. The placement of the sun in the sky was how they told time. Yes, it was Thursday, which meant Alex planned to go back to Calm Waters, but she wasn't ready to tell her mother or sisters yet. She couldn't pinpoint the reason why she didn't want to tell them, other than that the meetings felt private, so she kept it to herself.

"I'm heading into town to grab a few groceries," Alex said. That part was true at least. She would pick up some things after the session. She poured water into the coffeemaker and heaped several scoops of fresh grinds into the filter.

Sam seemed to accept the answer. She cut her bagel, gave half of it to Molly and laughed when Molly's eyes widened.

"Do you remember the last time you felt that kind of joy from getting a bagel?" Sam pointed her chin in the direction of her niece.

"To be five years old again," Alex said.

After a while, Lucy, Ben and Mom got up and came to the kitchen for breakfast.

Alex tipped her head back to drain the last sip of her coffee. She put her empty mug in the kitchen sink. "I'm off to shower and head out."

Ben glanced up from his spot at the table. He and Lucy had started a game of Yahtzee because heaven forbid Lucy had nothing to do for a single minute of the day.

"Need anything from the store?" Alex asked.

He shook his head and went back to the game.


Grief was heavy on every face in the room. Alex shifted in the hard metal chair and scanned the circle of people at Calm

Waters. She recognized the woman with the beautiful white hair. Next to her was a tall, burly man with a thick beard and a ball cap. Michelle came through the doorway and took the empty seat across from Alex. She raised a hand in recognition and smiled.

Laurelle stood by the coffee station, but she came over now and placed a hand on the shoulder of the burly man. After she welcomed everyone, she took a seat and started the session. Alex decided she would just listen again.

As soon as Alex had woken up that morning, she'd felt compelled to go back to the counseling session. Something had stirred in her, similar to what she had felt when she was alone on the basement floor so many years ago. It was something unexplainable, but also frightening, so Alex knew she should go back.

After the session ended, a comfortable quiet washed over her, even though she hadn't spoken. She stood and folded up her chair, leaning it against the wall. Then she went to the coffee station to pour herself a cup.

"You're back." Alex looked up from stirring milk into her coffee and saw Michelle next to her, reaching for one of the small paper cups.

"I am," Alex said. She looked around her at the rest of the members. "Am I allowed to keep coming if I don't share anything?"

"Sure. You'll be ready when you're ready." When Michelle spoke, some of her hair shook. She eyed Alex. "Are you from around here?"

Alex tilted her head. "No. Why?"

"Oh, I've lived in the area all my life. I thought you looked familiar, but I know most locals. Not many vacationers come to these meetings."

Alex looked away. She didn't feel like giving away her life story. Things had been easy up until now; she went to school, got married, had kids, started her own successful online business and lived in the suburbs. In an instant, it had become complicated. Alex couldn't help but think if only her father had burned those damn notes, all of this confusion wouldn't exist. If only she hadn't found them, she could have carried on with her grief, feeling it subside little by little each day, disappearing like smoke.

Only, she had found them, and now she was another person. A new Alex. She supposed she would now mark time as before her father died, before she knew about what he had done, and after. Already the "before" was filled with odd, ghostly memories and flashes of happiness she wanted to hold onto.

"Sorry, I didn't mean to make you uncomfortable. I like to talk." Michelle adjusted the purse on her shoulder.

They left the building at the same time, walking out onto the sun-filled street. It was the type of day where the sky looked like a vast blue dome overhead, bright and cheerful, and the air was already hot. There was a bench to the right of where Michelle and Alex stood on the sidewalk, in the shade under a tree.

"Want to sit for a minute? It seems a shame not to enjoy our coffee," Michelle said.

There was no need to rush, summers were for moving slowly without a schedule, so Alex nodded. She perched on the edge of the bench and looked out at the cars driving by, the people window shopping.

"You look young," Michelle said. "I have a daughter probably close to the same age as you. Maybe she's a bit younger."

"Oh?" Alex didn't know what else to say to that.

Michelle cleared her throat. "Did you lose your spouse?"

"No, it was my father." The back of Alex's throat was dry. She glanced at Michelle from the side of her eye. "It's a little complicated. He left behind some unresolved things."

"Death is complicated, isn't it?" Michelle sat back against the bench. "Do you have kids?"

She nodded at Michelle. "Two girls."

"How nice. Kids are the best thing ever, hey?"

Alex sipped her coffee. She thought of Lucy and Molly and the little things that made them up: their big, wide eyes and thick eyebrows, the way their noses became dotted with freckles each summer, the roundness of their cheeks.

"How's your daughter handling all of this? You said it was your husband that passed away?" Alex asked.

"It's complicated, too," Michelle answered. She crossed one of her legs over the other. "He wasn't her father. She misses him, though."

Alex looked across the street, away from Michelle. Her face went flush with embarrassment. She shouldn't have asked such a personal question.

"I haven't spoken to anyone much about it, but it feels good to get it out in the open." Her voice was rich with emotion. She seemed like the kind of person who was easy to get to know. "That's why I like this place." She gestured back towards Calm Waters again.

"It's helping," Alex said. It was the surprising truth. Even though she was only attending and not sharing, the heaviness in her body lifted a little each time she left a session.

"The only problem with living in such a small town is that you keep running into everyone." Michelle squinted an eye as she took a sip of her coffee. "There isn't much privacy. I see Laurelle everywhere. I see the other people, too, and we all kind of nod and then look away from one another, not wanting to acknowledge that we know each other's innermost thoughts or one another's pain."

It hadn't occurred to Alex that you couldn't get away from the smallness when you lived in town. She felt sorry for

Michelle. Summerville had always been an escape for Alex and her sisters.

"That's hard," Alex said.

Michelle adjusted her position and reached for her bag. "It is what it is. Anyway, I should get going. It was nice chatting with you."

"See you next week?" Alex said. She immediately wondered why she'd committed herself to another session. It wasn't like her, especially when she didn't know this woman. On the other hand, maybe it was okay to accept that she was doing this for herself. For one short hour once a week, she put herself and her grief first. Maybe she would eventually find it within her to forgive her father. Although, she wasn't going to hold her breath on that.

Twenty minutes later, Alex stood in the middle of the grocery store, eyeing the chocolate bars and graham crackers conveniently placed next to one another at the end of the first aisle—a fine display of product placement and marketing. It worked on her. Alex was trying to decide if she should make the impulse purchase and surprise the girls with the ingredients to make s'mores. She had a bag of marshmallows in her hands when she looked up and saw Michelle walking down the aisle, a basket hanging on her arm with only a few pots of yogurt in it.

"Hello again," Michelle said. "We can't get enough of one another, it seems."

Alex pushed her cart to the edge of the aisle and smiled. She held the marshmallows up. "I'm deciding whether or not I should spoil my kids."

"In summer? I vote yes."

Alex glanced down at the nearly empty basket in Michelle's arms and felt a pang for her, the kind of pang that comes with loneliness. Weekly grocery shopping had to be a regular, upsetting reminder that it was only you in your house. She made a mental note to do her mother's grocery shopping for the rest of the summer for her.

"The weather's so gorgeous today," Michelle said.

Alex nodded. "It is." Small talk was painful, and Alex wasn't quite sure why Michelle was attempting it. She hadn't expected this kind of awkwardness with Michelle when their conversations had been easy so far.

"What are you up to for the rest of the day?" Alex asked. A chill rippled through her body from her neck, down her spine and out her legs. The air conditioning inside the grocery store had been cranked. She hugged her arms to her chest and rubbed at them.

"Actually, I'm planning the Celebration of Life I'm holding for my partner," Michelle said. Her eyes brightened like a good idea came to her. "I know we've only just met, but I'm inviting our Calm Waters group to it, if you wanted to drop by?"

"Oh," Alex said. "Sure. Yes." It came out before she had time to think. A Celebration of Life was too intimate. Alex shouldn't be there when she barely knew Michelle, but she didn't know how to say no politely.

"Great." Michelle took out a piece of paper and scribbled on it while she spoke. "It's at the Legion. This weekend. Here's the date and time and the address."

Alex took the piece of paper and folded it, placing it into the front pouch of her purse.

"See you there," Michelle said. She waved before turning and walking away, down the aisle in front of Alex.

Alex tilted forward at the waist to put her weight into pushing the massive cart in front of her but stopped when she saw a younger woman approach Michelle. They were familiar with one another, Alex could tell by the way they stood, how close they were and how their shoulders brushed one another comfortably.

Alex stayed and watched them. She normally wasn't nosey, but something compelled her to stand in place. At one point, the girl turned her head and looked directly at Alex. She had incredibly blue eyes that Alex could see even from a distance. Alex jerked her head back and shuffled her things in her cart, pushing the eggs to one side, putting the bread on top of the milk. Her face flushed at being caught staring.

When Alex looked up again, the girl was back talking to Michelle; this time she seemed tense and rigid, her arms folded across her chest. Her face was twisted into a grimace, like she was upset. Michelle, on the other hand, appeared patient, calmly answering the girl with words Alex couldn't hear. The girl said something else to Michelle—her hands bunched in fists when she spoke—and turned on her heel to storm away. She left the aisle toward where Alex was standing.

A shot of adrenaline coursed through Alex's body. How uncomfortable, to be seen watching someone's private conversation.

The girl studied Alex again, one of her perfectly shaped eyebrows arched as she got closer. She held Alex's gaze as if she was going to say something.

Did Alex know her? She searched her memory, frantically thinking about who this woman could be, if she was supposed to know her. Was she from Calm Waters? Alex was fairly certain she'd never seen her before. It was only the way the woman stared at Alex that made her doubt herself.

The woman got closer still, and Alex thought she was going to stop, but she continued walking, straight out of the store.

Alex shuffled to the right to hide herself behind the row of chips. She didn't consider herself to be a busybody, and she didn't want to give Michelle the wrong impression.

Eventually, Alex picked up the chocolate bar and the bag of marshmallows and put them in her cart, knowing the girls would be thrilled when she got home. She went up and down the rest of the rows, filling her cart with food and trying to avoid coming across Michelle again. When she made it out of the store, she was grateful she managed to escape without getting caught up in any further awkward exchanges.

At home, Molly bounced up and down at the sight of the marshmallows.

"Can we stay up for the campfire tonight?"

"Sure, I don't see why not," Ben said. He glanced at Alex for confirmation. She nodded, but she wasn't listening when he kept speaking. Her mind was still back at the store, thinking about Michelle and the woman with the deep blue eyes.

# TWENTY-ONE

## SAM

When Wes called, his voice was tinny and far away.

"I've been thinking. We need to talk."

Sam's stomach flipped, but not in the way she would have liked. She waited, standing next to one of the comfy chairs in the living room. It was Monday when they'd last spoken; it had only been three days since then. Sam wondered how much thinking he might have done in that time.

"I'm pretty sure I can't do this," Wes said.

"Can't do what?" Sam asked.

"Be a father. I can't be a dad, Sam. I'm not ready for it."

Sam's arms hung at her sides. Her vision went cloudy from the tears, not for herself, but for her baby who was already being rejected.

"You don't think you can do it," Sam repeated.

"I know it's complicated because of everything that's happening with your dad. It's all so confusing, but I can't." He took a long breath.

"I really don't know what to say."

"I'm sorry," Wes said, as if that would help at all.

"Don't you think you should consider it a little longer?" She hated the desperation in her voice. It was a last-ditch attempt to save what might be her new family. She was disappointed in herself for that, but she couldn't take it back.

"I'm going away." Wes spoke quietly now. "I'm going to travel for a bit. Try to get my head straight."

Sam's nostrils flared and there was a pounding in her ears. His life was going to continue unchanged. He had the luxury of going away to get his head straight. Meanwhile, Sam had to figure everything out for herself and for another person. Their child. They had both made this baby, yet Sam would be the one to have to explain why Wes wasn't present; she would have to be everything to this child.

"That sounds nice." She didn't try to hide any of the bitterness in her tone.

"It's not like I wanted this," Wes said.

Her legs buckled. She sat in a chair, her body curled in on itself. The anger was dissipating and was being replaced by humiliation. How utterly humiliating to be so unwanted.

"I have to go," she managed to say. Her head was throbbing.

"Wait. I didn't mean to hurt you. I promise." Wes's voice was low on the other end of the phone, a heaviness settled into it.

Sam couldn't find the right words, so she said nothing. She hung up and wasn't surprised when Wes didn't call back.

Outside, the sky had started to turn to shades of gray as evening crept in. Sam's head was foggy while she walked to her car. She had slipped out of the cottage before anyone had noticed. Getting into the front seat, she lurched the car out of the driveway and down the road. She tried her best to focus on the route in front of her, but her brain was firing in all directions.

Thankfully, the road was flat and familiar, she'd done this drive so many times, going back and forth to and from town, she didn't need to think in order to navigate her way. She would arrive in the middle of the quaint streets of Summerville, nestled on the edge of Shadow Lake, as if on autopilot. Along Main Street were the shops with T-shirts and hats for souvenirs, restaurants with open windows, the place to get good coffee, the bakery with the incredible butter tarts. All of them familiar markers along her route.

At a red light, she shifted in her seat so that she was more upright, and tilted her shoulders forward a little. Sam breathed in and then let out a yell that clawed at her throat, making it sharp with pain, like shards of glass scratching their way up her trachea and out her mouth. She yelled because of the heaviness, because of the feeling that everything in her life was so forever and unchangeable. Having a baby, being alone, being unsure of what path she should take, or who she even was. This was her life now. Letting it all out helped a little, and despite the throbbing in her head, she could admit she felt somewhat better.

When she got to town, Sam picked up an ice cream milkshake from the dairy and walked to the edge of the bank. She slid her feet out of her sandals, dug her toes into the sandy ground and slurped her milkshake the way kids did.

She heard movement behind her. "Which flavor's your favorite?"

She turned. Hunter stood over her. She noticed his tall frame even in the dim of the evening.

"I'm a chocolate-peanut butter girl. You?" She tried to be light and casual when she spoke.

"I'm partial to pistachio."

Sam crinkled her nose. People actually ordered pistachio?

Hunter noticed and laughed.

"Can I join you?"

She nodded and gestured to the spot on the sandy ground beside her.

He took his hands out of his pockets and sat. "Everything okay?"

"Am I that obvious?" She wiped at her eyes with the back of her hand.

"They're pretty red," he said and handed her a napkin. When their hands brushed one another, Sam did her best to ignore the jolt of electricity shooting up her arm.

She looked down and noticed her chewed fingernails were in need of a decent filing. Her fingers were long, but her hands weren't delicate. They were big and thick, with short, uneven fingernails. Maybe if she was more feminine the men in her life would stay with her. Most of the men she'd dated in the past were mostly interested in short-term flings—a few months was the longest relationship she had had. When she was a teenager, she'd had plenty of boyfriends in school, and had flitted from relationship to relationship so much so that Alex used to tease her. She thought she was having fun, but now that she looked back on it, it would have been nice to have someone love her long enough to stick around for a while. Someone to love her despite all her faults.

Sam opened her mouth to speak and then closed it again. She needed a moment before her voice would come out clear. It would only betray her if she tried using it. She hadn't planned on telling anyone about Wes yet, not even her sisters. It was too embarrassing to admit that he was leaving her and didn't want to raise his kid, but there was something about Hunter...

He propped his elbows on his bent knees, leaning slightly forward. He looked in front of him, examining the lake. "You don't have to say anything. I can just sit here with you. Unless my presence makes you want to throw up." He glanced at her sideways, a small smile on his face.

Sam laughed, finally. That was the last time she had seen him, wasn't it? When she'd stood in front of him and thrown up on the edge of his porch. He had reacted swiftly, gently taking hold of her hair, placing a hand in between her shoulder blades while she bent over, getting her water afterwards. She had been mortified, but Hunter had been calm and kind, like this happened to him all the time.

"Nope, it's not you. It's me," she said, stretching her legs out flat in front of her. "I'm pregnant."

Hunter's body straightened in surprise, as if a rope were attached to the top of his head, pulling him upright. "Oh. Wow. Uh—congratulations."

She let out a sharp, loud laugh, almost like a bark. Another one of her not-so-feminine traits. "I don't know," she said. "Are congratulations in order when your boyfriend tells you he wants nothing to do with you or your baby? We weren't together long, but he didn't even really give me a shot."

Hunter's face went grim. "Wes? Really?"

"Yep."

He didn't say anything for a while, his forehead furrowed. "I guess he did seem a bit—"

"Like a complete ass?" Sam said. She bowed her head and looked at the condensation running down the outside of her milkshake cup. She touched it with the tip of her finger, swirling it around in a circle. "I swear I'm smarter than this."

"You don't need to explain anything to me." He put his hands behind him now, holding up his body on the grassy bank. "You've been given some tough circumstances—that doesn't mean it's your fault or has anything to do with how smart you are."

Sam appreciated his kindness, but she didn't look up from studying the cup. "Are we the weirdest neighbors you've ever had?"

"You might be." He shifted in his seat. "But it adds to your charm."

She laughed again. "You don't know the half of it," she mumbled.

Hunter didn't seem to hear. She turned to him and found he was already looking at her, unblinking. The sudden temptation she had to lean over an inch was surprising. Her face went warm. She looked away.

"If there's anything I can do," he said. "I don't know how long you're staying, but I'm around for the summer if you need anything. Maybe even longer." He folded one leg underneath him. He seemed awkward, but it was endearing. What could Hunter do for Sam, a single, pregnant woman?

Then again, she had already planned on staying here with her mother to help her get sorted and settled, to keep her company. Maybe this was a sign. A reason to slow down, search out the quiet life and stay for a while. Pregnant women needed low-stress environments, didn't they? Being around Hunter seemed to lower her blood pressure. He was so calm, and interesting. The sound of his voice, the way he said things, it sometimes caused her stomach to flip, but she hadn't taken the time to think about what that meant yet.

It was quiet here, on the sandbank in front of the water, Sam and Hunter sitting side by side, and Sam thought it could only be a good thing to stay for longer than the summer. She had accrued enough vacation time at work, so maybe she could even take an extended leave.

"Actually, I think I might stay for a while, but I don't need help. I can manage, thanks." She turned towards him and lightly tapped his elbow, hoping he would know she appreciated the offer. When he smiled back at her, she couldn't help but notice the way her heart sped up.

# TWENTY-TWO

## ALEX

After dinner on Friday evening, Alex sat in the living room, legs curled under her and a book on her lap, while the girls were in the other room playing a board game with Ben. They were nearing the end of Alex's second week in Summerville, the first full week of having the girls and Ben with her, and today had been a long day in the sun for all of them. Alex wanted Lucy and Molly to get to bed early. That would mean they would have to start the bedtime routine soon. The process of getting them changed into pajamas, brushing their teeth, reading them stories, maybe singing a song and asking the girls over and over to please stop talking and go to sleep was exhausting. Alex planned to read for a few more minutes to work up the mental energy, but a knock on the door interrupted her. She glanced at Jess on the other couch, laptop open and clicking away at the keys.

"I'll get it." Sam came into the room from the kitchen. She opened the door and greeted someone Alex couldn't see yet. "Mom?" She turned and called, and then turned back again. "Please come in."

An older woman entered the cottage and stood in the doorway, her hands clasped together in front of her.

"Maria! So nice to see you." Mom came into the room and moved closer to the woman. She leaned in for a hug and a kiss on the cheek. "Girls, have you met my friend Maria? She has a cottage on the lake as well."

Alex thought the woman looked familiar, but couldn't place her. She stood up and went to the door to be polite.

"These are my daughters—Samantha, Alexandra and Jessica," Carol said. It was always odd to hear their full names.

"Maria Fraser." The woman held out her hand to Sam first.

And then it dawned on Alex. The woman who had commented on her father's photo.

"Nice to meet you," Sam said.

Jess came over and held out her hand, a polite smile on her face.

Alex nodded and pressed her lips together when it was her turn to say hello.

"We're going to have a glass of wine down by the lake," Mom announced. She turned to Maria. "Just one minute." And then she disappeared into the kitchen.

Alex, Sam and Jess stood in a semicircle, awkward and silent. It was usually Alex who kept the small talk going, but she was too busy studying Maria.

"I'm so sorry for your loss," Maria said to all of them.

"Thank you," Jess answered.

Alex put a hand in her pocket. "Did you know him well?" She knew her voice wasn't warm, she could tell by the way Jess shot a sharp glance in her direction.

Maria shifted in place. She ran a hand through her hair. Was it a nervous gesture? "We were friends."

*We*. Alex thought of the little 'xo' she had used in her comment. A coincidence with the notes? "You mean the three of you—you and my mother and father were friends? Or—"

"Yes, of course. We were all friends." Maria appeared ruffled, or was it confused? It was hard to tell.

Mom came back into the room then, an open bottle of wine and two glasses in her hand. "Let's go have a chat." She gestured toward the door to Maria. "Excuse us, girls."

Maria nodded at Carol as she whisked past them and opened the screen door. Before leaving, Maria turned again and glanced directly at Alex. The smile faded from her face.

When they were safely out of earshot, Sam turned to Alex. "What was that about?"

"That might be *her*," Alex said. There was something in her gut telling her not to trust Maria. Something was off.

"Alex, don't be ridiculous. You can't go around thinking everyone Mom and Dad knew is the woman who Dad had an affair with," Jess said.

"Why not?"

Jess went back to the couch and sat down, crossing her legs and placing her computer back on her lap. "Because that's not rational. We have no idea who she is."

"I have a gut feeling," Alex said. She sat across from Jess. Sam stood at the edge of the doorway, glancing out the window, frowning.

"You can't accuse someone based on a gut feeling." Jess's voice was impatient. She looked down at the keys on her laptop.

Alex's instincts were telling her to look into this further, though. She frowned at Jess. "This is something. I can't ignore it."

"Dad had an affair. It's awful and it was wrong and it's messy, but he's gone now. He's gone," Jess said, looking from Sam to Alex. "Is this the part of his life you want to focus on?" Her voice went high-pitched and uneven.

"Okay." Sam's voice was gentle in contrast. "You're right." She always tried to be the voice of reason when things got tense.

Alex shifted in her seat and strained her neck to look into

the kitchen. Ben and the girls were still preoccupied with their game. "I want answers. That's all. What if this woman lives somewhere close by?"

"So?" Jess said.

"We should know so that we're prepared for whatever else we have to face," Alex said. "Like, what do we do if he had another family?"

"We would know if there was another family." Jess rubbed her forehead, pressing her fingers into her temple and kneading the sides of her head.

"We didn't know about the affair. We went our entire lives not knowing that he was cheating on Mom," Alex replied. "Why would you think we would know about him potentially having other kids?"

Jess let out a small gasp. Her eyes were focused on her computer screen.

"What?" Alex asked.

Jess snapped her laptop shut and stood up. "Nothing. It's nothing. I just can't listen to this anymore. I have a headache, I'm going to bed." She stormed out of the room.

Alex jerked her head back. "What was that about? What is going on with her lately?"

Sam shrugged and came to sit down on the couch. "I don't know. Give her time."

Alex couldn't believe that Jess didn't want to pursue this. All this time, something had been going on and they were in the dark. Now there was a little glimmer of information, a potential lead, and Jess wanted to ignore it. It baffled Alex, but it wasn't enough to make her stop. The oldest child often knew better than the younger siblings, so she wasn't about to leave this alone. She was determined to see what she could find out about Maria, but it would have to wait until after bedtime. She got up from the couch. "I've got to get the kids to bed."

Sam nodded in response.

In the kitchen, Alex stood over Lucy and Molly and watched while they rolled colorful dice, pounding their markers into each box as they counted and moved through the board game.

"Time for bed," Alex said.

"Wait. Not yet. I'm beating Daddy."

"We'll finish this in the morning," Ben said.

Lucy and Molly flashed an irritated look at Ben and then reluctantly stood up.

"Can I have a snack?" Lucy asked. Classic stall tactic.

"You can have a piece of fruit."

"Never mind," Lucy mumbled.

Ben stood up and stretched. "Nice try," he laughed. "Go brush your teeth."

As soon as Lucy and Molly were out of the kitchen and halfway down the hall, Ben turned to Alex.

"Who was that out there?" He nodded at the doorway.

"A friend of my mother's came to visit." Alex rested a hand on the cool countertop. She lowered her voice. "I think there's a chance she might be the other woman."

Ben rubbed at his chin. "The other woman? What makes you think that?"

"I have a hunch."

"A hunch?"

Alex rested her free hand on her hip. "Why do you keep repeating what I'm saying?"

"Alex—"

"I think there's a chance she could be the one from the notes. I want to look into it."

Ben pursed his lips. He studied Alex for a moment. "Are you okay? You're not quite yourself."

"There's a lot on my mind," she said. He knew that.

Ben seemed to accept it. He walked past her into the

hallway towards the bathroom, brushing his hand on her lower back as he went by. "Be careful."

Alex had been careful all her life. This wasn't the time for that.

# TWENTY-THREE

## ALEX

Inside the Legion where the Celebration of Life was being held, thick, humid July air smacked Alex in the face. There wasn't a huge crowd, but the room was small and the atmosphere felt oppressive. This might not be the best idea she'd had, but it felt too late now.

Alex spotted the bar in the far-left corner. She decided to head straight there to ask for a glass of wine. Situations like this, where she was at a social gathering alone, always made her incredibly uncomfortable. A glass of wine would help.

"White, please." Alex pointed to a wine glass. She suspected that at a place called the Legion the choice would be between red or white, and not the type of grape or region of wine country. She was right. The wine was good, though. Crisp and fresh, with only a hint of sweetness, a dash of tartness on her tongue.

She turned around and spotted a tall, round table a few feet away that was empty. Alex set her glass down and rested one elbow on the edge of the table. The gathering was noisy, despite it being small and intimate. People greeted one another with long hugs, men slapped one another on the back and chatted loudly. There were women with loose-fitting printed tops and strappy sandals, men with polo shirts tucked into khaki slacks, all too tanned or burnt, noses red and forearms leathery from the sun. They smiled and kissed each other on the cheek with the sides of their mouths. It was definitely a celebration. It was actually quite nice.

"Alex?" Someone's hand was on her arm, gripping lightly. Michelle stood beside her. She had on a black flowing skirt and a black T-shirt. She looked casual and elegant. "Hi! Thank you for coming."

"Hi," Alex said. She wasn't sure what else to do in the moment, so she found herself hugging Michelle. "I'm so sorry for your loss."

"That's sweet of you," Michelle said after they had pulled apart. She smelled light and fruity, like champagne. "I see you've already located the refreshments." She nodded at Alex's glass of wine.

"Yes, thanks." Again, Alex wasn't sure what to say. It struck her that before this summer, she hadn't been to a visitation or funeral in a long time. Now she was at her second. It was hard to know how to act. Death made Alex uncomfortable. "This is a lovely gathering."

"Nice, hey? I didn't expect this; most of my friends never met my partner but they knew how important today was for me. I'm lucky they're here to show their support." Michelle had too much makeup on today, foundation and blush and eyeshadow caked on thick.

Alex looked away. When she turned back, a woman was approaching. She had a guarded expression on her young-looking, familiar face. It took Alex a second, but then she placed her. It was the deep blue eyes that tipped her off. She was the woman from the grocery store, the one Michelle had had an argument with.

"Hi, honey," Michelle said. She turned back to Alex. "Alex,

I'd like you to meet my daughter, Becky. Becky, this is Alex. We met at Calm Waters."

Becky nodded, but remained quiet. She didn't show any sign that she recognized Alex. She stood close to Michelle, touching her forearm, placing her hand on her mother's shoulder in a protective manner. Her dark hair fell in soft waves over her shoulders and her deep blue eyes looked even more vibrant close up. They were accented by the beautiful, bright summer dress she was wearing. It was the kind of dress that fit perfectly and made Alex want to ask where she got it from, but that obviously wasn't the right thing to do here.

"I'm sorry for your loss," Alex said instead.

"Thanks." Becky's tone was flat, her face unreadable. "He wasn't my father." She turned back to Michelle. "Can we start the speech?" A microphone was set up at the front of the room next to a podium.

"Soon." Michelle nodded at her.

Becky let out a low huff, an exasperated puff of air.

Alex turned her head away from them so Becky wouldn't see her raised eyebrows. If they hadn't been gathered for a Celebration of Life, Alex would think Becky was almost hostile.

"Becky." Michelle spoke with a stern voice. "Please."

"Fine, but I have to leave as soon as this is done. I'm meeting Dad."

Michelle turned to Alex. "My ex, Becky's father, wouldn't come today," she said. "I thought he should be here for Becky, but he didn't care much for John. We had an unconventional relationship and didn't get to see each other often; Becky's dad worried about the disruption and the impact on her. Thought she needed consistency."

Alex flinched. She was embarrassed at the intimate details—

*Wait. Did she say John?* It was a common name, of course, but still.

"*Mom,*" Becky hissed. Her face flashed with annoyance.

"Sorry," Michelle apologized. "I'm flustered. You know that."

"Can we do this, please?"

Michelle nodded again and tapped her daughter's slender hand. Her smile was tired, and her face resigned.

Becky leaned over and said something Alex couldn't hear in a low voice to Michelle and then nodded at Alex once more before she turned and left, disappearing into the crowd.

Michelle's cheeks were pink when she turned back to Alex. "Becky is handling grief in her own way, I suppose," she said. "She's angry."

Alex couldn't help herself. "Why?"

"Oh, it's complicated," Michelle replied shortly. "John and I —she never really approved. Anyway, I've got to go say hi to some other people, but please grab yourself some food, have another glass of wine. It was nice of you to come." She smiled and touched Alex's arm lightly.

Alex watched Michelle go. She likely wouldn't stay long enough to have another glass of wine, or to hear anyone speak. She had come to show her support for Michelle, but now that they had spoken, she wanted to leave. It wasn't right for her to be here. Death was intimate, and she was a stranger. Alex tipped her head back to drain the last sip of her wine and put the glass down on the table.

On her way through the group, Alex noticed a few people gathered to her left in front of a table. The table was set up with framed photos; next to it were a couple of large displays of pictures on two easels. Her eye caught something odd. Alex did a double take, and then her heart thrummed in her chest. She scanned the photos again.

It was her father.

Her breath hitched. Before Alex had a chance to absorb it, for her brain to make sense of what she was seeing, her body moved forward as if on autopilot. She looked over her shoulder, searching for Michelle, and then turned back to the photos again. One of them was instantly familiar. It was an old one. Her father was standing in the kitchen at the cottage—*their family cottage*, surrounded by their family's things. The clock on the wall, the mugs her parents always used for coffee, they were in the picture. Her stomach lurched at the way her father smiled directly into her eyes.

She squinted to get a closer look at the bottom edge of the photo. Something was cut off, something dark and shadowy. Her eyes widened when she realized what it was. Only she would recognize it, but it was undeniable to her. That was the top of her head—it was her hair, a nest of frizz from the humidity and the lake, tangled because she rarely ever brushed it in summer.

"What the hell?" Alex said.

A woman nearby glanced at her and frowned before moving away.

Alex recalled Michelle's words again. *John and I.* Her underarms went damp, but the back of her neck was chilled. She scanned the room, confused and dizzy, desperate to carve out a clear path to the exit among the bodies of well-wishers.

She couldn't get her mind to work properly. There had to be an explanation. Michelle couldn't be the woman from the letters, there was no way. But there were so many photos of her father. Smiling, holding a fishing rod, next to Michelle. That one was the most painful. There was the one of him holding up an ice cream—from his profile photo.

Her chest ached. She needed air. Alex turned, looking for the doorway, hoping to slip out before Michelle started speaking, but the room felt crowded.

She was almost at the doorway when she heard a tapping on the microphone, followed by Michelle's voice.

"Excuse me? Excuse me, everyone."

The chatter quieted to a lull. Alex turned to see Michelle standing at the podium, tugging at her shirt, brushing her hair off her face. She winced, searching for a way out, but people stood directly in front of the doorway. She was stuck; she had no option but to listen.

"I want to thank you all for coming. John would have been happy." Michelle's voice wavered, shaking for a moment as she pulled out a piece of paper and smoothed it onto the podium in front of her. "We weren't married—obviously most of you know that—but he was a big part of my life. He was my rock. We had so much fun together when we could." She searched the crowd, looking at Becky pointedly when she said it, and then her eyes darted back down to the paper. "I won't say much up here, it's not really my thing, but I did want to say that love is love, no matter how it comes into your life. And we really loved one another."

Alex inhaled sharply. Her breath caught in her throat. Her entire childhood was a lie. It was crystal clear to her. The happy family she thought they had been wasn't real. Her father was leaving them to have sex with *Michelle*, who knew how often. Or maybe even worse, they likely spent time walking around hand in hand, making each other coffee in the morning, talking about their weekend plans. All the things he did with their mother. A thought struck her. *For how long?*

Michelle's voice reverberated through the room again. "He was kind and sweet and funny and he was everything I ever wanted. When I thought of him and I growing old together, I imagined us living together, sitting on our porch, watching the lake as we sipped coffee and talked."

"No," Alex yelped.

A few people turned to look at her, kind expressions on their faces. They must have mistaken the tears in her eyes for grief. They didn't know this was wrong. They shouldn't be openly celebrating the life stolen from a family.

From a few feet away, Becky glared at Alex. There was no sorrow in Becky's face. It was cool and calm, not grief ridden. Alex's mind worked it over. How well did Becky know Alex's father? Was he a big part of her life? The thought of sharing him, even now that she was an adult and he was gone, was sickening to imagine. She couldn't stay here a second more.

Alex pushed her way through the group of people next to her who grumbled and shot her disapproving looks as she went. She didn't care. She moved as quickly as she could to the door, out the front steps and then closed her eyes for a second. It was a relief to feel the fresh air on her skin again. To smell the freshly mowed grass and hear the cicadas buzzing. She turned to the right, ready to force her shaky legs to carry her across the parking lot and into her car, but something was in the way.

Standing directly in front of her, about to head into the Legion, was Jess.

# TWENTY-FOUR

## JESS

"Alex?" Jess stumbled back a few steps. What the hell? Her mind raced, but she couldn't make sense of it.

"Jess? Why were you going in there?" Alex's voice was shrill. Her face and neck went pink and splotchy. She came down the steps that led to the Legion and stood in front of Jess, eyes narrowed. "What on earth are you doing here?"

Jess could ask the same thing. She glanced over Alex's shoulder as the door creaked open, a small blonde child escaping the hot room behind her. The sound of someone's voice amplified by a microphone came floating out the front door.

"I—I don't know. Wait. What are *you* doing here?" Jess asked.

"This is a Celebration of Life," Alex said. "For *Dad*." She raked a hand through her hair.

Jess closed her eyes briefly. She knew what it was. Becky had emailed to tell her about it. *I thought you should know*, she had written. *I tried to convince her not to do it.*

"Why are you here?" Alex asked again.

"I came... to see it," Jess replied.

Alex stared, unmoving. She opened her mouth like she was about to speak, but then closed it.

"Did you know about Michelle?" Jess asked. Her pulse sped up. Maybe she hadn't been the only one shouldering this burden.

"What? No." Alex shook her head. Then her eyes widened. Her voice was low and steady when she spoke. "How do you know Michelle? I've been going to a grief support meeting. I met Michelle there, but I had no idea she was the woman from the notes. What do you know?"

"Everything. I knew everything," Jess said. She had to tell Alex now. All of it.

Alex's face went dark, her mouth stretched into a thin line across her face. "You what? What does that mean, exactly?" Her tone was back to shrill.

"I've known about Dad's affair since we were kids." Jess slumped onto the bench nearby. Alex took a seat next to her, watching her every move.

"What?" she asked. "How old were you?"

"I don't know, about seven or eight? I overheard him talking to someone in a way that wasn't right. Someone who wasn't Mom. I put two and two together eventually. His business trips. His long work hours." She paused and wiped at the edge of her damp eyes. "Then I followed him into town one day and I saw them."

Alex leaned forward, her head bowed. "This whole time? You kept this from us. You didn't tell Mom?"

Jess crossed her arms over her chest. The accusation, the anger in Alex's voice, it made her heart thunder. "I didn't know how to handle it. I didn't say anything to anyone."

It came back to her in flashes of memories. The way she would follow him into town and would sometimes see him meeting up with her. Every time they would get into one another's car and drive off somewhere together, Jess's stomach would lurch.

"I met her daughter one day. By accident."

"Becky?" Alex asked.

Jess flinched. Alex already knew so much about Michelle. How?

"Yes. Becky," Jess said. "I was in town once and saw Michelle. She was walking around with a girl who looked like she was my age. They were holding hands, browsing outside the shoe shop. I was with Dad at the time."

"Oh my God," Alex said. She had the decency to finally seem concerned for Jess. "What happened?"

Jess could still remember the cold wave of anxiety that came over her back then. She could still feel it.

"Dad was awkward. He had a terrible poker face. I guess I had one, too, because Becky caught me staring at her. When Dad and Michelle tried to pretend they were window shopping so they could talk, Becky cornered me and asked me what my problem was."

"What did you say?" Alex asked.

"Nothing, really. It's hard to remember." That wasn't true. Jess remembered that day like it was etched into her skin. She could still recall the recognition that dawned on Becky's face that afternoon. Even at a young age, Jess knew Becky understood what was going on. They both did. The way Becky's eyes had narrowed, the way her chin had jutted straight out in front of her in a mixture of anger and defiance.

"You don't belong here," Becky had said. "This is where we live all year long. You only come up in the summers, don't you?"

Jess had nodded.

"This is our home. You should leave."

"And you never said anything to him?" Alex asked. She stood from the bench and crossed her arms over her chest.

"I wanted things to go back to the way they used to be," Jess said. "I was desperate for our old life. I thought if I didn't say anything, maybe we could pretend it never happened. Obviously, that didn't work."

Jess didn't mention that, later, as time went on, she would run into Becky every now and again in town in the summers. They slowly, eventually, exchanged names and started talking. Becky was reluctant at first, they both were, but theirs was a shared pain. It didn't happen often, but as they grew, when they saw one another, they would talk. Stilted and short conversations to begin with, and then a little more. Their need for someone to talk to about it was greater than their anger, and when they got older, they exchanged email addresses.

Now, they rarely ever spoke. How long had it been? Becky wasn't living in Summerville anymore and Jess didn't come here as often as they used to. That's why the email from Becky the other night was a surprise.

"Nobody ever called him out on his lies," Alex said. "Why didn't Becky?" She was still standing, her back straight and her shoulders raised around her ears.

Jess thought about Becky. She was kind, Jess knew, underneath the anger. She shrugged. "I can't speak for her. She dealt with it her own way. But we were only kids at the time."

"Why didn't you say anything when I found the letters? It's been almost two weeks. You could have told us," Alex said.

"I wasn't ready." Jess still wasn't ready for everyone to know. "We can't tell Mom yet. I need to figure out how to talk to her about it."

Alex scratched at her neck. She pressed her lips together. "Did you ever go to therapy?"

"I did for a while. It helped."

"I don't understand how you never told Mom."

Jess bristled. She pushed her hair off her face and gathered it into a ponytail, then let it fall over her shoulders again. "I wanted to protect her."

They were silent for a while, exhausted by their knowledge, and then Jess spoke again.

"I'm ashamed of what I've done. I wasn't strong enough to be honest with everyone, to call Dad out on it and tell Mom. But I didn't want our life shattered. I was only a kid."

What she would never tell Alex was that, back then, she worried more about him than their mother because she could see a sadness threatening to drown him. It was heavy and forever present. It took her a while, but she could recognize it in him, because it was in her, too.

Alex folded her arms over her chest. "This is a lot to take in."

"I know."

"I don't think we should tell Sam yet. It's too much stress for her with the pregnancy," Alex said. She reached into her purse and pulled out her sunglasses, placing them squarely on her face. "I think I need to be alone now. Will you be okay?"

Jess folded her arms across her chest and nodded. "I'll be fine."

Alex turned and trudged down the street, hunched over.

"I'm sorry," Jess said, mostly to herself.

# TWENTY-FIVE

## SAM

It had been only a week since Sam first suspected she was pregnant, a little less than that since she confirmed it with a test. She chewed on the end of her pen as she smoothed the calendar out in front of her onto the kitchen table, resigned to the fact that she had to be responsible. Now was as good a time as any. She may not have been overly excited about having Wes's baby, but she was going to do the right thing.

Sam roughly calculated that she must be about six weeks pregnant at this point. If she had been at home, she would have already made her first prenatal appointment with her doctor. Since she planned on staying here for a while, she had called the midwifery practice that served Summerville and the surrounding area to get on their list. She didn't tell them she wasn't completely sure where she would be when she had the baby. That was a detail she was fairly certain could be hammered out closer to her due date. For now, she had an appointment to see Claire, the midwife, in four weeks. While she waited, Alex had informed her it wouldn't hurt for Sam to keep track of her diet, her water intake, how she was feeling. Sam had already bought a bottle of prenatal vitamins, the same kind Alex had taken when she was pregnant with the girls.

She pushed the wall calendar away and stood up to stretch, pressing her hands into the small of her back.

"You've got to read this when I'm done with it. It's so good." Carol held a book up in the air as she walked into the kitchen. "You should read as much as you can now because once the baby arrives, it's really hard to focus." She nodded at Sam's stomach.

"Really? I don't know. I don't plan on letting this change my life completely."

Carol froze in place, her eyes bulging. Then she let out a loud, exuberant laugh. She bent at the waist and held onto her stomach, wheezing and chortling for much longer than necessary, Sam thought.

"Oh sweetie, I'm sorry. I'm sorry. Those are very famous last words. Listen, if I can give you any piece of advice, and goodness knows you'll get lots and lots from many well-intentioned people," she said as she swiped at a tear at the edge of her eye. "My advice would be to never say never. Don't try to predict how motherhood is going to be and the right way to do things, because once you've mastered one stage, it all changes and you're back at square one, unsure of what to do next."

"Really?" Sam frowned. She had seen what life was like with Alex and the girls, but Alex made it look much easier than that.

"Yes." Mom's voice was softer now. "But don't worry, because you'll figure it out. That's what we do." Carol brushed a piece of Sam's hair out of her face. "My baby having a baby. It feels different to me this time than it did when Alex was pregnant."

"Why?"

"I don't know." Carol shrugged. "Maybe because I didn't think you'd have kids."

"You didn't?" Sam said. Her mother's words stung, but she couldn't pinpoint the reason. It was an innocent enough observation, and yet, it felt like Alex was held to a different standard. Alex was the oldest, the shining star who did everything to make a parent proud—she got good grades at school and then settled down and got married, had kids, moved to a nice home, started her own successful business. Mom didn't see Sam achieving all of that too?

"You've always seemed like a free spirit, I suppose," Carol said. "I never knew where you would end up. I wasn't sure what your place would be."

Sam moved to the other side of the kitchen and pulled a piece of bread out of the plastic bag, popping it into the toaster. She turned around and leaned on the edge of the counter, folding her arms across her chest. She wondered if the way she was floating through life with no solid plan bothered her mother. Then again, maybe all her mother wanted was for Sam to be happy. The trick for Sam was figuring out what that meant.


Later, when Sam went outside to sit by the water, she saw Hunter down on his dock, placing a fishing pole and tackle box into his tin boat. She'd noticed that most days at dusk, Hunter went fishing, often alone. He seemed to be a solitary kind of person, so it surprised Sam when he approached her dock in his boat and came to a stop.

"Want to come with me?" he asked.

His tanned forearms were splashed with droplets of lake water. Something about the way they shimmered made Sam want to touch them, brush her hand over them.

"Sure," she said.

He stood in the boat and placed one hand on the dock, his other hand stretched out toward her to help her inside. He was gentle with her, careful to make sure she was seated before going back to his spot by the engine. Then he smiled at her, his white teeth illuminated by the stubble across his chin. He was so handsome.

A swooping sensation went through Sam's stomach, up into her chest. It was inconvenient. This wasn't the time.

"Ready for this?" he asked.

Sam nodded. Who knew? Maybe she was.

After they had been in the boat for a while, after choosing lures and casting their lines, waving at other boaters who passed across the lake, Hunter turned toward Sam. "Hey, can I ask you something?" His eyes went back down to his fishing rod almost as quickly as they had been directed toward Sam. He pulled one lure off and put another on.

Sam leaned her body to one side and let her hand dangle over the edge of the boat to feel the cool lake water. "Sure."

"What's been your best day?"

"My best day? This summer? Or, in general?" Sam asked.

"In your life. The best day in your life. Can you think of one?" Hunter still wasn't looking directly at her. It was an odd question that came out of nowhere.

"I've never really thought about it. Do you have one?"

Hunter looked up. "There was one summer, my parents took my sister and I to Europe for a few weeks. It was an extra special trip, they kept telling us. They had saved up for ages. They wanted us to really experience it, so they showed us all these amazing things, like ancient ruins and cathedrals and castles and buildings that had been there for centuries." He pulled on his fishing rod and started to slowly reel the line in. A small smile appeared on his face. "At one point, my parents took us to this regular old restaurant for dinner and the place happened to have blue cake for dessert. Later on, my mom and dad told us it was the only thing my sister and I would talk about afterwards. We were in Europe on the trip of a lifetime, and our best memory was the blue cake."

Sam laughed. "Oh, your poor parents." She rested her fishing rod on her lap. "So that was the best day of your life? Blue cake?"

Hunter shook his head. "Only part of it. The next morning, after the restaurant, my mom woke me up early. It must have been six in the morning. I was worried something was wrong, but she only asked me to follow her to the kitchen of the little apartment we had rented. She poured me a bowl of cereal and we went out to the balcony and chatted as the sun rose. She wanted to watch it with me alone." Hunter smiled. "We had cereal together and talked, in Europe, watching the sun. Our little secret. The blue cake always reminds me of that now."

There was a soft pull in Sam's shoulders. What a beautiful memory. She leaned in closer to Hunter, but she wasn't close enough to touch him. She wanted to be.

"I don't have a blue cake story," she said. She wished she could think of one, but nothing came to her.

"Maybe it hasn't happened yet. Someone like you will have one. Probably lots of them," he said. His eyes sparkled when they looked at her.

"Someone like me?" Sam wasn't sure how to take that.

"You seem like you have a big heart, like you really feel things. You're a special kind of person. You deserve a million good days." A flush came to his tanned face. He looked down and cleared his throat. It only made Sam feel more for him.

"Thank you," she said. "I'm not sure anyone other than my parents has ever said something so kind to me."

"It's true." His voice was quiet.

They sat in silence for a moment, and Sam enjoyed it. This feeling was interesting, like she couldn't quite catch her breath but didn't want to. Was this how it was supposed to feel? She'd never had it before. Then it struck her how unfortunate it was, to meet someone like Hunter right after learning she was pregnant with another man's baby. How could this work?

"It's getting dark. I should go back," Sam said.

Hunter looked up, and she thought she saw a flash of surprise, maybe even hurt, in his eyes.

# TWENTY-SIX

## ALEX

Now that it was nearing the end of July, Lucy's skin was starting to turn golden brown, which made the tiny hairs on her arms and legs shine white in the sunlight. Alex imagined she would never stop marveling at her daughters' perfect little bodies. Their soft, smooth skin, their rounded bellies, their shiny hair that fell in sheaths down their backs. For the past two weeks, Lucy and Molly had spent the summer sand-covered and barefoot, smudges of jam on their cheeks, hair tangled and unwashed. Lucy wandered around the cottage wearing tiny pairs of shorts that somehow made her look so grown up, then she wore tie-dye T-shirts she had made last summer at day camp, or one of her many tank tops with rainbows and unicorns, and suddenly she looked like an eight-year-old again.

Alex had never been the type of mother who wanted to freeze time. She always thought her daughters kept getting better and better as they got older, more like little people and less like babies that relied on her for everything. Early mother-hood had been draining and exhausting for Alex, such long stretches of sleeplessness and always having someone attached to her. But now she watched the girls in their perfect little-kid messiness and she actually did want them to stay that way. She didn't want them learning about all the complicated adult worries her family was struggling through. One phrase spoken out of turn and their whole view of their grandfather could forever be altered. It was too much pressure.

Alex spent most of that day sitting on the Adirondack chair watching the girls build sandcastles and moats in the sand leading down to the shallows of the lake. It had been two and a half weeks since she had run out of the Celebration of Life. Two and a half weeks since she had seen Michelle and listened to her say all those awful things. She hadn't been able to shake it since then.

Ben tried to comfort her discreetly whenever they were alone, so nobody else would notice and think something was up. He would grasp for her hand to stop her from rushing around the cottage, getting food for the girls or searching for their goggles and towels. He would hold Alex's gaze and then press his lips to her cheek, her forehead, her jawline, the edge of her neck. Ben showed comfort by being physical. Alex appreciated it, but she needed to think right now, not touch.

She could hear someone approaching from behind her chair, though she didn't need to turn around to know. Ben had a familiar sound. When he got close enough, she watched him sit in the chair next to her, sticking his legs out in front of him and reclining into it as much as he could.

"How are you doing?" he asked.

"I'm okay."

Ben leaned over to rub her arm. "Alex." His voice was firm, but not unkind. He turned to her. "You haven't been yourself at all. Maybe it's time to let this whole thing go. Or maybe you should talk to your mom. Get all of it out in the open."

"Maybe," Alex said, even though she didn't mean it. She

looked out at the lake, not meeting his eye, and squinted into the warm breeze. She hadn't spoken much to Jess about it yet, let alone considered telling her mother anything. The timing didn't feel right. Then again, when was the right time to blow up someone's entire past? Jess had been mostly quiet around Alex, and Alex had surprised herself by keeping quiet, too. Although, her mind had been constantly whirring, trying to work out the details of how Jess could have known all this time and kept all of it to herself. She was only a kid then. Alex's mind flashed with a memory of Jess the way she remembered her as a child— wearing a bathing suit, up here at Shadow Lake, hair in her face, quiet and thoughtful, but smiling. Was that before or after Jess found out? It felt like a memory from another life now that Alex knew.

"Daddy! Do you want to see what we're building?" Molly's eyes flicked from her sand village to Ben, her face breaking into a proud smile when she noticed him.

"Sure." Ben paused for a beat and then stood up, almost as soon as he had sat down. He went to Lucy and Molly's side, sitting cross-legged in the sand next to them, and listened to them explain every intricate detail of the village they were building.

"Do you know about the origins of moats?" he asked Lucy.

"No. What's an origin?"

Ben laughed before launching into a lengthy description of the term origin and then where moats came from.

Alex was lucky to have chosen such a good man to be her husband and the father of her girls. He was so good at father-hood. Like most parents, he had times when he got overly frus-trated and fought little battles that Alex would never have chosen to fight with the girls. He sometimes could be heard telling them absurd things like, "Baths are not for splashing," but for the most part, he was the one who would get down into the sand and listen to his daughters talk for ages about whatever was interesting to them that day.

Alex watched him, thinking that he could never in a million years be the type of man who would carry on an affair for their entire marriage, or lead a double life. But, then again, her mother must have thought the same thing about her father. She frowned to herself and crossed her feet at the ankles.

"You okay?" Jess appeared and sat in the now empty chair next to her. She kept her eyes out on the beach, watching Lucy and Molly.

"I don't know. How about you?" Alex glanced sideways, studying Jess's face. She felt a pang of something for her sister—what was it? Sadness? No, it was heavier than that. Grief for her childhood.

Jess sighed. "Same."

"I'm thinking of going back to grief counseling. To see her," Alex admitted. She almost couldn't believe she was saying it, but she had been contemplating doing it for a while now.

Jess leaned forward slightly in her chair. A pinched look appeared on her face. "Why would you do that?"

Alex shrugged. "She doesn't know about us, does she? Did Becky ever tell her the truth about you?"

Jess shook her head, eyes still focused forward. "No. Becky and I both kept everything to ourselves. Dad didn't know that I knew anything, Michelle didn't know that Becky and I spoke. I have no idea what she knew about us, to be honest."

"Good," Alex said. She had wanted to talk to Michelle again, to find out more, but she wasn't sure why. All she knew was that Michelle could know nothing about who Alex really was. "You shouldn't have gone to the Legion," Alex remarked. "She might have recognized you."

"From when I was a kid?" Jess said. "I doubt it."

"You never know. She doesn't know me at all, though. I can talk to her again."

"Seeing her is a bad idea, Alex." Jess's voice was low. "You only want to go because you think it'll make you feel better somehow, but you're going to end up feeling way worse. You're going to end up hurting people."

Jess seemed so certain of the outcome.

Alex opened her mouth to protest, but then closed it again. A stiffness formed around her jaw. She said nothing more about Michelle to Jess.


In the lobby of Calm Waters, the friendly woman sitting behind the desk nodded at Alex. "Welcome back." She smiled and her eyes flicked to the doorway to Alex's left. "They're getting started in a minute."

Alex went through the door and down the hallway, stopping before she pulled on the handle. She smoothed the front of her shirt that had now wrinkled from being in the car. She had become sweaty while driving over, not only because it was the end of July and the heat had never agreed with Alex, but because this was all still so distressing for her. She thought knowing who the other woman was would help, but Alex only felt waves of unease.

When she finally went into the room, nobody noticed. They were all milling about, the meeting not started yet.

Alex's eyes darted around until she spotted her. Michelle. She was moving like she hadn't a care in the world—a living, breathing reminder of her father's betrayal. Alex didn't know what she was expecting to feel. There was nothing but a confusing fluttering in the pit of her stomach.

Now what? Alex didn't have a plan. She stood still, placing both of her palms flat onto her thighs and breathed in through her nose, out through her mouth, the way her mother had taught her to do when she was anxious and upset.

Michelle caught sight of Alex and her eyes widened, her

face brightening. "Hello! I haven't seen you in a while." Michelle came over to where Alex was standing. "I wanted to thank you for coming to the Legion, but you disappeared."

"Sorry, I wasn't able to stay long."

Michelle waved a hand. "No problem. It was nice of you to come and show your support."

The hairline at the back of Alex's neck went damp.

"What happened to... to him?" Alex asked. "Your husband?" The words came out of Alex's mouth like someone else was speaking them. Her voice sounded so far away and foggy.

"He had a heart attack. I wasn't with him at the time." Michelle's eyes clouded over, rimmed with red in an instant. She shook her head. "I guess he wasn't my *husband*, husband. We never made it official. I considered him mine, though."

Alex's throat constricted. She tried to hide it by shifting her stance. She had to move to keep the anger at bay, so she found herself swaying back and forth slightly, the way she used to do when she was holding Lucy or Molly as babies. The mindless rocking of new motherhood. Alex was doing it now, as if trying to soothe herself, while wondering what kind of a woman could claim a man—a husband to another woman and a father to three kids—as her own? He wasn't hers, he never was. She knew she needed to ask more.

"He wasn't your husband?" Alex said.

"Well, no," Michelle said. "But there was so much passion. So much hope and promise as to what could come of our relationship."

Alex was dizzy. Nausea rolled through her. She froze on the spot and tried not to give herself away.

Michelle kept going. "He was a good man. We were together for almost thirty years."

Alex's grip on her purse tightened. A chill ran through her, despite the fact that she had been sweating only moments ago.

Thirty years. For most of Alex's life, her father had been with Michelle, and she never knew. She couldn't make sense of time then, it was all a confused jumble. She was how old when he'd met her? When Alex had graduated, got married, had Lucy and then Molly, how long had Dad been dating Michelle then?

Now Michelle had a distant look on her face. A small smile settled across it. "Anyway, how are you doing? You haven't been here for a while. I've been thinking about you."

"Why?" It came out of Alex's mouth before she could stop herself, before she even knew what she was saying. It was hard to make sense of anything. She was standing in front of her father's mistress of thirty years.

Michelle's head jerked back slightly. "Well, because I know you're struggling. I can see it in you." She shifted her purse on her shoulder. "I care about you. You remind me of Becky."

It struck Alex in that moment that Michelle was a fellow mother. Michelle had known the worry, the love, the heartache of having kids. It wasn't what Alex was expecting, to find a real person like this in front of her. She had assumed she would walk into the meeting and see Michelle anew. Alex had been certain she would see her for what she was: an unfeeling, horrible excuse of a woman who ripped people's families apart without a second thought. The other woman. It was such an awful thing to be.

Instead, despite seeing something raw and painful, she saw the Michelle she first met. A mother, a woman dealing with her own grief, smiling kindly and looking directly into Alex's eyes when she spoke.

Maybe it was the effect of being in the middle of her favorite little cottage town carved out of water and sand, where it was serene and calming, that caused Alex to stand there and not react. Alex didn't want to be calm, though. She wanted to be angry and hot, enraged by Michelle and what this woman had done to her family. She wanted to see fury and fire when she watched Michelle walk around the room, getting herself a cup of coffee, sitting and listening to Laurelle and the other people at Calm Waters. She wanted to be repulsed by the other woman, but she wasn't. And that was even more confusing to Alex than everything else.

# TWENTY-SEVEN

## SAM

Sam watched Jess as she wandered around the cottage like a lost puppy. She wasn't sure why, but her sister seemed adrift lately. Jess had sat by the lake for hours the other evening, staring and frowning at nothing in particular out in front of her. Though she loved Jess very much, Sam didn't want to be like that. She didn't want to be uncertain about anything, she wanted purpose and a strong sense of what she was doing, where she was going. She had to pull it together for her baby.

Sam slipped into her flip-flops by the front door that Thursday afternoon and glanced over her shoulder, telling anyone who could hear that she was going over to Hunter's.

The air outside was thick today. She could feel the humidity in the bend of her elbows and the top of her lip. Sam knew her hair was getting bigger by the minute, her curls turning into a frizzy tangled mass around her face. The sky was a whitish-gray band stretched over the top of Summerville, no sun in sight. These kinds of days offered a reprieve from sunburn and heat at least, but Sam hated the humidity more than anything else. It wasn't only because she had curly hair, but also because it made you feel slow and heavy, like you were trying to run through sand.

When she arrived at Hunter's place, she poised her fist a few inches away from the door, ready to knock, but he swung it open before she could say a word, a broad smile on his face. "Hey. I saw you coming."

Sam lowered her hand. Everything between them so far had been nice—and also confusing. Like this moment. Her body almost burned at the way he stood close to her, his head down so he could look into her eyes. He was so close, she could smell him, earthy and woody, like coffee and campfires. She liked being around Hunter, it was physical, but also he was kind and smart. He said things to her that were sweet and thoughtful. At night, Sam had found herself thinking about how much she wanted something to happen between them, but then she would be reminded of how impossible it was. She couldn't start something new right now—pregnant with another man's baby. It couldn't go anywhere, and would only end up hurting.

"Come in," Hunter said.

She followed him down the short hallway back to the main room overlooking the lake. She could see his tin boat tied to the edge of the dock. The other day came back to her and how comfortable it had been. She took in a breath before sitting on one of the couches in his living room.

"What's up?" Hunter took a seat across from her. Good. Sam needed the space to do this.

"I love spending time with you," she said and then hesitated. It must have been long enough for Hunter to know something was coming. His face fell.

"But?" he said.

She gestured to her stomach. "We met at the wrong time, I guess. I'm pregnant with another person's baby. I'm going to have to figure out how to do this on my own."

Hunter's jaw flexed. "Sam, I like you. I like being around you." His voice was quiet.

The nerve endings in Sam's body tingled. She cast a furtive glance in his direction. She already knew she liked a lot about him, too. She was undeniably attracted to him: his strong, tall body. She liked how calm and steady he was, quiet and understated. He radiated confidence but not in a showy way. But she was pregnant and had no plan for her life. The only thing she knew was that she had to focus on her baby. She sure as hell wasn't in the right place to merely have fun.

She ran the edge of her fingertips over her bottom lip. It was best if she came right out and told Hunter that this wouldn't work before they got any closer.

She turned to face him. "I like you, too," she said. She wanted to also say that although she was attracted to him, she wasn't in the best place to start something, that she should prepare for having a child. She couldn't ask him to be a part of raising the baby. She didn't even know if she wanted that.

But she didn't say any of that. Instead, she crossed the room and sat next to him. Her fingertips radiated with heat when she touched his hand, and the words wouldn't come.

# TWENTY-EIGHT

## JESS

For the last few weeks, Jess had kept thinking about the moment she saw Alex outside the Legion. After a lifetime of carrying the burden of the secret to herself, she'd finally let it out to her sister, and she still didn't feel any better. She'd expected there would've been more of a release.

Since then, she'd tried to act like everything was normal. She ate cherries right from the fridge, she wandered down to the beach and sat in one of the big chairs to watch the water, she went for a swim, she hung around the cottage. Even today, as she went to town for groceries, she tried to pretend that nothing had changed. But she couldn't stop thinking about how she felt and what she should do next.

They wouldn't be able to keep it from Sam and Mom forever. Maybe that was where the twisting feeling in her stomach came from. She thought it would feel good to let go of her secret, but there was still so much unsaid.

Jess was in her car winding down a road surrounded by tall trees and green grass, rocks edging the asphalt, on her way into town. In the quiet, she chewed the inside edge of her lip, thinking. It felt like she was always thinking, but not doing.

When she got into town, Jess parked and walked along the bustling street toward the bakery. The sidewalks were full of people wearing large hats and sunglasses, licking the edges of melting ice cream cones, enjoying the last few days of summer.

Jess stopped to flick a pebble out of her sandal that was digging into the bottom of her foot. She leaned one hand up against the stone building next to her and when she stood upright again, Jess saw them across the street.

Michelle was outside the giant shoe store, looking at the sidewalk display. One of her hands held the strap of her cross-body purse while the other touched the shoes in front of her. Becky was a few feet away, in a breezy sundress, holding a toy truck in one hand and hanging on to a little boy's hand with the other.

Jess's pulse sped up. She moved toward a lamppost to try to hide before she could be seen. This was ridiculous. She knew she should stop hiding and get out of there, but something held her in place.

*I'll only stay for a second*, Jess told herself.

Michelle picked up a pair of plastic sandals, turning them over in her hand. She placed them back down again and looked up quickly, as if she had been startled, glancing around her. The little boy leaped towards Michelle, grabbing onto her with his chubby hand and, even from across the street, Jess could see Michelle's face light up.

Michelle and Becky chatted for a little while and then turned away from the shoe store, heading down the sidewalk toward the locks, the little boy racing for the bridge ahead of them.

Jess was struck by how relaxed they both looked, strolling arm in arm. She frowned. Their lives hadn't been drastically changed by the death of John. They were grieving, yes, but life would keep on going. They would be okay with a little bit of time. The thought made Jess's chest hurt.

Maybe Michelle and Becky would stand on the bridge and watch the boats for a while, maybe they would get ice cream after. One thing Jess was now certain of was that they both appeared to be completely content. They seemed to be able to let go and move on in a way Jess couldn't.

Jess moved from her position behind the lamppost on slightly unstable legs. It threw her off to see Michelle and Becky again. She glanced at them once more and then made her way to the bakery. She would have to force herself back to normal. She would pick up some scones and cookies, maybe a few of those incredibly rich brownies the girls loved, and then she would head back to her family and keep pretending.

When she got back from town, Jess found the cottage empty. Everyone was out somewhere. She went straight to her bedroom to change into her swimsuit.

Down at the dock, Jess tossed her towel on the chair and stood at the edge, her toes curled over the creaky wood. She looked at the water below her. It was breezy today, which meant waves rolled into shore a little louder than usual.

Jess took a step back and then launched herself off the dock and into the lake. She swam. It could have been for fifteen minutes, it could have been forty-five. It was hard to say. Jess pushed and pulled her limbs forward and back, gliding through the water until her arms started to tire. She flipped onto her back and let her head drop to the surface. Her shoulders and back floated on top of the water. It was then that her mind finally quieted. When she was weightless like this, her ears just below the surface of the water, her eyes closed, she almost forgot where she was. How long could she stay this way before she decided she had to go back?

When she was a kid, she could stay forever. She never tired of being in the water. This was such a gift, back then. When

Alex and Sam and Jess were kids, they would spend most of the summer in the lake. If they weren't swimming, they were often barefoot, with dirty fingernails and hair crusty with sand and lake water. They spent hours unsupervised, riding bikes along the roads lined with cottages, into town for ice cream or to fill a little brown bag with ten-cent candies. They wore shorts and tank tops that were often mismatched, but mostly it felt like they lived in their swimsuits. Sometimes they would play tag or hide-and-seek until the sky darkened, only popping back into the cottage when they were hungry. Even once Jess knew about Dad, she could keep it buried and almost forget about it entirely while she was with her sisters. Things were simpler then. There was nothing simple about being an adult.

Jess flipped over and swam back to the dock. She heaved her body out of the water and reached for her towel to dry herself off. After she wrapped it around her body, she went back to the cottage, into the living room. It was still quiet inside, which suited her fine. She thought about getting dressed when a sound came from behind her.

"Oh. I'm sorry." It was Hunter's voice.

She flung herself around to face him. "Hunter! What are you doing in here?"

"I'm so sorry, I don't normally let myself into places." He stood by the entranceway, fumbling over his words. "It looked like nobody was home and I thought I would drop off the flashlight. I was going to put it on the counter and then leave again."

Jess pulled the towel tighter around her body. She eyed the flashlight in his hand. "Thanks," she said.

"Hey, can I ask you something?" he said as he moved a step closer.

"Sure." Jess's pulse sped up a little. She took a breath in.

"It's about Sam."

Of course it was.

She let the breath out slowly. "What's that?" she asked.

"I'm having trouble reading her. Sometimes it seems like she's interested in something more happening between us, but at other times, I'm not sure. I think she came to tell me we couldn't see one another, but then..." His voice trailed off.

Was something happening between them? That was the first Jess had heard of it. She had been so preoccupied by Alex these last few weeks, she'd almost completely forgot about Hunter and whatever it was he and Sam did or didn't have. She was glad he'd stopped himself from saying more, she didn't want to know.

"She's pretty much an open book," Jess said. "You get what you see." She shrugged, to indicate she couldn't help him with this. She didn't want to be a therapist or a mediator or whatever else he was looking for. Except, when he looked at her, he had such a genuine expression on his face. He liked Sam. He was a good person. Sam deserved to have something special like this.

When they were growing up, Sam was the one who would speak to Jess in soft tones if she was upset, she was the one who always made time for Jess, always listened to her, could calm her down quickly with her soothing voice, her tight hug. As they'd got older, the tables had turned a few times. The bond they had was special, it was one Jess didn't quite have with Alex, which is why it surprised Jess now that she knew nothing about what was going on with Sam and Hunter. Then again, Jess supposed, she hadn't asked. When was the last time she and Sam had had a deep conversation? She had to be a better sister.

"Do you want me to try talking to her?" Jess asked.

Hunter smiled a little shyly. "Only if you don't mind."

"No problem." She tugged at her towel again. "I should probably go get dressed."

"Right. Sorry again." Hunter went for the door, pulled it

open and then stopped. "You're a good sister. They're lucky to have you."

Jess didn't answer him. The tiny flicker she felt when he turned and looked at her once more made her feel not so certain about that.

# TWENTY-NINE

## SAM

Two weeks later, well into the second week of August, Sam wriggled her toes in bed and looked down at her feet. Were her ankles swelling up? Could that even happen this early? She pushed her pajama shirt up and studied the smoothness of her stomach. It was still flat, but Sam wondered when it would start swelling, showing a tiny, telltale bump.

She rubbed her hand over the top of her skin and closed her eyes, wondering if the baby would have her curly hair. Poor thing if it did. She was teased about it as a kid, though it was one of the things Mom used to say made her unique.

"Standing out from the crowd is a hard thing to appreciate when you're young, I know. But you're so lucky to be you and nobody else," Mom would say.

Sam wanted to feel that maternal connection, that bond with the baby, but she didn't have it yet. She was trying not to let the unfortunate complexities of her situation bother her, but it *was* bothering her, and it was getting in the way of her enjoying her pregnancy. She tried to forget about Wes completely and tried not to think about her and Hunter and how that couldn't work. She was failing for the most part.

Today, however, she had her first midwife appointment, and she vowed to focus only on her baby.

Swinging her legs over the edge of the bed, Sam launched herself up to standing and walked to the bathroom. It was quiet, which meant everyone else was likely still asleep. She splashed her face with water, then twisted her hair into a bun on top of her head.

After she was dressed, Sam went to the kitchen, opening the fridge and staring at the contents. The thought of coffee still bothered her enough that she avoided it first thing, and the food aversions she currently had made choosing breakfast difficult. Cereal was now a no-go; the milk was gross. The texture of oatmeal was disgusting. She still liked bagels, but they didn't have any today.

"Good morning." Carol walked into the room, interrupting Sam's train of thought. "How are you feeling?"

"Not bad," Sam said. She noticed she had already been asked how she was feeling often, even this early into the pregnancy. She supposed that came with the territory, but it was clear now that her mother was standing in front of her that everyone should be asking Carol that, not Sam. Sam could take care of herself. Her mother, on the other hand, still looked weak and tired. Her eyes had dark circles underneath them. "What about you? Are you okay?"

"I'll be just fine." Her mother's voice was soft. She took a mug down from the cupboard. "It's you girls I'm worried about. You all seem so distracted lately. I feel disconnected from the three of you."

A pang of guilt shot through Sam. They were supposed to be here for their mother. Sam didn't mean to be wrapped up in herself and her own problems. She would have to talk to Alex and Jess about this. Their mother needed them.

"We're okay," Sam said. "Promise. And you need to take care of yourself, not us."

"You never stop taking care of your children."

Sam looked down at her stomach again. She said, "I better go into town to find something to feed this little one, then. There's nothing here I feel like eating. Do you want to come?"

Carol shook her head. "I'm not dressed and I'm feeling lazy. You go and get some breakfast. And don't worry about me. Please."

Sam touched her mother's arm as she left. She made a mental note to bring this up with Alex and Jess later. For now, she decided to head to the bakery in town to grab herself something to eat on her way to the midwife.

When she walked inside the small bakery, Sam was met with the warm, slightly sweet, yeasty smell of fresh bread. It was incredible. Finally, a food smell that didn't disgust her. She ordered an everything bagel and a half-dozen cookies for Lucy and Molly to have later.

The food aversions were only the tip of the iceberg when it came to how strange pregnancy was and the things it did to her body. How bizarre that a human being could grow inside her, and her organs would move and rearrange themselves to make space for a person. She wished she could be happier about each new discovery, but she wasn't. No matter how much she tried to pretend, she wasn't pleased about this whole thing. Poor kid. It already had a subpar mother.

At the midwife's office, Sam met Claire. She looked to be in her early forties and was average height, with a short bob of curly hair. Sam felt an immediate kinship to anyone with curly hair. This was a good start. Claire had bright blue eyes and large teeth that showed every time she smiled—she never seemed to smile closed-mouthed.

In the office, Sam sat across from Claire, dutifully answering her questions about Sam's age, her height, her last menstrual cycle. Claire smiled after each question, nodding encouragingly when Sam answered, as if she needed validation to continue.

"And how about the father? How's your relationship?" Claire asked.

Sam rubbed her forehead. "He's involved. Sort of," she lied. "But we're not together."

Claire nodded, making a note in her book, revealing nothing in her expression.

"Okay, and how do you feel about the support you have? Do you have family you're close to?"

"Yes," Sam said without hesitation. She didn't want Claire to think she was a total basket case. "I have two sisters, and I'm staying with my mother for a while. My sisters, my brother-in-law and nieces are all staying at the family cottage with us for the summer, too. Oh, and I have a friend. He's already offered to help." She surprised herself by mentioning Hunter, but she wanted Claire to know she had people she could rely on. She wasn't completely alone.

"That's great," Claire smiled. More note taking.

"So, what do I do now?" Sam asked.

Claire laughed a little, not unkindly. "Well, you should take care of yourself. Eat nutrient-rich foods, drink lots of water, get lots of sleep. Those kinds of things."

Sam could do all that easily.

"And you'll come and see me every month until thirty-six weeks, when you'll start coming every week. We'll check your weight, your blood pressure, have a chat about how you're feeling. And then we can listen to the baby's heartbeat."

Sam gaped at the thought of a heartbeat. It hadn't entered her mind until Claire said it out loud. That would be possible already?

Claire gave Sam a knowing smile. "It's as awesome as you can imagine." She snapped her file shut and rested her hands in her lap. "But it's too early for most women to hear at ten weeks."

Sam's shoulders dropped and her body curved inwards on itself. She had thought she didn't feel connected to this baby, but then she had been so hopeful about hearing its heart.

Claire noticed and let out a small laugh. "I knew I shouldn't have mentioned the heartbeat yet. This always happens."

Sam was silent. She folded her hands together and placed them on her lap.

"Okay, okay. We can try, but I'm warning you, it's very iffy this early."

Claire pulled out a handheld device she referred to as a doppler and, after Sam had reclined on the couch, moved it over Sam's exposed stomach.

Sam held her breath at the sharpness of the cold gel. She watched Claire's face intently. What did her frown mean? Why wouldn't she look at Sam? Was she avoiding her gaze on purpose?

Claire expertly directed the doppler back and forth, back and forth, as she looked across the room at nothing in particular in deep concentration. They both listened for what felt like forever until Claire paused and stopped her arm, tilting her head to one side as if that could help her hear.

"I think I heard something," Claire said.

A very faint, barely audible whooshing sound.

"What is that?" Sam asked.

"That's it. That's the heartbeat." Claire held her hand very still.

Sam closed her eyes, hoping it would somehow make the sound bigger, and listened as the whooshing came and went. For a brief moment, it made a rhythmic pattern. A steady, beating heartbeat. Her baby. There was an actual, real person inside her. Someone who would be part of her forever.

Fat tears rolled down the side of her cheek and into her hair.

They were tears that confused her. Sam was overcome with both the miracle of her baby and the sadness of bringing a helpless being into a world where their mother didn't particularly want them at first, and their father had no interest in raising them at all.

Claire handed her a tissue and smiled. She must have thought they were happy tears. It only made Sam sadder.

# THIRTY

## ALEX

Sometimes, the way Molly and Lucy moved would bring tears to Alex's eyes. Watching their arms sweep through the air gracefully as they spun around, twisting their bodies in the way kids do, for no real purpose, but because they want to move.

It was watching them grow that did it. These amazingly independent kids who had come from her and Ben were their own little people. They spoke and acted of their own free will and the fact that Alex had any part in raising them, was able to guide them and watch them, well, it could be overwhelming if you thought about it too much.

Today, Molly was sitting at the spot on the beach where the sand met the lake, her legs splayed out in front of her, head bent in concentration. She was building a little sand village with houses and castles, with pebbles for gates and leaves for the trees. Lucy was gathering water to make the sand mucky and sticky so the homes would stand up. It was one of those rare perfect moments when both girls got along like they were best friends, whispering and giggling, building on one another's ideas.

Alex watched them from her favorite spot under the ash tree next to the beach. It was cool in the shade, but she was treated to a warm breeze that tickled her legs and arms, blowing over her skin and through her hair. She sipped her late-morning coffee. Ben came and joined her.

When Alex turned to smile at him, she saw a frown on his normally relaxed face. Her chest tightened. "What is it?" she asked.

"We need to talk."

A jolt went through Alex's body. Those words never came before something good. "Here?"

"Might as well."

Alex glanced out at the girls. They were busy, heads bent in concentration.

"You have to stop this." Ben leaned forward and rested his forearms on his knees.

"Stop what?"

He tilted his head up and gave her a knowing look. "You know what I mean. I know you went to the grief counseling again without telling me about it. And the fact that you didn't tell me leads me to believe you have something to hide."

Alex stiffened. "That's not true. I'm not hiding anything."

"Alex. Come on," Ben said, a touch of impatience in his voice.

"How did you know I went anyway?"

"Jess just told me. In the cottage."

A shot of annoyance went through Alex like a flash. Why was Jess meddling? She would have to deal with her later.

"I wanted you to go to grief counseling for yourself," Ben said. "But the last time you went, Jess said it was only about seeing her."

Going to Calm Waters felt like a deep betrayal of her mother, but Alex couldn't seem to stop herself. Finding out about Michelle and then discovering the fact that Jess had known all along was devastating. It was even harder to learn it had gone on for thirty years, right up until her father's death. What other secrets could he have possibly been hiding?

Alex knew Ben was right that she wasn't going to the sessions for herself anymore. Everything she was doing was wrong: befriending her father's mistress, not telling Sam what she was doing, not telling her mother anything at all—but hearing the judgment in Ben's tone made her stomach drop. He was supposed to be her support, always on her side.

"Whatever it is that you're searching for," Ben said as he shook his head, "it's not right to lie to everyone. This isn't you, Alex, and I don't think you'll be able to properly grieve if you keep digging up the past."

"I feel like I don't have the whole truth yet," Alex said to Ben. "Wouldn't *you* want to know more if you found out your entire childhood was a lie?"

Ben sat back in his seat and let out a sigh. "You're being kind of dramatic, don't you think?"

Alex sucked her cheeks in. Her body went hot. Ben knew her better than anyone, so for him to question her like this was painful.

She assumed that her digging would lead to answers. When seeing Michelle again hadn't quelled the twisted, confused feeling in her chest, Alex had kept having coffee with her after the sessions at Calm Waters, talking with her and hoping she would find answers about her father, about why he had chosen to risk everything he had worked so hard at building up. She both hated Michelle and was drawn to her. Over and over again, these past few weeks, Alex kept finding excuses to chat with Michelle and kept coming back from it the same as before, with no answer. Deep inside her, there was a truth she would never admit to anyone. Alex liked Michelle. The shame of it was overwhelming.

"Let it go, Alex. You're different these days." When Ben

looked at her, his face was missing the warmth she was used to. "You're distracted. You're digging up nothing but pain. What if your mom finds out? What do you think that will do to her? And you're so focused on finding out about your father's past that you're not present with the girls. You're missing important moments with them. Do you want the girls to look back and remember this as the summer Mom was distant?"

Alex flinched like she had been hit in the face. He had never called her parenting into question before. She was a good mother. She knew this. What she didn't know was why her own husband couldn't see that she wasn't able to wrap this all up like a neat package and set it aside until she found what she was looking for. The questions would always hang there in the air in front of her. When she went about her mornings getting the girls ready for school, standing at the grocery store in the milk aisle, tapping away on her laptop, her mind would always be partially preoccupied by the question: Why weren't we enough of a family for him? Was she ever enough?

Ben stood up. He put his hands in his pockets and looked down at Alex. "If this is how it's going to be, I'm going to go home and take the girls. I don't want them noticing that something's wrong with you. They ask a lot of questions, and I don't want to lie to them."

Alex held her breath for a minute while she tried to think of how to respond to that. Ben had never threatened to take the girls away from her before. It was hard to understand why her husband couldn't support her. She needed him to be by her side, to tell her it was going to be okay, to agree with her choices. Instead, he was threatening to go home and take the girls with him. His words set off the most guttural, innate protective feeling inside Alex. She had been careful with her children before, when kids were mean to Lucy and Molly, when they were out in public, she would grasp onto their hands tightly in crowds, but she had never felt something like this, least of all with Ben.

Alex had once told Lucy that she loved her and Molly more than anyone in the world. Lucy had looked at her with her wide eyes and said, "Even more than Daddy?" Alex had smiled and leaned closer to Lucy, whispering conspiratorially, "Even more than Daddy." Lucy's freckled nose had crinkled up, her thick eyebrows creasing. "How rude," she had said. Lucy was protective of Ben. It was cute. But now, Alex realized, it was true—she didn't love anyone more than her daughters, not even the man she had spent most of her life with.

"Don't you dare," she hissed. Ben's face flashed with confusion. "Don't ever use our kids as a threat." She glanced at the girls and then stood up and faced Ben. She didn't trust herself to say anything else. She hesitated only for a moment, and then she said, "You should leave."

"What?" Ben's eyebrows shot up. "Leave? Like, go home? You can't be serious."

"I don't mean go home, I mean go somewhere else. Anywhere. I don't care what you do, but leave me and the girls. Now. I need to be alone for a while."

"Alex."

"No," Alex said sharply. She glanced over her shoulder to make sure the girls weren't listening. "I can't believe you would threaten me with our children." Alex thought of how the girls would come to her side of the bed automatically at night when they had a bad dream. They would whisper for her, ask her to lie down with them, and Alex always would. She would wait until she could hear their steady breathing again, until they had relaxed and calmed, their long eyelashes settled onto their round, freckled cheeks before she would leave them. The girls would always come first.

She thought Ben understood her, but he obviously didn't.

He didn't know how much it hurt her to learn that her own father didn't love her the way she loved her daughters. He didn't understand any of her choices or her pain. She turned to face the lake. Behind her, she could hear the sound of Ben's slow footsteps as he walked away.

# THIRTY-ONE

## SAM

On her way down to the water, Sam saw Ben going to his car, his head bowed and hands stuffed into his pockets, and a small alarm instantly sounded in her head.

"Ben looked pretty distracted. Is he off somewhere?" Sam asked when she took the seat next to Alex along the edge of the beach.

"It's nothing. It's fine," Alex said. Her shoulders were hunched over, her chest caving inward.

"It doesn't look that way." Had the two of them had a fight? How many times had Ben and Alex fought over the last twenty years? It didn't honestly seem like it happened all that often. Ben was very easygoing. He was the ice to Alex's fire. It's why they worked, Alex always said.

"I don't feel like talking about it." Alex had a pinched expression on her face.

"Okay," Sam said, although she knew it wasn't okay. Talking about things was what Alex did. A different approach would be needed. "What's going on with you lately? Have you found out anything new?" Sam asked.

Ever since her mother had mentioned it in the kitchen, Sam

had also noticed the space between them all. For the past few weeks, both her sisters had been distant, but Sam didn't know why. Of course, the baby preoccupied her, and so did Hunter, but it wasn't an excuse. She'd found it easy to forget about Dad and push the thought of his betrayal of Mom down, so she didn't have to face it. But she should be there for her sisters, especially when they needed each other. A wave of guilt came over her.

"No. Nothing. Why?" Alex turned her head sharply, her eyebrows bunching into a knot.

"I'm concerned about you, that's all."

"You don't have to be," Alex said. She turned her head back to the water to watch Lucy and Molly.

Sam sat back in her seat. This wasn't going to go anywhere, she could tell by the cool tone in Alex's voice. After she stayed silent a while, Sam told Alex she was going inside to get something to eat. It was an excuse to leave Alex alone. She would have to try talking to her again later. For now, maybe she could find Jess.

Inside, Jess was lounging on the couch, her feet up on the coffee table in front of her. "Hey, you," Jess said. "How are you? I feel like we haven't talked in a while."

Sam was struck by how relaxed her sister looked. She hadn't been this way all summer. It warmed Sam's heart.

"I know. We've all been busy, I guess. And I think the Dad stuff has us all in a bit of a tailspin." Sam paused a moment. "I'm sorry."

Jess shook her head. A small frown appeared on her face. "You don't need to apologize."

"Okay." Sam took a seat on the couch and touched her stomach. "I heard the heartbeat."

Jess's eyes widened. "You did? At the midwife appointment?" Jess's hand went out to Sam's stomach, as if by instinct, and then she stopped herself.

Sam nodded at her and smiled. There was nothing to feel, her stomach was still relatively flat. She looked like she had eaten a big meal at most, but it felt nice to have Jess's hand on her. The closeness between them was like it had always been. Sam missed this.

"I still can't believe you're having a baby. Have you thought of names?" Jess asked.

"Not yet." It felt too soon. Although, after hearing her baby, something in Sam had changed. A click, like she understood how big this was. Sam had never been the kind of girl who always wanted to have kids. She thought she might at some point, but it hadn't been her end game the way it had for some of the other girls she grew up with. She had always thought that maybe when she was much older, she would finally get herself a house and have kids, but a husband had never really entered the equation in her mind. As she had got closer and closer to forty, she was fine with where she was. Some of her friends and coworkers, even her sister, loved being mothers and couldn't imagine their lives any other way. But some of her friends seemed to have regretted having them so young, it was obvious in the way they spoke about their lives. Other people she knew had said they never wanted kids. The world was made up of all kinds, and there was room for everyone. It didn't affect Sam's life or her decisions one way or another. Which is why she was so stunned to discover now that this tiny heartbeat was exactly what she wanted.

Jess shifted on the couch, until she was close to Sam, right next to her, their hips pressing up against one another. She leaned over and rested her head on Sam's shoulder. Sam didn't want to move, she was so taken aback. Jess used to do this when they were little. If Sam were on the couch watching TV, Jess would make her way closer and closer until she was draped onto Sam's upright body. Sam always let her because she was Jess, and she was the baby. Anyway, it felt good to have someone want to be close to you, to be comforted by your physical presence.

"Hunter was looking for you today," Jess said.

A tiny shiver went through Sam. She realized it was laced with desire. His name could do that to her? That was surprising. It was getting harder and harder for her to try to forget him or the hope she had that something would happen. Although Jess's hand on Sam's stomach reminded her that it was too complicated.

"Oh?" was all Sam said.

"He seems like a really decent person."

"It's too difficult," Sam responded, although she was touched by Jess's words. The confusing feelings, the ones where Jess felt things for Hunter, too, sat between them unspoken for a moment until Jess said it out loud.

"It was a mistake that afternoon when I kissed him. I was sad. It was nothing."

"It's okay," Sam said. "You don't have to explain anything."

Jess lifted her head and looked at Sam. "I feel like I do. You deserve something good, Sam. Maybe your situation with him would be unconventional, but so are you. You should have seen the way his face softened when he asked about you."

The bloom of desire went through her again. It was hard to ignore. Sam had spent most of her life giving off the impression that she was easygoing and free. She didn't make many plans, she flew by the seat of her pants, she didn't want to do what everyone was doing, which was why she didn't see herself settling down and having a family. Then Hunter came along and it was all thrown into question. The undeniable fact was, she liked him a lot.

"You should give him a chance. At least go talk to him," Jess said.

It was partially that Sam was caught up in this moment with Jess, being close, talking like they used to, not wanting to let any of the outside sadness into their little circle. It was also partially that Jess was right. She should give Hunter a chance, she should give them a shot.

Sam patted Jess's knee. "Okay."

She stood up and Jess sat upright on the couch, her eyes widening again with surprise. She was probably shocked she had convinced Sam of anything.

Jess smiled and then settled back into the couch. "Good. Now go."

Outside, Sam went quickly over the soft ground between the cottages. She was there, knocking on his front door within minutes. When Hunter opened the door, her body hummed.

"Hi," he said.

"Hello."

"Want to come in?" He smiled. His shoulder rested on the edge of the doorway.

Sam took a step forward. Hunter must have understood. He lowered his head just as she got close enough. She pressed her lips against his and found them to be softer than she expected. His kiss was gentle at first; his arm went around her, his hand lightly touching her lower back. She reached for the side of his face, placing her hand on his cheek, and he wrapped his other arm around her, squeezing her softly. A rush went through Sam's body. She ran her hand through his soft hair. This was good. It was exactly what she wanted.

They pulled away for a moment and blinked at one another.

"Now what?" Sam asked.

"Should we go inside?" Hunter's voice had a shy edge to it. His cheeks were pink, his hair ruffled from where Sam had run her hand through it.

"I think so."

·   ·   ·

Afterwards, back at the cottage, Sam knew what had to be done. She hadn't spoken to Wes in ages, not since he had dropped off the face of the earth after finding out she was pregnant, probably somewhere across the world having a fantastic time, but she really didn't care.

"Hey. It's me," she said into the phone.

"Hey." Wes's tone was bored, and it set off a mild irritation inside her.

"I'm not going to call you again after this. I wanted you to know that I've got a handle on this. I don't need you."

"Sam..." Wes said warily.

"No, I mean it," she interrupted him. "I'm in control here. I can have this baby and create a good life for it without having everything all lined up. It doesn't have to be perfect, it only has to be me." Sam could hear Wes take a breath in, as if he were about to speak, but she didn't want to hear it. "This is your out, Wes. Enjoy your life, honestly. I'm fine with it because I don't need you. I've got my family to think of now."

She didn't wait for him to speak again, instead she hung up the phone and placed it on the table in front of her. She only let herself wonder what Wes would have said for a brief moment before she crossed her arms over her chest. She *could* do this. Her will was strong and her instinct even stronger. Wes didn't have anything she needed.

# THIRTY-TWO

## ALEX

A few days after their argument, Alex's anger with Ben had begun to fade. It always went like this. She was fiery and angry initially, but with time, the fight went out of her. After a week had passed, she knew he was right; it was time to let everything be over with. She shouldn't see Michelle again.

Over the last several days, Alex had kept busy, watching the girls at the beach, making lunches for everyone to eat outside, throwing loads of dirty and sandy towels in the wash, folding the girls' clothes and putting them in their suitcase. They planned to leave next week, the second last week of summer, to give them time at home to get the girls organized before school started.

Today, she stood in the middle of the kitchen, looking around her, surveying the empty cupboards and the nearly bare fridge. She should go into town and grab some groceries for Mom, maybe stop by the bakery for fresh bread and those soft cookies everyone loved, but she worried Ben would be suspicious.

She touched her forehead. *So, this is where I've arrived now?* This was the point in her marriage where things felt shaky and unfamiliar. After Ben had threatened to take the girls home with him, Alex had worried about every move she made and whether or not he would be judging her. She tried to seem more engaged, but she knew she was still being quieter than usual with the girls.

For a while, Alex and Ben only communicated in one-word answers or short sentences. Then Alex had warmed up, and Ben didn't hold a grudge. He never did. It was a good quality of his. At some point, they would have to have a much deeper, longer talk about it, but she didn't have the energy yet this morning.

Later that afternoon, Alex sat on the dock sipping a cold beer, enjoying the hoppy taste as it washed over her tongue. Ben sat with her. She worked up the courage to say what was on her mind.

"I know you want me to be done with the searching, and I agree, but I think I need to go and see her one last time," she said.

"See who?" It was Sam's voice. She had appeared without Alex or Ben sensing it.

Alex whipped her head around to face her sister, her throat tightening. Sam's hair fell around her face, the curls extra bouncy today from the humidity. She made her way around the edge of the chairs and stood next to Alex, looking down at her.

"Hey." Ben turned in his seat to face Sam. "How are you feeling?" He was trying to change the subject, bless him. It didn't work.

"I'm good, thanks." Sam smiled at Ben and then took a seat in the empty chair next to him, leaning her head forward and craning her neck to look at Alex before asking again, "Who do you need to see?"

Alex pressed her fingertips to her closed eyelids. She couldn't outright lie to Sam's face. At least before, she had merely been avoiding the truth, now it would be much less forgivable a thing to do. She was so tired of the secrecy and lies. It was all getting to be too much. "I met the other woman. From the notes," Alex said. "Her name is Michelle."

Sam took a sharp breath in, and then her lips pressed together into a tight line across her face. "You did what?" she asked, her voice hoarse.

"I've been going to grief counseling and met her there, but I didn't know it was her at first."

Ben raised his eyebrows at Alex.

"And then she invited me to go to the Celebration of Life she was holding for her partner, and I went." Alex paused. She looked at Sam, directly in the eyes. "It was a Celebration of Life for Dad. That's how I found out who she was."

Alex waited for Sam's typical reaction—a mess of big emotions. When they were little, Sam would laugh with her entire body when she was happy, her shoulders shaking, her torso twisting from side to side, a smile on her face so wide it looked like her face might split into two. When she was mad, her face would go as red as a beet, her eyebrows narrow, and her mouth turned downwards right before the shouting began. Now, her face contorted, but not in anger. Her expression was pained. The back of Alex's throat hurt. She looked down at her feet.

"That's messed up," Sam said. "I don't know what to think."

"I know. It's very confusing," Alex agreed.

"Wait. You said you wanted to see her one last time. Why the hell would you want to see her again?"

"I want to see if there are any other secrets I need to know about."

"She wants to see *you*?" Sam asked.

"She has no idea I'm Dad's daughter."

Sam stood up and moved around the dock. Her eyes were wide, her face twisted down into an odd frown.

"Maybe you should sit down. You shouldn't be under stress," Ben said, but Sam didn't respond.

"Alex, can you hear yourself? This is so messed up. Have you told Jess? Am I the only one who didn't know?" The questions came out in rapid succession.

Alex rubbed her forehead. The secrets were all mixing into one now. She couldn't remember who knew what, or what needed to be kept hidden. Ben knew it all, Mom knew nothing —but how much did Jess know again? Now Sam.

Alex looked at Ben. He shook his head.

"Jess knows," Alex said.

Ben hung his head, his eyes closed.

"She's known since we were kids," Alex continued.

Sam slumped into her seat again. An odd sound, something like a choked cry, came out of her mouth. Then she was silent for a long time. When she spoke, her voice was low and shaking. "She what...? What are you telling me right now?"

"You should probably talk to Jess." Alex thought Sam should hear the full story directly from Jess, the way she had herself.

Sam seemed to consider that for a moment. Her eyes darted around and then settled back on Alex again. "Where is she?"

"I don't know. Inside, I think."

Sam was silent for a while. "Why didn't you tell me? We could have figured this out together. Why was I the only one left out?"

Alex hadn't considered figuring things out with her sisters, but now she couldn't think of why. She had been so wrapped up in her anger, her intense curiosity, that she'd gone into autopilot. Sam, although fiery, could sometimes be calm under pressure and always had a lot of good ideas. She could have helped.

"I guess I didn't want someone to talk me out of it." Alex glanced at Ben. He frowned back.

"This is not some little *thing*, Alex." Sam's voice rose. "This is a big deal. He was our father, too, not just yours."

Her shouting made Alex nervous—what if Mom overheard?

"Calm down," Alex said. She knew full well that Sam hated it whenever those words were directed at her.

Sam shot her a look with cold eyes and then paced across the dock again. "You're telling me everything. Right now."

"Don't tell me what I'm doing," Alex said. She was aware of Ben's head snapping back and forth, watching the conversation between Alex and Sam like he was watching a tennis match.

"You are telling me everything!" Sam shouted again. She was close to a level usually reserved for meltdowns.

"Okay, okay." Alex held her hands up in surrender. She only agreed to stop the shouting. Alex's eyes went to the girls on the beach. They had come down for a swim and appeared to be blissfully unaware. Thank goodness their little ears weren't listening the way they often were.

"Start by telling me about her." Sam's voice was cold and low.

Michelle was like most older women their mother's age, Alex supposed. She wasn't the awful caricature of a home wrecker Alex had wanted her to be. She was a mother, a grandmother, she wore too much makeup sometimes and her voice was a little annoying, but she was kind, Alex couldn't deny it.

"I don't know," Alex said. "She's a woman who Dad found interesting, I guess."

Sam closed her eyes for a long time. When she opened them again, she looked out at the lake. She crossed her arms over her body. "I don't think any of this is right," she said. "But if you're going to go see her again, I'm coming."

Alex sighed. "There's more."

Sam's eyes widened, as if there couldn't be more, it was bad enough.

"Michelle and Dad were together for thirty years. Right up until he died."

Sam's face turned pale, like she was going to be sick. "I can't even understand what you're saying," she sputtered.

"I know."

"Why would you still see her after finding out who she was?" Sam asked. "What did you expect?"

Alex looked down at her feet. It was a question she hadn't been able to answer for herself, as much as she tried. "I don't know."

"That's not good enough, Alex."

An uncomfortable silence sat between the three of them, broken only by the sound of Molly shouting as loud as she could. She ran straight for them, soaking wet from the lake. "Mommy, Daddy, Auntie Sam! Watch me!" She appeared in front of them, dripping water onto Alex's lap, a grin on her face.

"What? What are we watching, Moll?" Ben reached for her, trying to direct her backwards a few steps so she would stop soaking them.

"Watch!" she squealed again before turning around and hightailing it back into the lake. She skipped and hopped into the shallow water, then threw her body forward, into a wild bellyflop that created an impressive splash. When she came back up again, her smile was even larger than before. They all dutifully cheered for her from their chairs. Molly laughed and Lucy swam around in circles.

Alex sat back in her chair and felt her shoulders soften. The warm breeze danced across her bare arms. Somehow, the kids were always able to bring levity, to put things in perspective for her.

"I promise no more secrets from you," Alex said.

"We've had enough of them by now." Sam lifted her chin.

"I know."

"But I'm still coming with you to see her. And this doesn't mean I forgive you," Sam said.

Alex didn't say anything in return. She deserved that.

# THIRTY-THREE

## JESS

Everything was unraveling.

It was clear as soon as Sam came into the cottage. She let the screen door smack loudly behind her and stormed directly to the kitchen.

"Where's Mom?" she asked.

"In town," Jess replied. Sam's cheeks were pink, her mouth turned down at the corners. Jess didn't like where this was going.

"I know about Alex and the woman from the notes. I overheard Alex talking to Ben and she had to tell me." Her tone was loud and sharp. She was angry.

Jess pressed a hand to her temple. She didn't have the energy for an argument, but she could sense one brewing.

"How much did she tell you?" Jess asked. She closed her eyes.

"Everything," Sam said.

Jess's heart thrummed in her chest. Her hands fell to her sides. When she opened her eyes again, Sam was glaring at her.

"Why didn't you tell me? How could you keep this from me?" Sam asked.

"I was a kid, Sam. I didn't know what to do."

"I'm not talking about then. I mean this summer. You and Alex both knew about this together." Her face sagged. There was a dullness to her eyes that caused Jess's breath to hitch. She hated it when she hurt her sisters, especially Sam.

"I'm sorry," Jess said.

Sam crossed her arms over her chest. "It's not okay. You shouldn't have kept this from me. I'm your sister, Jess. When are you going to let me in?" She watched Jess for a moment, her head jutting forward from the neck. When Jess didn't say anything, Sam left the room without another word.

Jess clutched the edge of the kitchen sink. Why did their family have to be like this? Well-adjusted families didn't keep enormously heavy secrets from one another. She was no better than her father. She stood grasping onto the counter tight enough to make her fingernails turn white. Then she took a deep breath in and pushed it out from down in her belly.

"Are you okay?" Alex's voice came from behind her. She stood by the doorway, her forehead creased with lines.

"I don't even know where to start," Jess said.

"I know." It was Alex's version of I'm sorry. She rarely ever said the actual words and everyone gave her a pass for some reason. It was acceptable in their family because it was known that Alex couldn't apologize. That wasn't enough for Jess anymore. She hated confrontation, but she hated who they were all becoming even more.

"You told Sam before I was ready."

"Jess, she should know," Alex started.

Jess shook her head. "No. Don't tell me how things should work. You don't get to make all the decisions."

Alex flinched. Jess couldn't understand how this could be surprising to her sister. Alex was always taking charge without giving others a say. At some point, people were going to get angry.

"I'm not making all the decisions. We were sitting on the dock, and she overheard me talking to Ben. It was bound to happen," Alex said. She was standing inside the kitchen now. She looked over her shoulder to make sure nobody else was around.

"But you told her," Jess said. "It was for me to tell, Alex. When I was ready."

The other night, Jess had had a dream. It flashed through her mind again. Jess had been standing on the edge of a cliff in Ireland, looking down below her into a vast darkness, trying to see something. A panicked, anxious feeling settled into her bones in her dream. *Isn't that odd,* Jess thought, *how you can feel such real things in a dream, like anxiety?* She had been there with her sisters, but she couldn't find them. When her head had whipped around to look behind her, when she had turned and gone in search of them, she'd got nowhere. She had walked and walked across springy grass and found herself in the same place. A stunning, isolated landscape. Completely alone. Jess shivered at the memory.

"Sam deserves to know. This is huge," Alex said. "Besides, you told Ben about me seeing Michelle again." There was an edge to her voice.

Jess's cheeks went warm. She *had* told Ben, but it was justified. She was only trying to save Alex from herself.

"Don't deflect," Jess said.

Alex crossed the kitchen to stand next to Jess. She pulled a piece of bread from the plastic bag and placed it into the toaster. When she opened the fridge, she leaned into it. She eventually took out the jam and placed it on the counter. Then she turned and rested the small of her back against the counter, waiting.

Anger flickered inside Jess at the sight of Alex making toast, as if they weren't here discussing the unraveling of their family. Sam was furious at both of them, they were still hiding a terrible secret from their mother, and just as it was coming to a head, Alex decided to make toast.

Jess stared at her sister.

"What?" Alex asked. She crossed her arms over her chest and shrugged one shoulder.

"I can't believe you," Jess said.

"Come on, Jess. Don't stand there like you're perfect and I'm the villain. You can't keep burying your secrets forever. You'll regret it."

"Jesus. Do you think I'll ever be able to do things the way I want? When I want?" Jess snapped. "Am I allowed to have any control? Or does everything have to be your way?"

"What on earth are you talking about?" Alex asked.

"I wanted Sam to know when I was ready. I wanted her to hear it from me." Jess eyed the toast, blinking back tears. She didn't want to cry right now. Not in this moment when she was trying to finally stand her ground with Alex.

"It had to come out. It was the way the conversation was going. I couldn't lie to her face." Alex turned to the toaster. She looked down towards the counter and busied herself with the toast. Even the way she so casually dipped her knife into the jar of jam infuriated Jess.

"You see me as a little kid who doesn't know what's good for me, who always has to do what you say, but what about what I want?" Jess glanced out the large windows that overlooked the lake. She could see the gentle sloping beach, with Lucy and Molly in the middle of it. Ben was still watching them. Mom was with him now, having got back from town. They would have to finish this up quickly.

"Oh my God. You're not seriously going to make everything about you, are you?" Alex said. "You're the baby. You've *always* gotten what you want."

"You think I wanted to know about Dad? That I wanted to carry it around my entire life?"

"I think you like the attention now," Alex said. The words hung in the air between them.

Jess's stomach hardened. She pulled herself upright. She lifted her chin and told herself she wouldn't react. When her hands shook, she placed them in her pockets so Alex couldn't see. She wouldn't let Alex know that she had the innate ability to create a heaviness in Jess. If your own family thought the worst of you, how could anyone else love you?

Jess realized that Alex knew exactly how to get to her, and now she had very little fight left inside her. Years of therapy and for what? Her sisters were still mad at her, they were all lying to their mother. It was coming back: that uncomfortable anxiety, the tightness in her chest that she thought she had gotten rid of so long ago. Jess turned and left the room without saying anything else and Alex didn't try to stop her.

Outside, Jess considered getting in her car and driving away. She could leave and nobody would notice, probably until hours had passed. But her sense of right and wrong stopped her. Jess would never leave her mother and her sisters with no explanation. She wouldn't cut them out of her life in some dramatic move. That wasn't her.

She was contemplating the driveway in front of her when she heard someone.

"Jess. Hey—Jess." It was Hunter. He stood in front of her in a loose, gray T-shirt and a pair of dark shorts.

"Hey." She tried to smile.

"How are you?"

Jess let out a long sigh. "I'm fine." It was easier than the truth.

Hunter held her eyes, like he didn't believe her. He tilted his head a little.

Jess relented. "Actually, I'm not great. Family drama. I don't want to bother you with it."

He nodded. "I've had my fair share."

"I'm going for a walk." Jess motioned toward the road at the end of the driveway.

"Mind if I join you?" Hunter asked.

Jess did mind, she would have preferred to be alone, but something stopped her from saying it. Instead, she half shrugged in response.

Once they fell into silent step with one another, Jess wondered if Sam had told him anything about their situation. The notes, the affair, the betrayal. It was embarrassing to think about.

"Do you want to talk about any of it?" Hunter asked.

Jess shook her head. "No. Not really."

Hunter nodded.

Jess's lips felt dry. She licked them and then looked down at her feet. "What's going on with you and Sam?" It was forward of her to ask, but she was looking for something to talk about. Anything, really.

Hunter's back straightened. "I'm not really sure. I'm trying to go with the flow. Why? Has she said anything to you?"

Jess laughed in spite of herself. Hunter looked like a lost puppy. "We haven't talked much about it."

Hunter waved his hand. "Right. No, of course not."

"We probably won't be talking about much of anything, I guess." Jess wasn't sure why she was revealing this to him. Normally, this would be something she would keep to herself. But she had a need to let it out suddenly, like a pressure cooker releasing its steam.

"Why's that?"

"We got in a huge fight. We're all fighting." She stopped walking abruptly. Something held her there, unmoving.

Hunter turned to look at her.

To Jess's horror, she started to cry deep and heaving sobs, the kind that make you choke on catching your breath. Everything felt so insurmountable: the issues with her family, the fact that she still didn't know what the hell she was doing or who she was. She put one hand over her mouth to cover up the ugly grimace she was certain she was making.

"Hey," Hunter said. He reached his hand out to her and then brought it back down again.

Jess sniffed and swiped at her eyes with the edge of her hand. "Don't worry. I won't try to kiss you."

Hunter laughed. Thank goodness he laughed. Jess laughed, too. Maybe now they could be friends. There was nothing else there, Jess knew.

"You know, all families are messed up," Hunter said when they resumed walking.

Jess appreciated it. She wasn't sure how true it was, but she appreciated him trying to help her anyway.

# THIRTY-FOUR

## SAM

With the baby growing, Sam felt an uncharacteristic need to take control. She had to get to the bottom of the situation with the other woman and put the past behind her if she was going to soon be responsible for a human being.

Sam ran her hand over her stomach. She was only about eleven and a half weeks now. The baby was the size of a fig, she had read in the weekly emails she had signed up for. They were always so cheerful. *Your baby is now the size of a fig! You may be excited for all the changes you're experiencing, or slightly anxious. Get rest, eat well, get some exercise, and share your feelings with someone you trust.*

*Easier said than done,* Sam thought. Then again, this was a positive experience from day one for most women. Sam couldn't imagine bringing this little fig baby into her world with the way things were, with Wes and Hunter and all the uncertainty. Not to mention what was happening between her sisters. They were fighting so much. Sam needed to get herself together, she needed a solid plan, and she definitely needed to try to fix things as much as she could with her family.

"Ready?" Alex popped her head around the corner of the

bedroom where Sam had been standing, looking at herself in the mirror and fiddling with her hair.

Molly squeezed through the gap between her mother's body and the doorframe into the bedroom. She rushed to Sam's side. "Auntie Sam, I want to come with you!"

"Molly, I already gave you an answer," Alex said, a stern tone to her voice. It was her mom voice: slightly exasperated, but firm. Sam took a mental note.

"But I want to go." Molly had wrapped her arms around Sam's hips, burying her face into Sam's soft middle. Sam ran her hand through Molly's hair, liking the way it felt so smooth in between her fingers.

"I wish you could come, but this is grown-up stuff. How about if I bring you back a treat?"

Molly's eyes widened. Sam could almost see her niece's brain working, thinking about the possibilities.

"She doesn't need a treat just because we're going into town," Alex said, although Sam knew it was hard for Alex to say no to Molly and Lucy. Sam had learned over the years that Alex was a soft touch when it came to motherhood. She had rules and routines for the girls, and the kids were pretty well-behaved, but Alex almost always said yes to the little things. Sam found it a surprising trait in her big sister. It was endearing.

"Yes, I do need a treat!" Molly protested, looking up at her mother.

"What would you like?" Sam asked before Alex could object again. She would probably get in trouble for that later.

"Wait until you have your own and someone overrules your decisions," Alex said pointedly.

Molly, ignoring Alex completely, put her finger and thumb on her chin and tilted her head, deep in thought. This kid. She cracked Sam up the way she looked so grown-up sometimes, a tiny body mimicking adult things. "Surprise me!"

Sam laughed. "Okay, I will." She bent over to kiss the top of

Molly's head and left the bedroom, following Alex out to the car.

The drive was quiet. Sam settled into her seat and watched the road outside, taking Alex's lead when it came to silence instead of talking. It was familiar, the grassy ditches next to the thick forest of trees that they passed. There wasn't much to see but scenery—giant rocks, gravel-filled shoulders of the road, the lake peeking out from the trees in the clearings, shining like glass under the afternoon sun. There were families that came to this lake, families like theirs. Sam could see some of them now, along the edges of the lake, stretched out on towels and sunning themselves under the bright August rays, watching kids splash in the water. Others were fishing or walking along the winding paths.

Sam glanced at the time on the dashboard of the car. It was eleven minutes past two. After Alex's last grief counseling session, she had made plans with Michelle to meet up for coffee today. Did Alex feel guilty about Sam coming? It was as if they were planning to ambush Michelle. Sam felt nothing but determination. It was odd how she wanted this so much. She needed to meet this woman, but was also terrified of what she would discover.

"We're here," Alex said flatly. She put the car into park and turned to look at Sam, her eyes falling to Sam's stomach and then back up again to her face. "Are you sure you want to do this?"

"We're here now. Might as well get it over with."

"Like ripping off a bandage." Alex smiled at Sam, but her face was sad. Maybe she was doubting all this now. When it became clear that Sam wasn't going to bend on coming to see Michelle, Alex had asked Jess if she wanted to come, too. Jess had declined. Just as well, considering they weren't speaking much yet.

Sam felt for Jess. She wasn't a monster, so of course it hurt her to hear that her baby sister had known about their father and Michelle her entire life. The thought of Jess carrying that around on her shoulders was awful, but it hurt even more to think that Jess didn't feel like she could come to Sam. She didn't know how to process it all just yet, so Sam felt it was for the best when Jess declined to come.

The coffee shop smelled rich and nutty and was bustling with people today. Sam still couldn't stomach the thought of drinking a cup of coffee, but the smell of it appealed to her.

"She's at the counter." Alex said in a low voice when they entered.

Sam's head jerked around to look.

"Not so obvious," Alex hissed.

Michelle was average height with a bob framing her face and the type of flat ass older women tended to get. Or maybe it was the high-waisted jeans she was wearing. Either way, Sam instantly disliked her, and then felt a twinge for judging a woman on her appearance. But she wanted to hate this woman. She did hate her.

"Let's sit down," Alex said. "Then I'll go say hi."

Sam followed Alex to a table on autopilot. She sat and tried to act normal, but her entire body was buzzing.

"What do you want?" Alex rummaged around in her purse until she pulled her wallet out.

"I'll have a tea."

When Alex approached Michelle at the counter, Sam watched. She kept watching when Alex spoke and Michelle's face lit up. They looked like old friends. It was sickening, but Sam couldn't look away.

*You can do this*, Sam told herself. It was merely having coffee with a woman who didn't know her. That's all this was. Simple. Yet her legs felt like lead even while she sat.

Alex and Michelle gathered the paper cups in their hands

and made their way toward the table. Sam fiddled with the zipper on her purse, looking down and then up again.

"This is my sister," Alex said. She gestured down at Sam. Her voice was heavy and she didn't sound like herself. Sam noticed she didn't offer her name to Michelle.

"Nice to meet you, hon." Michelle stood at the side of their table, a wide smile on her face, resting one hand on her hip. Sam hated grown women who called other adults they had never met before *hon* and *sweetie* and other pet names. It was juvenile and condescending.

"Nice to meet you, too." Sam found it incredibly hard to get the words out.

Alex shot her a look as she pushed Sam's tea toward her, then she slid her hands around her own coffee cup and took a sip. "So." Alex let out a puff of air. "How are you?"

This was going to be excruciating.

"I've been good," Michelle said. "Enjoying the last of summer." Her eyes flicked out toward the sunny street through the floor-to-ceiling windows. "When are you here until? You must have to head back to work?" She looked from Alex to Sam and then back again.

"We've got flexible jobs, but with school starting up soon, I'll have to go back to the city in a bit," Alex answered. She took another sip of her coffee.

Sam sat and listened, unsure what to say. It became clear then that she hadn't thought this through well enough. She was here, but now what? Small talk with a woman she despised? What on earth had she been thinking?

Michelle's phone rang and she grabbed it and clicked it on, holding it up to her ear. "Excuse me," she mouthed to Alex and Sam before she left the table.

"What are we doing? Are we going to sit here and make uncomfortable conversation?" Sam asked Alex as soon as Michelle appeared to be far enough away.

Alex glanced over her shoulder before speaking. "What were you expecting?"

"I don't know. Something else." Sam shrugged. "I don't understand why yet. Why her? What about her is better than Mom?"

Alex looked down at her coffee. "I had the same questions."

"And?"

"I haven't figured that out yet either. And honestly, I'm not sure what I want to do." She sighed. "Maybe we should leave it alone."

Sam didn't expect to hear Alex say that. She had been so hellbent on all of this, but now she seemed immeasurably tired.

"Maybe you're right," Sam started to say.

Alex's frown deepened. "Mom would be so mad at us if she knew we were here."

It was true, but that was why they were going to make sure their mother never found out. Anyway, Sam figured all of this—whatever meeting Michelle was supposed to be—would be done and over with after this visit. Was it closure? It was hard to say what drew Sam here, but now that they sat in the middle of the coffee shop, in the same vicinity as their father's long-term mistress, it was all so anticlimactic. Alex was right. Sam was ready to go. It was over, as far as she was concerned.

"Sorry, that was someone from the Legion. Loose ends after the Celebration of Life." Michelle smiled a weak smile. "I forgot some of John's things."

Sam's mouth scrunched up into a tight ball. Something swirled inside her. It must have been pure anger at hearing her father's name coming from Michelle that made her act. Sam looked directly into Michelle's eyes. "John London's celebration?"

"Yes."

Alex's eyes widened, a panicked look flashing across her features. Her mouth fell partially open.

"And who were you to him?" The words came out of Sam's mouth harsh and fast.

Michelle reached up to move a piece of her hair away from her face. She stopped and looked directly at Sam. "I'm not sure what you mean."

"Who are you to John? You're not his wife."

"How would you know who I am?" Michelle's eyebrows shot up and her head jerked back an inch.

"Because my mother is his wife," Sam said. "We're John's daughters."

The color vanished from Michelle's face. She looked from Alex to Sam and then back again.

"Alex." Michelle's voice was low. Now her eyebrows squished together like she was seriously thinking. "Alexandra?"

"And Samantha," Sam said.

Michelle stared at both of them like she was a deer in headlights.

"Sam and Alex," Sam spat. "John's kids."

Alex looked down at her lap as she shifted uncomfortably in her seat.

"John's kids?" The question came out in almost a whisper. "You can't be his kids."

"Why not?" Sam shot back. Wisps of jealousy and fury twisted in circles in her stomach.

"Because he said you died."

A shock of cold went from Sam's core out into her limbs. She couldn't have heard that right.

"He said what?" Alex choked out. Her voice was weak and frail.

Michelle's mouth opened, but nothing came out for a minute. Then she said, "He told me you died in a car crash. Your mother and all three of you girls. I didn't see him for a while after it happened."

Sam stood up, needing to move, to get out of there. She

couldn't make sense of the words; they were so dizzying. She lifted her hand to brush the hair out of her face and the floor shifted, swaying from side to side. Then she was falling and falling, wondering when she would meet the ground. Wondering if the little fig baby inside her would be okay.

# THIRTY-FIVE

## ALEX

The hallways in the hospital were cold. The kind of cold that seeps through your skin all the way down to your bones. Or maybe Alex was chilled because she knew she was to blame for all of this. It was her fault that Sam had fainted and crashed onto the floor. When Sam had come to and complained about her stomach cramping, Alex had panicked. She had cried out that Sam was pregnant. She had had easy pregnancies with no complications, no worries; she didn't know what to do when something like this happened. Luckily, Michelle had snapped into action, insisting that Sam stay still until paramedics arrived. To be safe.

Safe was how they should have treated the entire situation. They never should have been there at the coffee shop in the first place. Alex should have protected her little sister. It was her job, and she had failed. This thing with Michelle had gone much too far, and now here they were.

"Alex!" Carol rushed down the long, narrow hallway toward Alex, her hair flowing wildly around her face. When Alex's eyes met her mother's, she felt a deep surge of shame. She would have to explain everything.

"She's in here." Alex motioned to Sam's hospital room. "They've taken some blood tests and we're waiting for an ultrasound."

Mom and Alex hugged and then Alex stepped to the side to allow her mother into the room where Sam was stretched out.

"I think this is a bit of an overreaction," Sam said, reaching up for her mother's arms.

"Are you going to be okay?" her mother asked. She touched the side of Sam's face and held her hand there.

"I'm fine. I promise," Sam said. She looked at the doorway. "Where's Jess?"

"I couldn't find her. She wasn't home and she didn't have her phone on her." Mom let out a low sigh. "Have you noticed she's been different lately? Is she okay? Are all of you okay?"

Alex could see Sam's body stiffen even from where she was standing.

Mom must have misread Sam's reaction because she waved a hand at her. "Never mind about that right now. You don't need more stress or worry." She focused on Sam's face. "What happened?"

Sam looked like a child to Alex. It was the way she was laying there in the hospital bed with her head slightly bowed, like she was being admonished and she knew she was in the wrong. Earlier, in the ambulance on the way over, Sam had uncharacteristically taken a forceful tone and instructed Alex to tell their mother what was going on as soon as they saw her next. It was time to stop hiding everything from her.

"I found a pile of notes," Alex said before Sam could tell her again to explain.

Carol's forehead scrunched into a million fine lines. "I don't understand."

"They were love notes. To Dad. He was having an affair." Alex's limbs trembled as the words came out of her mouth. It was awful to say it out loud.

Carol's body went rigid. When she spoke, she was eerily calm. She always had a calming presence about her, but this was different. "Where? Where did you find them?"

"Does that really matter?" Alex asked.

"Where did you get them?" Carol repeated. Her voice was low and steady, the way it got when she was serious.

Alex's mouth twitched downwards. "In the shed."

"She found them in an old tackle box," Sam added.

Alex's legs were weak. Something wasn't right about the way her mother was speaking. This wasn't going how she thought it would.

"I thought I got them all," Carol said. "How much do you know?"

Alex froze. For most of her life, she'd taken comfort in knowing that she had a relatively normal and happy family. The Londons were considered to be good people, and Carol and John were envied because of their solid relationship. It was enough of a shock to learn her father wasn't the man Alex thought he was, but now it appeared her mother knew? Had she known all along? Anger and embarrassment welled up inside Alex. How could it not have crossed her mind that her mother would have known?

"What do you mean?" Alex choked.

Carol slumped into the chair behind her. "Please." Her voice was low and resigned. She waved a hand at them. "Tell me what you know."

Alex told her about first finding the notes and then the grief support and meeting Michelle, going to the Celebration of Life and seeing Dad's pictures everywhere and finally, at the end, she told her about Jess. She left out nothing.

They let it sit between them for a while before Alex spoke again.

"Now you."

"It was so long ago," Carol said. "I knew about some of it.

Your father had an affair when you were quite young, but he said it was over. He promised it was done and I believed him."

The weight of what her mother just admitted caused Alex to stumble back a step. She questioned the memories, the feelings, everything she knew to be true about her family. When Dad came home from work and played with her and her sisters, the way they would roll around on the floor, wrestling and laughing as their little sharp elbows and knees dug into him, was he just coming from being with her? Was he thinking about her?

"And you stayed with him. You didn't leave him. Why?" Alex couldn't understand. Her mother was a strong woman and had been their entire lives. She wasn't the type to take this kind of thing.

Carol lifted her head and gave Alex a look. "It's not so simple."

"It is to me. If Ben cheated on me, we would be over. Done. That's it." Her voice was cold, metallic. She didn't sound like herself.

"Alex," Sam interjected. She had been so quiet, Alex almost forgot she was in the room with them, but it didn't matter what she said. Alex wouldn't be swayed. She needed to know, to understand.

"How could you forgive him?" Alex asked. "How could you let him get away with risking everything?"

When her mother looked at Alex, her eyes were sad, but her face was determined.

"Not everything is as simple as you see it. Life isn't black and white. There are so many shady gray areas that nobody knows what to do with, and everybody has their own answer, especially when it comes to marriage and raising kids. Our marriage had its natural ebbs and flows, and I didn't want to give up when it got bad. I wanted to give him another chance and I wanted our family to have another chance. I'm sorry you had to find out this way, but this isn't something a mother tells her kids."

Alex thought about what a mother tells her children when they're adults. At what point does it become acceptable to treat them differently? She just wanted to be let in. She wanted her mother to tell her the truth. That was all she craved, but she didn't know where the deep need came from, only that it was there.

"I don't know what to say." Alex crossed her arms over her chest and looked down at the hospital floor.

"Then don't say anything. You have no right to judge me."

Alex's head shot up. It was so uncharacteristic of her mother to be so sharp with her words.

"Wait a minute," her mother continued, this time with an angry edge to her voice. "You spent all this time with *her*, keeping secrets from me and your sisters? What were you thinking?" Her face was grim.

Alex opened her mouth to speak, but Mom waved her hand in a dismissive way.

"No. No, don't speak right now." Her face was weary. "I'm so disappointed in you."

Alex's arms dangled at her sides. There was almost nothing worse than disappointing her mother, but she was still too angry about all of it.

"You're disappointed in me?" Alex said. She edged forward, closer to where her mother was. She was appalled with herself for being about to go where she was going, but she couldn't stop herself, not even when Sam shot Alex a stern glare as a warning. "How could you believe him that it was over? It wasn't over, it never ended. He was seeing her right up until he died. And he told her we were dead."

Carol froze. She opened her mouth and closed it again, like a fish.

"Alex!" Sam snapped.

Alex couldn't quell the anger inside her. She kept going. "He told Michelle we died in a car crash. All of us. Michelle knew about us at the beginning of their relationship, but then somewhere in the middle, he told her we all died. That's how much we meant to him. That's what kind of a man he was."

Alex's body shook. There was a heavy, crushing feeling in her chest. It hurt so much, but it was the truth and it needed to be told. John London wasn't the man they all thought he was. He was the kind of person who could hurt his family deeply, who could say terrible things about them like they were nothing. How could her mother accept that and live with it?

Mom's eyes welled up, rimmed with redness.

"Alex." Sam's voice was filled with pain. "Stop. Please."

Alex's phone buzzed in her pocket.

*On my way over with the girls to see you guys. Everything okay?*

When she'd called Ben earlier, Alex had given him the basic details. Sam was getting checked out, but she seemed okay. Ben had said he would get the girls dressed and head over as soon as he could.

*Okay.* She tapped into her phone with a shaking hand. All she wanted now was for him to pick her up and get her out of here.

She slipped the phone into her pocket and looked up at her mother. Her face was gray, her mouth a thin, white line across her face.

"I think I need some space. This is... this is all too much." Carol waved her hand around the room and stopped when it settled on Sam, gently touching her daughter as she was stretched out in a hospital bed waiting to find out if her unborn baby would be okay. A stab of guilt shot through Alex, finally calming the anger within her for a moment. Alex allowed Sam to come with her to meet Michelle. She never should have let that happen.

"I'll be fine," Sam insisted.

"But I'm not sure I will. Your father is gone, and I've been overthinking everything." Her mother's voice wavered. "Every morning when I get into the shower, I see the bar of soap he used to use. It sits there in its dish, getting smaller and smaller each day. One day, it'll be gone, but right now, it's one of the last reminders I have of him. Or his phone. I keep charging the damn thing. Can you believe it? I don't want it dying in front of me, but while I'm here worrying about ridiculous things like his soap and his phone, he was lying to my face, and you've been keeping secrets from me."

The image of her mother charging her father's phone night after night nearly broke Alex open. Exhaustion ran through her veins. She was so tired of what he had done to their family. The anger she had for her mother was misplaced. She shouldn't have spoken to her in that way. This was all his fault, not her mother's.

Across from Alex, Sam lay in her bed, her hair pressed to her head on one side, a messy tangle of knotted curls. Carol went and put a hand on Sam's face, running it over her cheek and through her hair, trying to fluff it for her. "You don't need more stress right now." None of them needed this. She looked back up at Alex. "I think you and I need space."

"You're not mad at Jess?" The sting of disappointment and rejection made the little hairs on Alex's arm stand straight up. Her mother had never said something to her like this before. "She knew about this, too. She knew her whole life." Alex couldn't help herself. It wasn't fair.

Sam's mouth hung open. "Stop it now." Her voice came out laced with both anger and pity.

Mom shook her head and then her face crumpled. "I know it's hard to believe, but your father loved me very much," Carol said to Alex and Sam. "And I loved him."

Alex couldn't help the bitter laugh that escaped her lips.

"Don't." Carol's voice was sharp. She pointed a finger at Alex. "Don't do that to me. I'm still your mother. And when all's said and done, he was a good father. He raised you girls well. This affair had nothing to do with how much he loved you."

The room went silent for a while, the sounds of nurses and doctors in the hallway filling the space.

"Give me some time," Carol said. Then she left the room.

# THIRTY-SIX

## ALEX

Later, after the blood tests and ultrasound came back okay, when Sam was getting changed and they were all getting ready to leave, Ben and the girls arrived in a flurry.

"I'm sorry we're so late. They were moving in slow motion." He leaned in to kiss Alex on the cheek, placing his hand on the back of her arm. "Everything okay?" This moment erased any lingering anger that remained between the two of them. A crisis made it clear that there were bigger things to worry about.

After her mother had left the hospital room, Sam had looked too drained to talk, so Alex didn't push it. Her body shook with exhaustion and nerves, too. They sat in silence until the doctors returned. Mom came back into the room to hear what the results were, but otherwise, they didn't speak.

Now, Mom was preoccupied with Lucy and Molly, bending down to hug them. When the girls had come into the room, her mother's face had lit up. Alex had almost taken it for granted, the way her mother's face did the same thing for Alex and Sam and Jess, too.

Ben gave Alex's hand a squeeze. "Alex? Is everything okay?"

"Sam and the baby are going to be fine." When she said it,

Alex's shoulders softened. She didn't want to keep fighting with her family. Her body was weak. It was slowly deflating, like a balloon. None of this had been worth it. Fighting with Jess, and having her mother mad at her. It was all awful. At least Sam and the baby were okay.

Ben nodded as Sam came out of the washroom. She smiled at Ben and leaned towards him, pointing her cheek in his direction and closing her eyes, waiting for his quick kiss. "I'm good," she said. Ben gave her a hug.

"I can take the girls back with me. I'd like the company." Mom took Lucy and Molly's hands in hers. "Maybe we can grab some ice cream on the way home." The girls whooped and cheered like they had been told they were going on vacation.

"Where do you want me to go?" Alex asked in a hushed tone so Lucy and Molly wouldn't overhear. She had no idea how space was supposed to work in their cottage, but hoped her mother wasn't about to tell her to go home early. That would be unprecedented.

"You can stay at the cottage, of course." Mom's tone was cool again. "But let's try and give one another a wide berth."

Pain crashed over Alex at the same time that relief flooded up from her toes. She wasn't being sent away, but her mother wasn't acting like her mother.

"Sam—" It was Hunter, rushing down the hallway toward them.

"Hunter?"

"Are you okay?" he asked when he reached her side. His face was drawn with worry. "I got here as fast as I could. I had been out, and my phone was at the cottage."

"I'm fine. I'll be okay. How did you know?" Sam asked.

"Your mother."

Carol was still holding onto Lucy and Molly's hands. "I'm glad you made it," she said to Hunter. Then she looked at Sam, her expression soft. "Are you coming with us?"

"I can take you home," Hunter offered.

"Thank you." Sam's face was pale, and her hair was a frizzy mess, a tangle of curls held together loosely on top of her head with a hair elastic. She would need help getting settled back at the cottage. Hunter would take good care of her, Alex knew he was that type.

She bent over and kissed the tops of Lucy's and Molly's heads. They each gave Alex a quick hug and then took Carol's hands again and went off down the long, stark hallway in their tie-dyed shirts and shorts, a splash of color in an otherwise drab setting.

When it was only Ben and Alex standing outside the hospital room, she hoisted her purse onto her shoulder. "Should we go?"

"Let's talk for a minute," Ben said.

Alex wasn't sure she could handle another conversation laced with disappointment, but she told herself to remain calm. She had no idea what he wanted to say. Ben touched her arm lightly and Alex gestured down the hallway. She said, "Let's walk and talk."

He followed her lead. "Is everyone going to be okay? Your mom looked pretty shaken."

Were they going to be okay? It was such a relative word. It was hard to know how easily everyone could forgive. Alex knew she wouldn't be able to forget the fact that her mother had known all along.

"I think she'll be okay, but I have no idea. This is all new territory."

They pushed through the large doors to outside and crossed the parking lot until they reached their car. They got inside and pulled out of the lot, heading towards the long stretches of narrow road that would take them back home. Alex rummaged through her purse on her lap, digging for her sunglasses. She was certain they were in there somewhere, but they always seemed to be getting lost.

"What are you looking for?" Ben glanced at her quickly before directing his attention to the road in front of him again.

Alex stopped digging. What was she looking for? What had all this been for? She had been so certain that she would feel better if she could find the truth behind the secrets, or the reason why her father had risked everything. She had made up her mind early on that she had to know because it would bring her closure. Everything would be okay with finality, but the truth was, everything wasn't better. At some point along the way, she had forgotten who she was and what she was searching for. She had gotten lost.

"I don't know."

"Your sunglasses? I think I saw them back at the cottage." Ben nodded down at her purse.

Alex looked at her lap. She started to cry.

"Hey, it's okay," Ben said. Alex didn't know if he meant the sunglasses anymore.

"I'm sorry," she said.

"For what?"

"For how I handled everything. I know I got so carried away."

"It's okay." Ben's voice was soft. "I know you wanted answers."

Alex shrugged. "Yeah, but I don't think I found them."

All this time, she was searching for proof that her life hadn't been a lie, that she was loved by her father. That her mother and her sisters were loved by him. She wanted to know she was valued, but she had thought she couldn't feel it unless she uncovered why her father did what he did. There had to be some reason. The truth was, the fact that her father had betrayed them wasn't what mattered in the end. It hurt, that was undeniable, and it would take a long time to forgive him, but she thought she could. Maybe she could because of what she had left.

She thought about what was waiting for her when they reached the end of this drive, and the night ahead of them. Lucy and Molly would ask her to lie down with them in bed. They would ask her to read to them, then they would turn off the light, put on their fuzzy sleep masks adorned with foxes and bunnies and hold onto Alex's hand. After stories and songs, Alex would lay there like she always did, on her back in the dark, each hand grasping her daughters' soft, chubby fingers. She wouldn't even think about the simplicity of it all. How all they wanted was her attention, her voice, her hand, her presence.

It was what they had that mattered. It was Molly and Lucy and Ben and the family they had created, it was Sam and Jess and their mother and the way she used to hold onto their hands, the way her mother's eyes used to fill with tears when she watched Alex sing, or Sam dance, or Jess tell a story. Family was messy and complicated, but it was also one of the only things she was most certain about in her life, one of the most solid things she had to hold onto when she was weak. When she had sat on that basement floor so long ago, unsure who she was or what she was doing, it was Ben who had reminded her. It was family.

Ben eyed her warily. "You're not going to keep looking for something else with Michelle, are you?"

"No, I'm done with that."

"So, what are you thinking about?" Ben reached over and placed a hand on her knee. Alex noticed he was back to touching and leaning in close when he communicated, and she could smell all of his familiar scents: shampoo and fresh air and laundry soap.

"I guess I've realized how lucky I am to have you."

Ben lightly squeezed her knee and Alex could feel the warmth of his hand.

"We're the lucky ones to have you."

Alex sat in her seat, eyes forward, feeling a little shaky. She had had so much anger up until now. About Michelle, her father, the way her sisters handled things, and then at her mother. She had lost sight of the fact that anger was only temporary, but her family was her family. The secrets and lies and disappointment wouldn't change what they had. All the memories, growing up, the family vacations, the time together, the trust. The unconditional love would always be there, Alex just had to remember to let it in.

# THIRTY-SEVEN

## JESS

After Jess got back to the cottage and found it empty, she waited in the living room, on the couch where she could watch for someone arriving home. She hadn't yet brought it up, but now she needed to see them, anyone, and find out if everyone felt the same way Alex did.

*I think you like the attention.* Nothing that had happened recently had hurt quite as much as Alex's accusation. What if her mother and Sam thought the same thing and nobody had told her? You think you know your own family and then you find out you don't. Why did it surprise her? She had known this to be true since she was a kid and discovered her father could be one person in front of them and a completely different one when they weren't around.

Hunter's car pulled into the driveway first and when Sam got out, looking so pale and exhausted, Jess panicked. She clambered to her feet and rushed outside.

"What's going on? Are you okay?"

"Didn't you get our messages?" Sam asked.

Jess hadn't looked at her phone since getting back. She shook her head.

"It's a long story, but I'll be fine," Sam said. "Let's go inside."

Hunter helped her into the cottage and Sam settled into bed. She convinced him he could leave and that she would call him if they needed him.

Jess stood by, desperate for Sam to tell her what was going on.

"Seriously, what happened? Are you okay?" Jess gestured to the hospital bracelet on Sam's wrist.

"I went with Alex to see Michelle. I got upset, I guess you could say. I fainted and Alex insisted I get checked out."

"And?"

"I'm okay. The baby's okay. I need to rest."

Every ounce of pent-up anger and resentment left Jess's body in that moment. She felt awful about not being there for Sam. Things likely couldn't get much worse. It had come to this: Sam ending up in the hospital.

"Thank goodness," Jess said. She reached out and placed her hand on top of Sam's. "Now this is going to end." She surprised herself with how firm she sounded, but she meant it.

She must have surprised Sam, too; her head tilted to one side.

"What's going to end?" Sam asked.

"The fighting. The secrecy. This isn't like us. This isn't who we are."

The sound of the front screen door opening came from down the hallway, followed by footsteps. Alex appeared at the edge of the room and leaned her hip against the doorframe. She pressed her lips together. "I'm sorry." Her voice broke.

Jess assumed she was speaking to Sam, but when she looked at her sister, Alex's eyes were on hers.

Jess nodded. She was too startled, too overcome to form a regular response.

"I know it'll take time," Alex said. "But do you think you can forgive me?"

Could Jess forgive? Could Alex and Sam and her mother forgive Jess? That was what families did, wasn't it?

"I want to. Otherwise, this is going to eat us up," Jess said. "I made a promise to myself a long time ago that I wouldn't hurt Dad, but in the end, the secret hurt you. It's hurt everyone. I can't do this anymore. I hope you can learn to trust me again."

"Of course," Alex answered. She pushed herself off the wall and came towards Jess. She reached out to her and placed a warm hand on the side of Jess's arm. "I'm so tired of all of this, too. Mom will need time, but she'll feel the same eventually. We all trust you, Jess."

Jess started to cry. It was so unexpected, none of them seemed to know how to react at first. Then Sam said her name, like she did when they were little and had so much innocence, like Jess was the baby again.

"We love you," Sam said. "We've been through the ringer, but none of us want this either. I don't want my baby to come into a family broken by anger and betrayal."

Jess wiped her eyes. "We won't let that happen."

Sam looked down at her stomach and touched it with the palm of her hand.


After they had talked some more and everything was out in the open, Jess finally felt the beginnings of a weight coming off her. It was a start. They were going to try to take the long road back to repairing their relationship as siblings. Now, Jess needed one more thing.

She found her mother down by the water, sitting alone on the edge of the beach. Jess sat next to her and leaned back into the chair.

They said nothing for a long time. When her mother finally spoke, it was controlled. "You shouldn't have had that on your shoulders your entire life. I should have protected you."

"You couldn't have, you didn't know. It's not your fault."

Mom reached out for Jess's hand to squeeze it. "I'm sorry, Jess. I'm sorry you knew and I'm sorry you carried that with you this whole time." Her voice cracked.

"I'll be fine. It's okay." They sat in silence for a moment, wiping loose tears from the edges of their eyes until Jess spoke again. "Can you forgive me for knowing all these years and not telling you?" She worried that what she had done was too unforgivable. As an adult, she still desperately wanted her mother's acceptance, but this seemed insurmountable.

"There's nothing for me to forgive." Mom sat up straighter. She pushed her knees together and turned her head to look at Jess. "You did nothing wrong at all, Jess. I should be the one asking for forgiveness. I had one job as a mother—"

"That's not true."

"No." Mom shook her head. "It is true. My job was to protect you. I had one job and I failed."

"You did not," Jess protested. "It's not your fault. It's nobody's fault, I guess."

"Except his." Her mother crossed her feet at the ankles.

Even though it was true, even though her father had put all of them through hell, Jess couldn't help but feel a hint of defensiveness. It was still uncomfortable to hear her mother's voice so filled with anger towards him. For some reason she couldn't explain, Jess still wanted to protect him. How messed up was that? After all of this, she was still thinking about her father.

"What do we do now?" she asked.

"We move on, I suppose. We try to put it behind us and live our lives."

Jess sat back again and thought about how she was going to do that, what that even meant. She tapped her fingers on the edge of the armrest. She was looking for the right words so she wouldn't hurt her mother's feelings.

"I want to go back to Ireland," Jess said.

Her mother seemed to think about it for a moment. "You should go. You should do what you want and need. I've got Alex and Ben and the girls and Sam and the new baby coming. I'm surrounded here. You should be surrounded by what makes you happy inside your heart right now."

"My family makes me happy," Jess started to protest.

"I know we do. That's the beauty of you—your heart is so full." She reached out and touched the side of Jess's face, the way she always had. "But we'll always be here, Jess. We're family, we're not going anywhere."

In Ireland, Jess remembered feeling calm as she stood surrounded by the cliffs. It was the same feeling she got when she was in Shadow Lake. She could almost taste the salty spray from the sea, feel the way it made the skin on her face dewy and cool while the sun warmed the bare skin on her arms and shoulders. Jess had been stunned silent by the beauty of the country. Now she wanted to go back. She wanted to pick up where she had left off. She wanted to wander and think and write, but, more importantly, she wanted to do it alone. Jess had a deep need to search for who she was outside of the London family.

The secret was no longer holding her here. She could be anyone. For the first time in a long time, she felt a certain kind of freedom.

The next afternoon, Jess found Sam in the cottage with Lucy and Molly who were spread out on the floor coloring.

Sam looked up from her place on the couch as Jess approached and grinned. "Do you remember how much we used to love this?" She gestured down at the array of markers and crayons, greasy pastels and thin pencil crayons spread across the floor.

Jess sat down next to Molly and picked up a crayon, rolling it around between her middle finger and thumb. She did remember. They used to spend hours together—Sam and Jess and Alex, even after they had gotten much older, they all still loved the quiet contemplative nature of the time they spent together, fingers splayed and tongues sticking out of the corners of their mouths as they colored large sheets of paper.

"Hey, can you come with me for a second?" Jess motioned for Sam to follow her. "Where's Alex?"

After finding her, the three of them walked out to the dock, where they took off their shoes and sat down, their feet dangling over the edge and into the water.

"When we have the fire tonight, there's something I want to do together. The three of us," Jess said. There were always many campfires near the end of summer. They roasted marshmallows, made s'mores, and sat in camping chairs talking until it was much too late. It was one of their favorite ways to say goodbye to another summer. This one would be different.

"What's that?" Alex asked.

Jess had a plan. "I want to get rid of the notes. I want to throw all of them into the fire." It wasn't enough to throw them into a garbage bin or rip them up, and it wasn't right to leave them there in the shed. Jess had thought briefly about asking Becky if she thought Michelle would want them, and then she thought better of it. There was a limit to her understanding. Throwing them into the fire seemed to be the only thing to do. Sam and Alex agreed.

Later that night, while their mother and Ben and the girls were still getting on their sweatshirts and gathering up marshmallows and roasting sticks, Alex, Sam and Jess stood in front of the fire that had already been built, watching the flames grow and flicker, feeling the heat on their shins.

Alex pulled the notes out from her sweater pocket and handed them to Jess wordlessly. Jess separated them into three piles and passed one of the piles to each of her sisters. She watched as Alex tossed the paper into the middle of the fire.

Sam followed. They both stood back, their faces softening, the creases between their eyebrows and around their mouths disappearing. They waited for Jess.

It was silent outside that evening, even though it was only dusk. It wasn't completely dark yet and the world hadn't gone to sleep, but the only sound Jess could hear was the crackle and hiss of the fire in front of them. Jess took a breath in. Her ribs were tight with tension. She threw the paper into the middle of the flames and watched as the notes turned from soft, yellowed paper into small pieces of red, glowing embers. Some of them floated up into the sky and cooled into gray ash before disappearing into the air. Alex reached for Jess's hand and Jess took hold of Sam's.

They watched as the fire flickered bright for a moment, roaring higher as if the wind had stoked it. And then it was over.

# THIRTY-EIGHT

## ALEX

A week later, outside on the driveway, rays of sun were fighting their way through the tops of the trees, shining down onto Alex's bare shoulders.

It was a tease that school was starting shortly when the days were like this. It felt like they should be swimming in the lake, eating ice cream after dinner and having a campfire late into the evening for weeks to come. Despite the end of August arriving and September being not far away, no change of weather had come with it. The days were still long and hot.

Earlier, Alex had wandered down the hallway of the cottage, looking for stray toys and books, hair clips and lone socks—remnants of the girls' stay here. It all needed to be gathered up. She had tossed what she could find into one of the open suitcases on the girls' bedroom floor. Once she had found everything she could, she had zipped it up and got ready to pack up. It was an odd sort of feeling. Alex wasn't merely packing up at the end of summer, like she had done for years and years. This time, it was like she was closing the door on a life-changing moment in time. Alex had hoped that for Lucy and Molly, they would remember all the things they usually did—the swimming, the staying up late by the campfire. But for Alex and her mother and sisters, this summer had been unlike any other summer. She would never forget it. She was a different person now, and this time had been defining.

At the car, Alex clicked a button to unlock the trunk, but paused with her keys held in mid-air when she heard the sound of gravel underfoot.

"Hey," the voice called.

The keys slipped out of Alex's fingers, landing with a soft thud on the gravel below as recognition dawned on her. Michelle was walking up the edge of the road toward her.

"Jesus," Alex whispered. She took in a sharp breath of air and looked from Michelle to the cottage and back again. What if Sam saw? Where was Mom—what if she came out here? Things had been cool between them since the hospital, and it was only recently starting to get better. The last thing Alex needed was another complication thrown into the mix. "What the hell are you doing here? You can't be here."

Michelle held up her hands like a stop sign. "I know, I know. I'm sorry. I wasn't sure how else to get hold of you."

It struck Alex that she hadn't thought about Michelle much since Sam had been taken to the hospital. She had tried to push Michelle completely out of her mind. After they burned the notes, and were repairing their relationships with each other, Michelle was the last person Alex wanted to think about anymore. It was over.

Michelle came closer and stopped in front of Alex. She had on an old pair of jeans with holes in the knees. Mom would never wear jeans with holes in the knees, it reeked of a desperation to hold onto a youth you no longer had. Although, as soon as Alex had the unkind thought, a stab of regret pierced at her. Michelle had always been kind to her, and now her face was tired and her eyes sunken.

"I did a little digging. I didn't have to search very hard." She sounded embarrassed, but Alex wasn't sure who Michelle was embarrassed for. "I could have found out all about John earlier, but I didn't want to."

Alex glanced over her shoulder again, checking to make sure there was nobody at the doorway or a window. "What are you talking about?"

"I may have made some bad choices, but I'm not stupid. I knew there must have been a reason why I never went to his house or his cottage. We carried on for thirty years, always on my turf. That sounds ridiculous, doesn't it?" She let out a small laugh and then looked directly into Alex's eyes. Michelle's smile faded as quickly as it had been there. "At first, after I thought you were all gone, I wanted to get to know him—see his things, be in his world. And then at some point, I stopped trying. He didn't want to allow me in, I could see that. I accepted whatever he was willing to give me."

"Why?" As much as it pained Alex to hear Michelle talking about her father this way, the woman in her, the part of her that understood how hard it was to find a good partner in life, was curious. Why would Michelle accept those terms? Alex never would have allowed it.

Michelle shrugged and turned her head to the side, looking at the trees set next to the dusty driveway.

Alex eyed her from where she stood, and her chest tightened a little. She couldn't help but feel something for Michelle despite how much she still wanted to hate her. "Did you know he was lying to you about us?"

Michelle lowered her head and clasped her hands together. She looked up again, directly into Alex's eyes. "I wasn't quite sure. I didn't care, to be honest. That sounds awful, I know. I wanted to have John in my life, on whatever terms. Now that I know your mother and sisters are here and have been so hurt..."

"What?" Alex asked. "Does it change anything?"

"No, it doesn't. I realize that. But I feel terrible. I'm human."

Alex frowned. Her head hurt, her limbs tingling from the anger and unease. She wasn't sure she could ever forgive her father for pretending they were dead. It was too deep a cut. Could she forgive Michelle for all of this? Did it even matter? Alex shifted on her legs and looked down at the gravel beneath their feet.

"Why did you keep coming to Calm Waters after you knew?" Michelle asked gently.

"I don't know, to be honest. I guess I was curious at first. I wanted to know who my dad would risk his family for. He could have lost everything because of you." She paused and stared at Michelle. Michelle held Alex's gaze. She wasn't backing down. "I guess I also thought I would be able to put you in the past and move on if I knew everything about you."

Michelle reached out and put a hand on Alex's arm. Alex wanted to recoil, but she didn't. "Listen, Alex. I'm sorry about what happened to your sister at the coffee shop. I hope she's okay?"

Alex nodded.

Michelle looked relieved, and then continued talking. "And I want you to know that I forgive you."

This time, Alex did recoil. She shook her head in disbelief. "What? I'm sorry—you forgive me?"

"Yes. I forgive you for lying to me all this time. You came to the grief counseling sessions in my town, even after you knew who I was. I didn't know who you were. That was unfair." She pushed her hair out of her face and stuck her chin out defiantly. "But I forgive you."

"You can't compare," Alex started. The words came out choked. Had she actually used the word unfair?

"I know." Michelle held up her hands again and waved them at Alex. "I wanted to get that off my chest. I know you and your mother and sisters will probably never forgive me, and I get that. That doesn't matter. I guess what you have to figure out now is if you can forgive your father."

Alex let out a bitter laugh, like a sharp huff of air, to cover up the jolt of pain inside her. She couldn't listen to Michelle any longer, talking about her father in this way, telling Alex what she needed to do. She didn't want to allow herself to really process Michelle's words or their meaning, but she couldn't help but realize that in all this time, throughout everything she had learned and gone through, she had never really thought about how good it might be for her health and state of mind to try to forgive her father.

She pulled on the trunk and lifted it up, leaning forward and shuffling some things out of the way—the old ice scraper from winter, the wool blanket in case they ever broke down in the car at night. Alex tried to make it look like she was making room for luggage, but she mostly wanted to hide her face.

"Wait. Please." Michelle put her hand out to the edge of the trunk.

Alex stood upright again and turned to face her. There was sorrow settled deep into Michelle's face. It was set into the lines around her mouth, the crease in between her eyebrows, like it was seeping into her pores.

"Even though it might not seem like it, your father loved you more than I could ever describe."

"Don't," Alex warned, shaking her head. "Don't do this just to make yourself feel better."

"I'm not. I promise. I'm telling you I could see it in him." She wrapped an arm around her torso. "It bothered me at first, the way I could see how his choice tore him up. How much I tore him up. I didn't want to be a bad choice, but I was secretly glad he was weak. If he were stronger, he never would have stayed with me. He never really did, if you think about it."

Alex put one hand on top of the trunk and the other on the edge of the car before looking away and out into the trees. Why was Michelle telling her this, and why wouldn't she leave already? Alex knew the story; they stayed together, her father didn't choose one or the other, he had both his family and Michelle until the end of his life.

"You know, there was this one memory I have of John." A small smile appeared on Michelle's face.

"Please," Alex said. She held up a hand and shifted on her feet. She glanced behind her again, hoping she could leave now without hearing the rest of it.

"Wait. This will be quick," Michelle insisted. "He told me once that when you guys were young, bedtime was his favorite time of day, and it wasn't because the kids went to bed and the grownups got a break."

Alex's face was grim. To tell this story was wrong. It was too intimate. But Michelle didn't pick up on Alex's signals and kept talking.

"He said he loved bedtime because he loved to watch your mother. It was one of the rare times he spoke about her to me."

Alex stiffened. That wasn't allowed. Michelle wasn't allowed to know who her mother was, or the way she looked, or how she treated her children. It should have been off-limits.

"He said that she would always crawl into bed with the three of you; no matter how tired or how long her day was, when you guys asked, she always said yes. He said that was when she was her most relaxed; at night, holding hands with you guys, listening to your stories from the day. That was when she seemed most at home."

Alex's head bowed. She thought of her earliest memory of her mother, of being on the bed, surrounded by Alex and Sam, baby Jess in her arms, and her patient, gentle voice. It had always been there, guiding her through her life. It was there when she was a kid and needed help with everything, the way her girls needed her now. It was there even when she was a teenager and wanted independence from her mother so desperately. She had been Alex's constant. Even now, they would overcome the anger and her mother would still be there for Alex. It was who she was.

There wasn't much Alex could say to Michelle then. Michelle didn't need to know anything that was going on inside Alex. She only nodded, reluctantly communicating her thanks. Michelle confused her so much. Alex had never known someone who could stir up hot rage in the pit of her stomach at one moment and then make her feel compassion the next.

"You know what I don't understand?" Alex said.

Michelle studied her. "What?"

"How could you do it? All these years, if you had a feeling we weren't really gone, how could you knowingly do something like this, especially when you're a mother yourself?" Despite the way Michelle looked on paper, she seemed too caring in real life for what she did and the way she acted.

"He was a good man. An easy man to love," Michelle said. "And I guess I'm weak, too."

Alex and Michelle stood in silence. Was that true about her father? It might have been for Michelle. It would take time for Alex to come to her own conclusion about her father's goodness.

Alex watched Michelle for a moment and then realized there was nothing else to say. She shut the trunk. She would come back and finish packing up the car later, and then they would leave. The summer would be over.

"I have to go."

Michelle moved out of the way. "Wait. One more thing. I spent my life with someone who was never mine. I hurt people and I was hurt myself. It's no way to live, but I have to move on now or I'll be stuck in my sorrow and pain forever." She looked directly into Alex's eyes and then said, gently, "Don't come to Calm Waters again."

Alex stood there, relieved Michelle was walking away. She took a final look and then turned around. She would likely never see Michelle again, but her face, the way she looked at Alex one last time with empathy behind her eyes, that would always be burned into Alex's mind. It would never escape her.

# THIRTY-NINE

## SAM

*Just under seven months later*

It was time. Sam didn't instinctively know it at first, the way she thought she would. In the movies, pregnant women had *the* moment. Water gushing onto the floor like the breaking of a dam, and suddenly they couldn't breathe, their faces contorted into odd expressions at the enormity of the contractions.

It wasn't like that for Sam. That morning, she woke up and looked at the ceiling of her bedroom like she had most mornings during the exhausting third trimester, contemplating how exactly she would maneuver her body out of bed. Her stomach was massive now, which meant the simple act of getting up out of bed each day was a complicated and arduous task.

The cottage was quiet. Mom was likely still asleep. They had both spent a lot of time napping, lingering in bed, as if they could sleep away the dreary days of February. It was the beginning of March now at least, and the promise of spring was on the horizon, finally.

Sam lifted one arm into the air to help with momentum and launched herself onto her right side, in line with the edge of the bed. Whipping the blankets off her legs and shoving them behind her with one arm, she prepared to roll. Her large, round stomach was in the right spot to fall over the edge of the bed without getting stuck on her mattress, which meant she could stand up without having to use any ab muscles. Thank goodness, because she had no idea where hers were hiding.

Sam stretched her legs and touched down onto the floor beneath her, standing in a bent-over position. When she straightened up, she felt a quick burst of warm liquid soak her underwear.

*Shoot. Did I pee my pants?* Sam froze in place. She hadn't had the type of pregnancy that left her with very little bladder control, and yet, Sam was sure that was all this small amount of warm liquid could be. It wasn't a flooding gush. In fact, it kept trickling down her inner thigh as she waddled to the bathroom to clean herself up, a single track of liquid like a raindrop shimmying down a windowpane.

After showering, drying off and putting on a clean pair of leggings and an oversized T-shirt—she was always hot these days—Sam made her way to the kitchen, quiet enough so she wouldn't wake her mother. With each step, she felt her underwear grow damp, another trickle escaping and sliding down her leg. She had no idea why she still appeared to be peeing, when it finally dawned on her.

*Oh.* She slowly put the pieces together, like an intricate puzzle. The little leak and the constant trickle was probably her water breaking, but where was the monumental gush or the immediate painful contractions? This wasn't what she had expected, but something told her it was time. Sam called Claire and they made plans to meet at the hospital in half an hour.

Mom was completely focused on Sam, rubbing her back, getting her water, packing up her hospital bag. She had already called Jess and Alex and they both were on their way over. Everyone had been on red alert ever since Sam had hit her thirty-ninth week, so they wouldn't be long. Hunter was on his way, too. He had been coming to his cottage off and on all year, mostly on weekends, but sometimes during the week to work remotely as well, and they had seen one another a lot. They still hadn't decided exactly what they were, but it suited Sam. She was lucky to have him in her life in any capacity, and she knew it.

When Alex arrived, she rushed inside like she couldn't waste a minute of time.

"Sam." She held onto her softly.

Sam melted into her sister's body. A painful ache took over her abdomen, increasing in intensity every second. She moaned and doubled over, which didn't seem to faze Alex. Alex gently rubbed Sam's lower back, in a methodic, firm motion. She spoke calmly to her in a low voice until the pain subsided.

"You've clearly done this before."

Alex laughed and let go of Sam now that she was able to stand straight again. "How have you lasted out here at the cottage this entire time? I would have gone mad, it's so dreary in the winter."

"I love the quiet life here," Sam said. "It's the perfect place to bring a London baby into the world, don't you think?"


After they got to the hospital, the pain increased. It came much faster than before, in waves that overtook her entire body. When it was time to push, Sam was relieved. She wasn't sure she could handle it anymore. Her groaning grew longer and louder with each contraction. Claire allowed her mother and Alex to stay in the room, thank goodness. Sam needed them. After the initial anguish of everything that had happened last summer began to wane, they had slowly found their way back to one another. And now, Sam needed them, and they were here. When Jess showed up shortly after, Sam could see that she felt helpless. Jess stood at the edge of the bed watching, her arms dangling at her sides. But she was here. Sam felt every emotion at the sight of her family.

When first asked if she wanted an epidural, Sam had decided to try to wait to get one for as long as she could, which she regretted greatly the moment Claire told her in a firm but soothing tone, "It's too late, Sam. We don't have time to administer it. A few more pushes and your baby will be here, I promise."

Sam glanced at Jess, who was frowning.

"I can't do this," Sam whimpered. Her face was hot, beads of sweat pooling at the edge of her hairline and under her nose.

"Yes, you can." Jess grabbed onto Sam's hand.

"You're the strong one," Alex said. "You're much tougher than Jess and I."

Sam choked out a sobbing laugh before the pain gripped her again. And then she was gone, her focus no longer on anyone in the room. She squeezed her eyes shut and forced herself to be strong and determined enough to push through the white-hot pain, enough to bring her daughter into the world.

A baby girl, coming into the world surrounded by the women of her family who already loved her fiercely.

Sam heard her mother gasp when she saw the baby.

*She's here. I did this.* Sam opened her eyes and lifted her head from the pillow. Exhaustion was setting in, but she was eager to hold her baby, feel her tiny body against her own skin.

In the flurry of excitement, Sam had a vague sense of what was going on around her. Alex and Jess held onto her mother, the three of them crying in between throaty laughs. They watched as Claire placed the soft, dewy baby onto Sam's chest.

"Oh my God," Sam whispered. She stared down at her daughter's perfect face. "Oh my God."

. . .

"What are you going to name her?" Alex came to Sam's side and touched her arm carefully. It could have been ten minutes or four hours, Sam was so exhausted. She raised her head to look at Alex and saw by the clock on the wall that it had only been half an hour. Thirty minutes with her daughter and already it felt like the most calming thirty minutes she had experienced in a long time.

"This is Emily Carol London."

Emily was a name Sam had loved ever since she was young. It was classic and beautiful to her, and she had never doubted for a second that she would pair it with her mother's name.

"It's beautiful," Alex said.

"I'm honored." Her mother wiped at tears with one hand and held onto Jess with the other.

When Sam motioned to Hunter that he could come into the room, he stood at her bedside and looked down at Emily, wrapped tight in a swaddle of blankets. Sam kept her eyes on her daughter when she spoke. "What do you think? Overwhelming, or what?"

Hunter laughed. "You are incredible," he said with a bewildered tone. "That's all I know." He put his hand out to her and she took it.

Claire came over to Sam and covered her with an extra blanket. She touched Emily gently. "Can I weigh her now?"

Sam nodded, her eyes following Claire as she held the baby expertly.

After a while, the weariness of what had happened set in. She was worn out physically and mentally and couldn't find the energy to talk. All she wanted to do was stare at her baby.

"We should go," Jess said. "You need your rest."

Alex hesitated but nodded in agreement after a pause. They gathered their coats and bags, said goodbye to Emily and kissed Sam.

In all of the bustle, as they were about to leave, Sam noticed

Wes standing in the doorway looking wary. She expected to feel something, surprise that he was there, or annoyance, but she didn't. She barely felt anything for him at all. She kept her gaze on Emily who was now back on her chest, snuggled in close to her warmth. "You can come in, Wes."

He could have been anyone. It didn't matter that it was Wes standing there by the doorway, looking sheepish. To Sam, he was so inconsequential now, dismissed to the back of her mind already, not even a mild concern. She was much too wrapped up in Emily and her tiny, plump body, her soft, smooth skin and the peach fuzz covering her shoulders. Emily was her focus.

"Can I see her?" His voice was low.

Sam looked up at him briefly and noticed how tired and waxy he looked. His face was ashen-colored, his long hair a tangled mop. She nodded and then lowered her arms, still cradling Emily, to allow Wes a better look at their baby. She felt enough for Wes to allow him to get closer, but she didn't offer Emily to him. He hadn't earned that right yet.

"This is Emily Carol London."

Wes sucked in a quick breath when he got closer to them. His lips parted and then a smile brightened his face. "Incredible. She looks like you."

Sam felt her shoulders loosen, but only a little. "And like you, too. She's a perfect mix."

Her mother, Alex and Jess were still in the hallway, milling about. They mustn't have been ready to leave Sam yet after they saw Wes, although Sam had never felt stronger in her life.

"How did you know?" Sam gestured to Emily.

Hunter had been at the edge of the room, about to go into the hall with Alex and Jess and Carol. He made eye contact with Sam now, eyebrows raised, his mouth a small line across his face.

Wes looked at him and gave a slight nod. "Hunter told me."

Sam stared at Hunter. How did he know how to reach Wes? And why on earth would he?

"Your phone rang earlier, and I saw who it was," Hunter explained. "I answered for you and told him what was going on. I thought he should know." He bowed his head. A wave of gratitude rolled over Sam because of how kind and compassionate Hunter was. He only wanted the best for her. Yet, it didn't change how guarded she was around Wes.

Sam turned back to Wes. "And you happened to call today?"

Wes put his hands into his pockets. "I've been meaning to call for a while now."

Wes's words had no effect on her. Sam had a laser focus, a purpose, and it had nothing to do with Wes or even Hunter.

Hunter pushed himself off the edge of the wall where he had been leaning and attempted to smile at Wes before turning back to Sam. "I think I'll run down to the cafeteria with your mom and sisters." He gave Sam a look, and leaned in. "You look like you've got everything completely under control."

"I do." Her eyes were set firmly on Emily.

Hunter leaned over and kissed the top of her head before he left the room.

"How are you feeling?" Wes asked, still standing slightly off to one side of the bed, as if he was waiting for permission to get closer.

"A little tired, but otherwise great."

"I can't believe you did this. You are such a rock, Sam. You carried her and had her and here she is. Our baby."

Sam stiffened at the words. *Our baby*. "What are you doing here, Wes? Why did you come back?"

"I realized I should be involved. It's the right thing to do, and I know now that I want to be in her life." He paused and looked at the doorway. "I guess you and Hunter are a thing now?"

Sam didn't hesitate. "Yes. We are." The past six months had been perfect, but she didn't want to explain any of it to Wes. She didn't have to.

"I still want to try to be a good dad, but I know where I stand. You're her mother and you can give her the kind of life I can't. I want to work with you on this. I promise."

Sam supposed that having more people in Emily's life to show her how much she was loved and adored was a positive thing. It was something her baby shouldn't be denied. "What about your drinking? I can't—"

"I know." Wes shook his head, cutting Sam off. "I know. I'm getting help."

Sam eyed him warily. He didn't look great, but he seemed to be trying. "I think it would be a good thing if you were in her life, but you have to promise not to screw it up," Sam said. "Messing up with me is one thing, but you won't mess up with my daughter."

The strength in Sam's voice startled him. She could tell by the way his body straightened, no longer lazily slumped to one side, but tall and straight, on alert. Sam didn't know she had it in her until she was holding Emily, but it was there. The desire to protect her child was innate and her need to comfort and hold her had kicked in the instant she had been delivered.

When Wes nodded, Sam relaxed back into the bed.


Later, after Wes left, her mother and sisters went back to the cottage to get it ready for Sam and Emily to come home. It was one of the great benefits of having a midwife deliver her baby— Sam could go home a few hours after birth and relax in the comfort of her own bed. Claire would be back to check on them in the morning.

Only Hunter hung around. He sat in the chair next to Sam's hospital bed. They looked like a happy little family,

Hunter and Sam and Emily, and Sam almost laughed at how complicated her situation was. She supposed it didn't matter what they looked like. Family was what you made of it.

Claire came into the room now, her gentle hands touching Sam's shoulder, running down Emily's back. "Are you ready?"

It was time for her to get up out of bed and get changed. Hunter looked flabbergasted. "Already? You had a human being come out of you."

Sam laughed and then winced at the pain in her abdomen.

"I can put Emily down in the cot while we get you into the washroom," Claire said, and then turned to Hunter. "Unless you wanted to hold her?"

Hunter looked from Emily to Sam. "I would love to."

Sam's stomach flipped. She held out her arms to him.

He came closer and then paused, turning to Claire. "Can you help?"

Claire gently but expertly took Emily from Sam's arms, placing her onto her chest softly for a moment before bringing Emily to Hunter and lowering her into the crook of his arms.

Sam watched the exchange from her bed. "Have you got her?" Her voice was laced with apprehension.

Hunter said nothing, his head bowed down toward Emily's small body.

Sam couldn't see his face to read his expression. "Hunter?"

When he looked up, his eyes were glassy, his mouth twitching with emotion into a crooked smile across his face. She had never seen him this way before, so at ease.

"This feels really nice." His voice was quiet when he spoke.

"Have you got her?" Sam repeated, though she had a sense she knew the answer. She had a vision then. It was of Hunter and Emily when she was older, maybe four years old, on the beach. Emily was shrieking with laughter as Hunter ran behind her, pretending to catch her, then playfully falling down again. Sam wasn't there, an outsider watching from the edges, but it was okay. It was all okay. A sense of calm washed over her. Hunter had Emily now in the hospital room and he would always have her. Sam was never more certain of something.

"I've got her." Hunter's voice cracked.

Sam allowed herself to cry for the first time since giving birth.

# FORTY

## JESS

Jess stepped lightly over springy grass. She kept an eye on the crowd in front of her and also on the ground, noting the pinks and purples of the wildflowers dotted among the vibrant green. Everything was so lush and colorful here for late March. That morning, she had signed up for a guided walk of the cliffs, something she'd wanted to do for a while.

"If you look to the left, you'll notice Doonagore Castle." Jess was only half listening to the tour guide, a friendly woman with a round body and bouncy hair under a giant hat. The details were interesting, but Jess mostly wanted to take everything in around her. The cliffs were so staggering, they didn't need an introduction.

She adjusted her own hat, feeling the wind whip through her hair when she took it off momentarily. It still took her by surprise sometimes, the fact that she was here and not home. She had been back in Ireland for a few weeks now while her mother and Sam were in Summerville, likely doting on Emily, or putting on sweaters and having coffee down by the beach, or watching the odd boat go by on Shadow Lake. She would go home and join them eventually, but not yet.

Alex would also be at home with her family, getting the girls to school, running her business, doing everything efficiently, because that was her way. Jess, on the other hand, was completely alone. It was perfect.

It didn't escape Jess that being alone felt right because of her family. They had given her a gift without realizing it. Once the secret had come out, they had all eventually learned to forgive one another. Jess had spent most of her life thinking her mother and sisters would find the way she handled things unforgiveable, but they had shown that they saw her for who she was, and they loved her. They accepted her. As a result, she had never felt closer to them. It was as if they had reverted to their childhood selves, as close as they were when they would sleep in the twin beds together, shoulder to shoulder.

She thought then of the novel she had just started writing— about a family nearly torn apart but brought back together. Jess knew how it was going to end. She had never been more confident in her writing.

On the cliffs, most of the tourists had stopped to snap photos of one another, using the shining ocean as their backdrop. Jess kept walking along the edge at the rock face. It was magnificent, stretching up towards the sky. She squinted in the sun, her eyes taking it all in, trying to make as many imprints in her mind as she could. She wanted to remember it; she wouldn't be here forever. She didn't need to be.

Jess took her hat off to feel the sun. It was a small mercy, the way it came out today, a spot of light in an otherwise gray, overcast sky. It warmed Jess's face, so she closed her eyes and tilted her head upwards. She could have felt insignificant here, a speck on the edge of this massive cliff, but she didn't. She felt good in her body, sure of herself. She was untethered, no longer holding onto the secret, no longer defined by her father and his mistakes.

Free.

# FORTY-ONE

## ALEX

"Can you make me my cereal?" Lucy's voice was still sleep-filled, her hair a matted mess on top of her head.

Alex put the can of coffee grinds down and turned to Lucy, wordlessly reaching her arms out wide for a hug, the way she always did first thing in the morning. A hint of a smile crossed Lucy's face before she lifted her arms to Alex and melted into her body, resting her cheek on Alex's chest.

"Mmm," Lucy hummed, her eyes closed and a small smile on her lips.

Alex's chest hitched at the unexpected emotion from her daughter. Her body warmed as she gently moved from side to side in a slow-motioned dance with her daughter. She rubbed Lucy's back, running her hand over the soft pajamas Lucy wore. She still liked onesies and had on her dark gray one that looked like a bear, with ears and a short, stubby tail. It was ridiculously cute, and Alex hoped Lucy wouldn't outgrow this stage for a while.

While she had been gone when the baby came, helping Sam adjust and get settled, Alex had missed the simplicity of these moments. She breathed in Lucy's familiar scent, warm and sweet, like home. Her daughter's thin arms felt good around Alex's waist.

Lucy gently pulled away. "Can you make my cereal?" she asked again.

Alex smiled and nodded. "Sure. How are you? How did you sleep?"

"Good." Lucy didn't waste time on elaborating. She was still waking up, so this was all the conversation Alex was likely to get. The good stuff came at night, when they were shoulder to shoulder in Lucy's bed before she drifted off to sleep. That was when Lucy would reveal details of her day, telling Alex about her friends, her teacher, what was happening in the book she was reading right now, what was on her mind.

Alex knew that an eight-year-old could easily pour her own cereal and milk. She also knew that she should let Lucy do it herself. That was what all the experts said. Her generation of parents were ruining children these days; the kids were spoiled and entitled, they didn't know how to do anything for themselves, they lacked skills when they grew up, couldn't handle disappointment.

Alex didn't see that when she looked at her daughter. She saw a kid who was sweet and smart, who loved to play outside and join clubs at school and behaved around adults but could come undone like the best of them around her family. She saw a kid who didn't always follow every rule to the letter but would and could do anything she wanted when she put her mind to it. Sometimes that kid wanted her mom to do something for her, like pour her a bowl of cereal when she was sleepy. Alex didn't care to teach her daughter an important life lesson at six thirty in the morning, standing in their dim kitchen. No, instead she did it for her, kissed her warm head and went back to making the coffee, confident that they would all be fine.

She dumped grinds into the machine, filled it with water and clicked it on, waiting for the gentle whir signaling it had started up. Alex leaned her back onto the counter as her mind went to what she had to do that day.

Now that she had been home for a couple of weeks, she was well into her regular routine. She would soon take the girls to school, and they would likely splash through every puddle they could find in their boots on the way. Alex made a mental note to leave a little earlier so they wouldn't be rushed.

Ben came into the kitchen then, pulling his shirt on, and mumbled something that sounded like a greeting. He wasn't a morning person.

"Hey." Alex leaned her body toward him, and Ben pointed his face to hers. A quick kiss, accompanied by a small smile and then he went to the cupboard for a mug.

"Coffee ready?"

Alex laughed at his inability to string words together coherently yet. "Almost."

He smiled at her and then took a step closer again, wrapping an arm around her waist. "Hello," he said. "I need a hug."

Alex went to him, resting her body against his. When they eventually parted, they saw Molly standing at the entrance of the kitchen from the hallway. A smirk was already squarely set on her face, her eyes shining. Molly was a morning person.

"Hi, Mommy!" She ran to join Alex and Ben, wrapping her tiny arms around Alex's legs.

Alex squatted down to get a better view of Molly. "Good morning. I missed you when you were sleeping."

"It was only one night."

"True. Still missed you," Alex said.

Molly giggled, and then her expression went serious, her eyes widening and the smile dropping from her face. "Mommy. Do we have time to make pancakes for breakfast?"

Alex marveled at what must be going on in a five-year-old's head. She smiled. "I think we can make time for that. Why?"

Molly's eyes flashed with excitement. She pumped her fist into the air. "Yes! I love them so much!"

Alex stood up and poured herself a coffee before pulling a mixing bowl out of one of the lower cupboards. She went to the pantry to grab the pancake mix and when she turned around, she was struck by everything around her. It was all familiar and ordinary: Lucy at the counter, hunched over, eating her cereal, Ben moving slowly, sipping coffee, and Molly skipping around on her delicate legs, her bare toes dancing across the floor as she anticipated a big breakfast before school. A calm came over Alex. Her body felt light. This was it. This was what she was searching for, something that could never be found in a note.

"Mommy." Molly tugged on Alex's hand gently, pulling her down to eye level. She reached out and put her soft hands on each side of Alex's face. "I want to help you."

Alex knew her daughter was only talking about the pancakes, but she couldn't stop her eyes from welling up.

"What are you thinking about?" Ben stood next to Alex now, reaching for the cereal.

She looked at him through blurry eyes. "You and Lucy and Molly."

He tilted his head, a confused smile crossing his face. "And? What about us? How wonderful we are?" he teased.

Alex ran a hand along his broad back, feeling the softness of his shirt, the warmth of his body. She didn't say anything, just kissed his cheek.

# A LETTER FROM THE AUTHOR

Thank you from the bottom of my heart for reading *Last Summer at the Lake House*. I enjoyed writing it so much, and I hope you equally enjoyed getting pulled into Alex, Sam and Jess's journeys. If you want to join other readers in hearing all about my new releases and bonus content, you can sign up for my newsletter.

www.stormpublishing.co/heather-dixon

I've sometimes been asked why I write, or how I can get up so early in the morning to write. The first answer I always give is because I love it. I can't imagine not writing. During the pandemic, it kept me focused and feeling grounded in a scary time. But there are also many other reasons I write as well. One of those is to understand and process emotions. Another is to explore 'what if?' Yet another reason, and I think the most important, is to entertain readers. For me, there's nothing better than being completely absorbed in a book and escaping to a world where I'm caught up in the lives of the characters. I love that feeling when you can't put a book down or can't wait to return to reading it. I love reading for the enjoyment of it—to be entertained, to feel things deeply—and I hope that I can somehow do that for others with my writing. When I set out to write this book, I wanted to tell a story of love, of family, of secrets. It's about life and loss and grief, but also about hope and forgiveness. It's about all the things that make our world scary and beautiful and worth living. I hope you felt all of those emotions and more as you read it. I hope you were entertained.

If you've enjoyed this book and could spare a few moments to leave a review that would be hugely appreciated. Even a short review can make all the difference in encouraging a reader to discover my books for the first time—and I find it so inspiring when readers get something from my books.

Thank you again for being part of this incredible journey with me. I love being a writer, and I love hearing from readers, so I hope you'll stay in touch—I have so many more stories and ideas to entertain you with.

Sincerely,

Heather

www.heatherdixon.ca

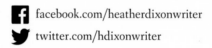

facebook.com/heatherdixonwriter

twitter.com/hdixonwriter

# ACKNOWLEDGMENTS

This book took many, many people to help craft it into what it is today, and I am forever grateful for all of you.

To my editor Vicky Blunden, and everyone at Storm Publishing—you are absolutely top notch. Vicky, thank you for your encouragement and expert advice, for helping me make this book even better than I could have imagined. It was an incredible experience to work with someone so clearly excellent at what they do. I'm in awe of how good you are at this, and I love what we achieved together. And to Oliver Rhodes and Kathryn Taussig, for taking a chance on a new author—thank you so much. I feel so lucky to be working with you.

To Amy Jones—thank you for reading a very early version of this novel and for meeting with me online, way back in March of 2020, when something "weird" was happening in the world. Your advice and feedback made such a difference.

To Michelle Meade—I feel like I wouldn't know how to tell a story if it wasn't for your help and advice early on! Thank you for helping to make me better at what I do.

To the talented Sarah Whittaker for designing a gorgeous cover. I love it so much.

To my early readers—Lauren Roberts, Julie Green, Jackie Khalilieh. Thank you for being among the first in helping me get this book to where it is now. And to my excellent writing group—Georgina Kelly, Lydia Laceby and Rosemary Twomey. This was written before we got the gang together, but I feel like you've always been a part of my writing journey.

The writing community overall has been so incredible. Karma Brown, Bianca Marais, the SPs, all the writers I keep meeting along the way—you've all been so kind and generous and have helped me become the writer I am today. And Liz Kessick, you are so talented at both writing and providing exceptional feedback and encouragement. I am lucky to have you in my corner.

To my incredible friends—the OG Bobcaygeon crew (Derek, Emily, Amanda, Corey, Jess, Gary, Jo, Larry, Laura and Chris), thank you for introducing me to the setting of my dreams. I love it so much, I made it a book! And to the Muskoka crew (Andrea, Chris, Marty, Aimee, Amanda, Amy, Clint, Derek and Emily) for keeping the party going! Thank you to my hockey family (Go Falcons! Go Cudas!) And thank you especially to Sarah Langley—for always listening to me talk and talk and wanting to hear about everything going on in my life. I will always feel the same way about you.

To my family—Chris and Melissa, thank you for all your support and interest in what I'm working on. Melissa, we're lucky to have you in our lives. Chris... they won't say it out loud, but I can tell this accomplishment makes me the favored child in Mom and Dad's eyes. Dad—thank you for always being up for celebrating my books with a good party! And Mom—I'm so grateful there's you. I love the way you support me, encourage me, take care of my children, take care of me (even though I'm in my 40s), and I love the way you love me. Thank you, always.

To Andrew, I'm glad we met when we were eighteen years old. I love our life. And to Anna, Lauren and Paige—the best three sisters there are. Your unconditional love has meant everything to me. I will never stop saying "Guess what?" and then telling you I love you (even though it makes you groan).

Writing a book and having it published has been a dream of mine since I was a little kid. It still feels surreal as heck to be writing these acknowledgements and seeing my dream come to life in front of me. Everyone who has helped me, asked me about my book, supported me... you have all made me feel very loved. I am so lucky. Thank you.

Manufactured by Amazon.ca
Acheson, AB